more of us

Love You More ~ Book 3

laura pavlov

More of Us Playlist

Four Walls ~ Broods
For My Daughter ~ Kane Brown
What Ifs ~ Kane Brown (featuring Lauren Alaina)
I Want More ~ Kaleo
Not Over You ~ Gavin DeGraw
Adore You ~ Harry Styles
Halo ~ Beyonce
Someone You Loved ~ Lewis Capaldi

Pathi & Nat,

This series would never have happened without you both. I cannot begin to thank you for all your love and support throughout this journey. Thank you for reading endless rewrites, cheering me on every step of the way, and for always believing in me. Most importantly, thank you for your friendship. You mean the world to me and I love you both so much! xoxo

If you love somebody, let them go, for if they return, they were always yours. If they don't, they never were.

Kahlil Gibran

one

. . .

Jade

WE'D BEEN in Honduras for just a few days, and I was adapting to my new environment. We'd flown into Tegucigalpa, the capital of Honduras, and driven endless miles on dirt roads to our compound. The building was surrounded by a large, cement block wall, which we were told not to leave unless we were with our group. There was no TV here, none of the modern conveniences we were used to, and every evening we all pulled out our prescription bottles and took our malaria pills—a daily reminder that we had entered a different world.

It couldn't have come at a better time. I was in desperate need of a change, which is why I'd signed up last minute to spend my summer here. I was sick of the drama that had followed me and Cruz, and I'd come to a fork in the road—and I'd decided to change my course.

My heart ached every day, and I hoped that once I immersed myself in helping those in need, it would hurt a little less. That was the goal. I'd found my rock bottom… it was lying on a hotel room floor after being knocked unconscious by my boyfriend's bandmate, all while Cruz, the love of my life, lie only a hundred feet away unaware because he'd decided to take prescription sleeping pills.

Did I mention he chased them down with whiskey? After he'd promised he would stop the pills and the drinking. It could have been worse. I could have died if I'd hit my head differently. And no one would have known.

It was time for a fresh start. No more crying over Cruz Winslow. I was sick of myself and sick of who we'd become. I still loved him. There was no denying it. But that didn't mean he was good for me.

He wasn't.

I'd known it for a while, but my traitorous heart had steered me wrong. But I wasn't thinking with my heart anymore. I was thinking with my head. I was a smart girl. It was time I started acting like it.

I'd done well on my MCAT, and I'd be applying to medical school in two weeks, pending we could find reception out here. My group leader, Richard, would also be applying at the same time, so he said we'd figure it out together, even if it meant driving into the capital to submit our applications.

Cruz had texted me daily since I'd arrived here, letting me know he'd started a thirty-day rehab program in Utah. I didn't have high expectations. He was continuing as the lead singer of Exiled, and I doubted he'd remain in this program for thirty days. Cruz was stubborn and he hadn't thought he had a problem before he found me lying unconscious on his hotel room floor, so what would make him think differently now? I wanted to trust him, but I knew better. I'd ignored his downward spiral for months, because I just didn't want to see it at the time. I didn't want to add to his stress. There had been signs and red flags—and I'd let him convince me over and over again that he didn't have a problem. That everything was under control. And I'd bought into all of it. Love had a funny way of allowing you permission to turn a blind eye when it was easier than dealing with the things life was throwing at you. But I'd taken off my rose-colored glasses, and I was seeing things clearly. I had no expectations anymore. It would be easier that way.

I needed him to stop texting me so often. I told him we could text once a week moving forward. I was determined to use this time to figure out who I was and find a new path—and he needed to do the same. Love wasn't enough. I'd learned that the hard way. I told him he was free to date other girls and do what he wanted. We were done.

Donezo.

Finit.

Although I thought I was tough and brave, honestly—the idea of him with someone else made me sick to my stomach. But it was a necessary pain. I needed to get over him, and I couldn't do that if we were still hoping to make things work. This was not our time and the sooner we both got on board, the better.

I had to be the strong one. Cruz wasn't. And at the rate we were going, we'd kill one another—if not physically, mentally. I'd finally realized that our love was not a good love. It was too intense, too overpowering and too toxic.

I shared a room with seventeen other girls from all over the United States. The compound was split in two. A girls' side and a boys' side. We'd all come on this medical brigade together. There were nine sets of bunk beds in my room, and Jessica and I shared the one in the back corner. I was on the top bunk because apparently Jessica is afraid of heights. I actually laughed when she told me. She wasn't kidding either, she couldn't even climb up there to sit and talk. I had to go down to her bunk if we wanted to visit. The window in our room faced the surrounding sugarcane fields, and it calmed me in a weird way. There were no paparazzi waiting outside for me, no gossip magazines spreading lies about me and Cruz, and no drama.

I was here to do something good with my life and help people that were in need.

I stepped in the restroom shared with seventeen other girls, with one shower and one toilet. You weren't allowed to flush the toilet paper in the toilet, and the shower water was cold at all times. It was a perfect daily reminder of my fresh start. Literally and figuratively.

I rinsed my mouth using purified water from my water bottle and quickly washed my face. I pulled my hair into a bun on top of my head, covered every inch of my body in insect repellant, and slipped into a pair of scrubs.

"You ready to go grab some breakfast before we head out?" I asked Jessica, and she set her journal aside and pushed to her feet.

"Yes. We officially start in our small groups today. I'm so glad we got placed together. And Richard seems pretty cool." Jessica grabbed her water bottle and we made our way to the dining area.

I chose fruit and cereal for breakfast, and we both tucked a peanut butter and jelly sandwich in our backpacks for lunch. The food trucks would come out mid-day and provide us with lunch, but Jessica and I liked to offer that meal to the kids we were working with, and we brought our own sandwiches to hold us over. My small group would be assisting at a dental clinic for the next few days, assisting Dr. Lingy with exams.

"Let's load up," Richard said, and we grabbed our bags and made our way to the bus.

The bus would drop each group at their locations. Ours was the farthest away, and I settled in next to Jessica for the long two-hour commute. The roads were bumpy, and she and I laughed a few times as we bounced out of our seats. I pulled out my mom's journal and read today's entry. I liked to read on the same date as she wrote it all those years ago. Even though she was gone, it somehow made me feel close to her.

May 19th

Dear Journal,

I am working full-time at the news station this summer, and I couldn't be happier about it. One of the news anchors told me that this was where he started. I have so many dreams, and I'm so ready to start chasing them. This is definitely the first one, and it's going better than I ever imagined. Sabrina, the lady who set me up with this internship, said that the producer was singing my praises, and she told me to keep up the good work. I definitely planned on it.

Jack and I are going strong. I can't believe how much I love him. Even when he drives me crazy, which of course he does, I love him. We will get to see each other more often now that I'm on summer break. Even working full-time, it's better than spending late nights in the library.

We have similar hours as he's training at the fire academy, and he's pretty wiped out at the end of the day. But I'm proud of him for chasing his own dreams. Of course, I'll worry once he actually has to run in a burning building, because who wouldn't, right? But we support one another, and I'd never try to stop him from doing what he loves.

I know I'm where I'm supposed to be, and I couldn't be happier. I need to get to work.

Ciao for now,

J.E.

"You two ready to kick ass today?" Richard asked, dropping to sit in the seat in front of us as the bus continued to bobble on the dirt road.

Jonah was asleep beside him with his head resting against the window. He also attended Northwestern with us, and he'd signed on for the summer brigade as well.

"Yeah, I'm excited to break into our small groups today," I said.

"Me too." Jessica leaned forward.

"I spoke to the coordinator, Jade, and we can go this weekend and submit our med-school applications. It's going to be a drive into Tegucigalpa, hopefully there will be Wi-Fi there. So, make sure you have everything completed and ready to upload," Richard said, running a hand through his dark hair. His brown gaze studied me. His white teeth were perfectly straight when he displayed his megawatt smile. He rocked that all-American boy look rather well, and the boy oozed charm.

"Okay, great. Thank you for setting that up. My applications are all ready to submit, so I can go any time."

"How many schools are you applying to?" he asked.

"Six."

"Six? That's not very many. I'm applying to twenty-eight. You're also young since you're graduating early, so you may want to up that number to increase your chances." He smiled, and I straightened in my seat.

"Yeah, I'm pretty set on where I'd like to go, and I'm not *that* young," I said. It came out sounding more defensive than I'd meant it to. The truth was, applying to medical school was expensive. I couldn't ask Dad for more money, because he'd funded my trip to Honduras as it was. Six applications would already be a small fortune, and I'd just have to hope for the best and pray that someone would accept me.

Richard held his hands up in defense. "Sorry, I didn't mean to come off like a dick."

"No, you didn't. Twenty-eight seems like a lot of schools to apply to," I said.

"It's pretty average actually. But you're a rock star, Jade, and I'm sure you could apply to *one* and you'd get in." Richard stared at me with an intensity that made me a little nervous.

Was he flirting with me?

Was I just out of practice with knowing how to read the opposite sex? Seeing as the last thing I was interested in was meeting anyone, I wasn't paying much attention.

"Far from a rock star but thank you."

"Don't you date some famous dude in a band?" he asked, and Jessica choked on her water beside me.

"No. We aren't together anymore."

But thanks for asking—this guy was batting a thousand. Throwing all sorts of salt in my wounds today.

"Ah, good to know," he said with a grin and pushed to his feet to return to the front of the bus.

"Well, that wasn't very subtle. I think he likes you." Jessica chuckled beside me. "He's super cute too."

"Not interested. Feel free to flirt away with him. He's all yours," I said, leaning back and reaching for my phone when it vibrated in my bag. We went in and out of service as we drove to our destination.

CRUZ

Just wanted you to know that I sat through a miserable three-hour session with Dr. Roberts, a.k.a. Dr. Evil. She really is a bit sadistic where I'm concerned. She seems to enjoy torturing me. Anyway, she thinks I should respect your wishes to give you space.

I smiled and rolled my eyes at the same time. Why did I have to love him so much?

How is this you giving me space?

CRUZ

You don't see my ass in Honduras, do you?

I think we should set some boundaries. We can text once a week for now.

CRUZ

For now? Until what??

Until you meet someone, or we both just move on.

CRUZ

I'm not going to meet someone, Jade. What are you on a dating quest in Honduras? I don't want to move on. Are you sure that's what you want?

My chest squeezed. *This* is what I *didn't* want. He had a way of pulling me back in.

Honestly? Yes. I desperately want to move on. But I didn't come here to date. I don't have to be dating someone to move on with my life.

CRUZ

I'm going to change, Jade. No more booze and no more drugs. I'll prove it to you.

My eyes welled, and it angered me that I wanted to believe him. But I couldn't invest in this relationship anymore. It had all but sucked the life from me.

I hope you do. But do it for you, not for me.

CRUZ

I'll do it for us.

> I have to go.

CRUZ
I'll text you in a week. I love you.

I sucked in a breath. He was making it tough to pull away.

> I love you. Goodbye, Cruz.

I turned my phone off and dropped it in my backpack. I swiped at the single tear running down my cheek before Jessica noticed. My chest ached. Everything hurt. It was like ripping off the bandage every time I talked to him. I missed him.

I loved him.

Focus, Jade.

You can do this.

Getting over Cruz Winslow was not going to be easy. But I'd traveled over eighteen hundred miles away to make it happen.

And I was no quitter.

two

. . .

Cruz

"GOOD. You waited the week to reach out to her again. That's a sign of maturity. You're putting her needs before your own," she said.

I stood at the window in Dr. Roberts' office, a.k.a. Dr. Evil, contemplating her words. I dropped down on the brown leather couch facing her. "Yeah. And it fucking sucks. She's pulling away from me and I don't know how to stop it."

"It's not up to you to stop it. Jade needs to make her own decisions. And right now, she's asking you to respect her wishes. She went to Honduras to take part in something bigger than herself. Bigger than the two of you. Let her go and spread her wings, Cruz."

"And if she doesn't come back?"

"Then she doesn't come back. It's something you'll have to live with," she said.

I pushed to my feet again. Aggravation coursing through my veins. I swear Dr. Evil liked to fuck with me on purpose. She got some sort of sick sense of accomplishment out of torturing me. I stared out the window at the lush grass area below. The trees were moving in the breeze and purple and pink blooms lined the walkway leading to the facility.

"That's shitty advice. *It's something I have to live with.* Way to throw in the towel, doc."

She chuckled. "I'm not suggesting you *throw in the towel.* If you love her, you'll give her this time. I know it's painful, but you have to remember why you're in this situation and accept the consequences that have followed *your* actions. She was left for hours on that hotel floor. I'm sure she's questioning a lot of things. It could have ended very differently. The situation has forced her to look at her own mortality. Question her decisions and choices." She leaned back in her chair and her glasses rested on top of her head as she studied me.

"Her decision to be with me?" I said, knowing exactly what she meant.

"Yes. Do you think that's unfair?"

"No. I just wish I could change what happened." I let out a long breath that I hadn't even realized I'd been holding.

"You can't change the past, but you can change what you do moving forward. And that's what you're doing now. But spending two weeks in a program does not make you reformed, Cruz. She needs to see it, and it's going to take time. So, instead of trying to convince her to take you back right now, because that's what *you* want...focus on being the best you can be. For you and for her."

"Fucking fine." What the fuck choice did I have? I ran my fingers over the new tat on my forearm. I'd permanently inked the nail marks that Jade left on my skin. It was a perfect reminder of why I could never go back to that lifestyle. Rock bottom was a dark, lonely place, and I wasn't going back.

She smiled. Which didn't happen often. Probably because she enjoyed seeing me suffer. Like I said, *Dr. Evil.* But unfortunately, she'd proven otherwise so far.

"Good, Cruz. Where do you want to start? What areas of your life do you want to focus on?"

"Well, I'm sober. That's one. And it fucking sucks because I have to feel all this shit. So, I should get some extra credit for that one," I said, with a laugh. "I've been writing a lot. Working on some lyrics. And I was online this morning finding the last two classes that I need to graduate. If I start my courses when I get out of here, I could graduate in December. And I found out I can actually walk at the grad ceremony at Northwestern because I completed the majority of my coursework there."

"Good, Cruz. I think receiving your diploma and attending the ceremony would give you a sense of accomplishment," she said.

"I never cared about that shit before, but graduating has been more of a challenge than I expected, so yeah, I don't mind taking a minute to celebrate it."

"Okay... you've got yourself some solid goals. This is a good start. Focus on *you*, and the rest will come."

"Alright. My brother is on his way, so I better head back to my room."

"Same time tomorrow?" she asked, pushing to her feet.

"Yep," I said, because fuck if I had a choice, but I would keep that to myself. I stepped into the hallway and made my way down to my room.

This place was nice, and I was fortunate that I had the resources to be here. The label had agreed to give the band a thirty-day reprieve from touring. We'd been dealing with a shit ton of drama since Dex left the band and Zach took his place. Dex had given multiple interviews about why he'd left, as if he'd had a choice. He'd claimed that there just wasn't enough talent in our group, and he chose to walk away. Fucking Dex. He failed to mention that he'd hit my girlfriend and left her for dead on the floor when he fled the scene. I fucking hated him. We didn't comment on his departure because I wanted to keep what happened with Jade out of the media. So, it was a good idea for Exiled to lie low right now. And being in this place—it allowed me to catch my breath. There was no press. No fans. No expectations. Aside from the ones I currently had for myself. And getting healthy and getting Jade back was all I cared about.

"Hey, douchebag," Lennon said when I got to my room.

I laughed. I missed him. Hadn't seen him in a few weeks. He looked good. The irony was not lost on me. Lennon was visiting *me* in rehab. I was now the one who had the problem. Never in a million years would I have thought our roles could be reversed. It was important for me to remember just how easy it had been to lose myself.

"What's up. Thanks for coming out. You here for a few hours?" I asked, dropping to sit on the bed when Lennon sat in the chair across from me.

"Yeah, I'm here until tonight."

"How's Bailey?" I asked.

"She's fucking fantastic." He laughed.

I rolled my eyes. My brother was one whipped motherfucker. And I couldn't be happier for him.

"Good. How's Zach doing at rehearsals?"

"Dude, it's so much better. You're going to be a lot happier. The vibe is just different with Dex gone. There's no tension. We should have dumped his ass a long time ago," Lennon said.

"Well, the goal was for me to leave. And obviously now that's not happening, but it was well worth the trade off. I couldn't let that fucker get away with what he did to Jade. No fucking way. And she and I aren't together right now anyway, so staying in the band a little longer isn't the end of the world."

He tilted his head to the side. "So, what's going on with you two? I sent her a text and just told her to be safe in Honduras. I didn't know exactly where you guys stood, but I wanted to let her know I was thinking about her. I'm still fucking pissed about what happened to her."

I pushed to my feet and paced the length of the small room. "I know. I fucking hate Dex. But I fucked up too, and now I have to just hope she'll forgive me eventually. She won't let me text her more than once a week, but she told me she loved me when I saw her at the airport, and when we were texting, so I guess there's hope."

He laughed. "Of course, there's hope. That girl loves your dumb ass. We all know it. But what happened to her was really bad, dude. It's going to take some time, which is good."

"Why is it good?" I narrowed my gaze at him.

"Because it gives you time to pull your shit together."

"You sound just like Dr. Evil. It wasn't so long ago you were the one in a shitstorm," I said, moving back to sit on the bed.

"You're right. And I found my way out, and so will you. You're not nearly as bad off as I was and being the stubborn asshole that you are—it shouldn't be as painful as it was for me. And you have something to work for." He chuckled.

"I'm proud of you," I said, staring at my little brother who was beginning to look more like a man than a boy. He had scruff on his face, and he looked… happy. And healthy.

"Proud of you too, brother. It was a big step coming here. You did the right thing."

"Yeah, thanks."

"So, we had a meeting, and I wanted to fill you in. We're cutting our tour schedule way back this year. I think we did too many shows last year, and the stress of it all took a toll on everyone. We're going to do half as many shows this time around, so we'll be able to spend our downtime in Chicago versus being on the tour bus."

An invisible weight made its way off my shoulders. I could focus on my classes and have some normalcy in my life again. And hopefully, I'd get Jade back in the process.

"That's really good news," I said.

"Agreed. And thank you, Cruz. I know you never wanted any of this, and you sacrificed a lot for me. I'm going to be there for you, you know that, right?"

"Don't go soft on me, asshole. But yes, I know."

"So, what does Jade say when you do get to talk to her?" he asked.

"She thinks we should see other people. She wants space from me. She's probably being hit on by all those nerdy fuckers on the brigade with her."

He laughed. "Dude, she's in Honduras on a medical brigade. It's not the Bachelor."

"She wants me to date, which is not happening."

"And why is that?" he asked.

"She ruined me. My dick is broken. It doesn't like anyone else."

Lennon fell back in the chair in a fit of hysterics. "That's rich. You really love her, don't you?"

"Obviously."

"Then get your shit together, brother. Because it's going to take a lot to win her back, but I know she loves your stupid ass, so you'll figure it out."

"Fuck you, very much."

"Dex reached out to Luke. He had the audacity to ask for a percentage of all our future earnings. Luke has legal on it now," Lennon said.

"Jesus. The dude is batshit crazy. After what he did, he should be sitting in a jail cell. But instead he's pouting that he isn't in the band anymore? He fucking assaulted Jade. He should have gotten a lot more than house arrest."

"We all agree with that. I blocked him because he was blowing up my phone. He's such an asshole," my brother said, studying my reaction.

"He pisses me off." I pushed to my feet and paced around the room.

"So, what do you do now that you can't go get drunk or numb yourself with pills?"

"I sit in this room and wallow in my misery," I said.

"I focused on music when I stopped drinking and getting high. You need to find something that gives you an outlet. Something positive."

"Well, sex is a good outlet, and I happen to be extremely talented at it. But I can't even do that at the moment." I dropped back on the bed and crossed my arms in front of me.

"Find something else, Cruz. Something that's just for you."

"Is Dr. Evil paying you to counsel me when I'm not with her?" I rolled my eyes.

A knock on the door interrupted us. I looked up to see Melody, the girl who runs the front desk.

"Hey, Cruz. Sorry to bother you. You have a visitor, and he wasn't on the schedule, so I wanted to check with you before allowing him back," she said. Her blond hair rested on her shoulders, and she formed a teepee with the tips of her fingers and rested her chin there.

"Who is it?" I asked.

"He says he's your father. Steven Winslow."

"Fuck me," I whispered.

"You don't have to see him. But if you want to, I'll stay right here. We can deal with him together." My brother's eyebrows pinched as he waited for me to answer.

"Yeah. Let's get it over with. Send him back. Thank you."

"What do you think he wants?" Lennon whispered.

Neither of us had spoken to our father since he'd sold bullshit stories to the press about me. He'd blamed my leaving the band on Jade, and he'd paid off Farrah fucking Clearwater to say she'd had sex with me, and I'd forced her to have an abortion. Luckily, Farah hadn't shared my father's twisted plan with the press, and she dropped her claim before it went that far. But it didn't mean my father hadn't made her an offer. The guy was a sick fucker. His world had crumbled due to his own selfish behavior, and he wanted to take everyone down with him.

"I don't know. How the fuck does he know I'm here?" I asked.

"I hired someone to find you," my father said, walking into the room and pulling out the desk chair before dropping to sit.

"You hired someone? Why the fuck do you care where I am?" I barked out a laugh. I mean, the dude tried to destroy me. He tried to destroy my relationship with Jade. And yes, I managed to do the rest myself, but my father is a sadistic motherfucker and I want nothing to do with him.

"Families fight, Cruz. You're both still my sons. I hired a guy to keep an eye on you two and when I realized I could get both my boys in one room, I jumped on a plane, and here I am. See, I'm not all bad," he said as he leaned back in the chair and crossed his feet at the ankles like he owned the place.

The room was suddenly too crowded. What's the saying? Two's company, and three's a crowd. Three was definitely a crowd.

"You have a lot of nerve coming here," I snarled.

"Well, you've both blocked my calls. Your mother isn't speaking to me. You didn't leave me much of a choice." He reached in his pocket and pulled out a flask before tipping his head back and taking a long pull.

Was he for real? Who comes to fucking rehab with a flask? Steven Winslow. That's who.

"I'm sure you can get your buzz on in a lot of other places," Lennon said, glaring at our father.

"Sure. But I'm not the one in the program, so it shouldn't matter. We're paying a lot of money for your sobriety. I'd hope that seeing someone have a drink isn't going to make you slip. If so, I'd say you're wasting your money, or *my* money, right?"

"You're such an asshole." I pushed to my feet and moved to the window. I didn't want a drink. I wanted to get out of this room. Away from this man. "Why. Are. You. Here?"

"Dex reached out to me. Apparently, we're both on your shit list. We have an idea that could be big for Exiled."

Lennon barked out a bitter laugh. "You're fucking serious?"

"There's been a lot of speculation over why he left. Bringing him back would have people waggling their tongues. It would be a media frenzy." His lips turned up in the corners.

"Get the fuck out," I said, walking toward the telephone in the room. I picked it up and spoke into the receiver, "Can you send security to my room, Melody. I need someone to escort my guest out."

Melody told me security would be on their way shortly.

"That's a tad dramatic, Cruz. Just think it over. It would be good press for Exiled. Just looking out for you. Luke's not taking my calls either for some reason, so you might want to remind him who introduced him to you. Don't bite the hand that feeds, right?" My father pushed to his feet.

I moved so close I could feel his breath on my face. "Dex fucked with Jade. He doesn't ever get to come back. And you fucked with everyone, so you don't get to come back either."

"Sobriety is really working for you, son. I think you could use a cocktail right about now." He chuckled and pushed his flask in my face.

An angry laugh escaped. "You think it's hard for me to have booze dangled in my face? You're wrong. I'm not you. I never liked the party. I liked numbing myself to forget where the fuck I came from. But not anymore. So, you can take your flask and your bullshit ideas and get the fuck out."

Security arrived at my door. "Is there a problem, Mr. Winslow?"

The man was speaking to me, but my father answered, "I don't think you want to throw out the guy who's picking up the tab."

"They don't care who pays the bill, daddy dearest. They care about their patient's sobriety. So, they'll have no problem escorting you out of here. I should know. I've been here more than once—you probably don't remember because you never came to visit during *my* stays here," Lennon said, nodding to the security guard.

"I won't put you in an awkward situation," my father said to the dude. "I can see myself out. I'm sure your supervisor wouldn't appreciate getting slapped with a lawsuit. One I could make very public, by the way. Think about my proposition, boys. I'll be in touch." He waltzed out of the room, and the security guard followed our father down the hall.

"Just when I think he can't get any lower—he surprises me." I rolled my eyes and stared out the window.

"Like I said. You need an outlet. You used to love all that martial arts shit when we were young. That's something positive," Lennon said, moving to the window beside me as we watched Dad climb into his waiting vehicle.

"Yeah. I used to be able to kick your ass with one arm tied behind my back." I laughed. "And I did enjoy it. I'll look into that."

"I'm going to call Mom and give her a heads up about Dad coming here. He might try to ambush her as well." Lennon dropped in the chair and phoned our mother.

I pulled out my laptop and Googled MMA trainers in the area. I read the reviews and sent a few emails to inquire about private training sessions. I'd need them to come to me here. This facility had a great gym, as well as outdoor areas that we could utilize.

I pulled out my phone and sent Jade a text. Technically, I was supposed to wait *another* seven days, but since I'd texted her this morning, it was still the same day so I thought it only fair that I could send more than one message.

> I'm getting my shit together. Don't give up on us.

The three little dots danced on the screen before they disappeared, and I tossed my phone on the bed. She'd probably make me wait another seven days before she responded. Patience was not my strong suit.

"Okay, Mom is aware of the situation. Apparently, she has a restraining order against Dad now. He legally can't just show up at her house." Lennon looked pleased with his words.

"Jesus. Our family is so fucked up. We need to remind her that he's not one to follow the rules. He thinks he's above the law. We'd all be wise to remember that," I said.

My phone vibrated on the bed and I reached for it.

MORE JADE

> Don't make promises you can't keep.

> Never. You're the only promise I've ever cared to keep.

Ain't that the fucking truth.

three

. . .

Jade

"YOU WANT TO DO THE HONORS?" Richard asked, and I reached for the last cement brick.

"Yes." I laughed as I pushed up on my tiptoes and set the final cinder block in place.

"Wow. This looks so good. I can't believe we actually built this," Jessica said, walking around the structure.

"It's impressive. Good work. I think we should celebrate tonight. I may or may not have some mini tequila bottles tucked away at the compound." Richard wriggled his brows.

"I'm so down. I could use a little fun," Jessica said.

"What about you? You've been here for six weeks working your ass off, you've submitted your applications to med school, I'd say your due for a little fun." He focused his attention on me. He and I had become friends, and we had a lot in common.

"Sure. I'm in," I said, bending down when Rosa came running toward me.

She crashed into my arms and I hugged her extra tight. Our time with this family was coming to an end, and I wasn't ready to say goodbye to her. Rosa Martinez was five years old and we had a huge language barrier—but we'd somehow managed to form a bond in the days since we'd arrived here to build her family a hygiene station.

"Poto poto ganzo, Jade?" she said, placing a hand on my cheek. She was tiny for her age, with bronzed skin, long dark hair and a beautiful smile.

Poto poto ganzo was the equivalent of duck, duck, goose back home, and it was her favorite game. Rosa, and her older brother Eduardo, would rush home from school each day to help us mix the mescula, the cement we used to seal the bricks in place, and watch as we built the structure.

"Si, mi amor." I smiled and walked to the area where we usually played and dropped down to sit.

Jessica, Richard, Eduardo and a few other members of our group came to join me when Rosa called out, "Poto, poto, ganzo."

I crossed my legs and wiped my hands on my black scrub pants. I studied the blisters and the small cuts covering my palms. They were my battle wounds for the work I'd been doing, and I was beyond proud to be here. Exactly where I needed to be right now.

I'd been thinking a lot about the miscarriage I'd had last year. It was still difficult for me to wrap my head around the fact that I'd been pregnant, and I'd lost the baby before I could even process what was happening. My heart ached for a child I'd never known. For what could have been. Something I wasn't ready for—yet I felt the loss deep in my soul.

"Ganzo," Rosa shouted out in laughter when she tapped the top of my head and took off running.

I hurried to my feet and pretended I was trying to catch her until she took her spot next to Jessica. She smiled up at me, her breaths coming fast and hard, and my chest squeezed.

Yep. I was exactly where I needed to be right now.

———

After I got out of the shower, I towel dried my hair and brushed it away from my face. It felt good to be clean, even if the water was ice cold. I slipped on a pair of shorts and a tank top and slathered my skin in lotion before applying more bug spray.

"Everyone's outside playing soccer. And did I mention there's tequila involved?" Jessica called out from the doorway.

I laughed. "Okay. I'll be right out."

"See you out there," she said before walking away.

I looked to see if we had any reception so I could check my emails. I wanted to make sure I didn't miss anything from the AAMC, the place I'd submitted my medical school apps, and our Wi-Fi was shoddy, so I checked often. So far, so good. It looked like my application was complete, and I was good for now. I sent Dad a quick text to tell him I loved him. I texted him every other day as promised to let him know I was doing okay.

A new text from Cruz popped up. It had been another week. He'd stuck to the plan to text weekly and not daily over the last few weeks, which was very *un-Cruz* of him. Patience had never been his strong suit. He'd finished his thirty days in rehab and was back on tour with Exiled. I was impressed he'd completed the program, but I kept our texts very much on the surface. He tried to take things deeper, but I didn't want to go there. He surprised me by respecting my wishes and not pushing.

CRUZ

Hey. How are you? What did you build
today? How's Rosa?

I sucked in a breath. Almost like I could feel him right here with me. There was a dull ache in my chest that hadn't left since the day I'd come to Honduras.

I dropped to sit on Jessica's lower bunk and leaned my back against the wall.

> Rosa's great. We only have one more day to finish our work for the Martinez family, so I'll be sad to say goodbye. We completed their hygiene station today. I'll send you a pic. It looks great. How are you? How's the band? Lennon? Adam? Are you still doing the MMA training now that you're on the road?

I had so many questions for him. I shouldn't ask. I shouldn't care. But I did. And I said we could be friends for now. And friends care about one another, right? Right.

CRUZ

> Lennon's still an asshole but he's doing great. He and Bailey are nauseatingly in love most of the time. You would love seeing him like this. Adam is good. Tory has been traveling with us, so that's cool. Yes, I'm training a lot. Five days a week. We brought our trainer, Gio, on tour, so everyone is working out now. LOL. I started another class and should graduate in December.

I swiped at the tear running down my cheek. I was proud of him. But it hadn't been that long. He needed time to get himself together and so did I. But it was so easy to fall back into needing him. And wanting him. I wouldn't allow myself to go there. I closed my eyes and remembered how it felt to wake up on that hotel room floor. After I'd been unconscious for hours.

Hours.

I could have died.

And Cruz was right there, in the next room. No. I needed to stay strong.

> That's amazing, Cruz. I'm happy for you. For all of you. How's your mom doing?

CRUZ

She's doing really well. She does yoga every day and she seems a lot happier. My dad is holding up their divorce, of course he doesn't want to make it easy on her. He's still an asshole.

He really is. He's put her through a lot. Please give her my best.

CRUZ

Your dad is really missing you. I was in town a couple days ago, and I met him for lunch. It was great to see him.

Yeah. He told me he saw you. How was he?

They'd been close when Cruz and I were together, and my dad had taken on a fatherly role with him.

CRUZ

Really good. I think he and Sara are getting pretty serious. He talked about her a lot.

My chest squeezed. I wanted my dad to find someone, and I loved Sara.

Yeah. I think it's been a long time coming. That was nice of you to go to lunch with him. I'm sure he appreciated it.

CRUZ

You know I love your dad. He's as salt of the earth as you get. Just like you.

"Jade, you coming out?" Richard peeked his head in the doorway.

I jumped off the bed and hurried to my feet. I don't know why I felt guilty taking a minute to myself, but I did. There wasn't a lot of alone time here at the compound.

"Yeah, I'll be right there."

He studied my face. "You okay?"

"Yep. I'm good. See you in a minute."

He walked away, and I typed out a quick message.

> He's the best. I hope I got some of that goodness from him. I need to go. There's a soccer game going on outside, and they're one man down.

CRUZ

> Okay, I love you, Jade.

My eyes watered and I took in a deep breath to try to push away the enormous lump in the back of my throat. Why did this always happen?

> I love you too. Bye.

It was the one thing I couldn't deny him. I loved him. I didn't say I loved him *more*, which had always been our shtick. I couldn't go there. But I also couldn't deny how much I loved him. But I could protect my heart from getting hurt again. The love was there. It always would be. It didn't mean it was good for me to act on it. It wasn't. And I wouldn't. But I could still feel it. I could still feel everything about Cruz.

I dropped my phone in my backpack and jogged outside. Back to my reality. My new normal. I shook off the sad feeling weighing me down and ran to the end of the field where Jessica and Richard stood.

"It's about time. Come on. Get in here. We're getting our asses kicked," Richard said. He raised his T-shirt to wipe his forehead, putting his chiseled abs on display for everyone to see.

I caught the ball with my foot when he kicked it to me, and I charged down the field. Well, I tried. Someone from the other team stole the ball about halfway down the grassy field and ran in the opposite direction, before scoring a goal.

"Moore, you were supposed to be our ringer," Richard bellowed out in laughter.

"What can I say. I'm better at school than I am at sports."

"You don't say," he said, rumpling the top of my head with his hand.

We played for another hour, and it felt good to relax and have some fun.

We grabbed dinner, and then a group of us settled out on the grassy field on a few blankets and passed around the mini bottles of tequila from Richard. Jessica moved to sit beside Dean. He was in our small group, and they'd been flirting for the last month. She liked him. She wriggled her brows at me from across the circle and I laughed. The area was lit by a few overhead lanterns, and the stars twinkled above.

I wondered what Cruz was doing. I wondered if he was dating at all. I told him he should date multiple times. I didn't want him to wait for me, because I didn't know if I'd ever be able to trust him again. I wanted to see what he did in our time apart. If he could stay sober. If he could be on tour without numbing himself to deal with the pressure.

"So, you and your boyfriend broke up before you came here?" Richard leaned close to me, so only I could hear him.

"Oh, yeah. We broke up before I left."

"How long were you guys together? I remember hearing he was some famous dude, but I don't really follow the tabloids. My room-mate pointed you out once on campus and said you dated the lead singer of a band."

I nodded. A lump formed again in my throat. It was still painful to talk about.

Painful to think about.

"We dated for a year and a half. He's the lead singer of Exiled."

"That's a long time. I can't picture you being a groupie," he said with a laugh.

I rolled my eyes. "I wasn't. I was with him before they went on tour. It's a long story."

"But you're single now?" His heated gaze locked with mine. He was cute. And charming. And super smart. But I wasn't ready for anything. A part of me wished I was. I knew it would be the easiest way to move on.

"I guess you could say that," I said, my voice just above a whisper. "But you could also say that my heart still belongs to someone else."

"I get that. I had a tough break up with my long-time girlfriend last year. We'd been together for years, and it was tough for a long time." He leaned back and picked at a few blades of grass.

"Why'd you guys break up?"

"She cheated on me. With one of my best friends," he said with a shrug.

"Oh, wow. That had to be tough. I can't imagine."

"Yeah. It sucked. But you get over it. Time has a way of healing. Did you get hurt in your break-up?" he asked.

"Yep. I think we both did." I turned my head and looked out at the sugarcane fields. I wished he'd change the subject.

"I hear you. Well, you know the easiest way to get over a broken heart?"

I faced him again and studied his features. Dark brows and full lips. Richard wasn't hurting for female attention. I wasn't sure why he was wasting his time on me. I hadn't put out any signals that I was interested.

"No. But I have a feeling you're going to tell me." I laughed.

"Meeting someone new. Someone charming and smart, maybe? Good looking, even," he said, and his lips turned up in the corners and he wriggled his brows.

I chuckled and squirmed a bit. I needed to be really clear. "You are all of those things, Richard, trust me. But I'm not looking to meet anyone. *At all.* So, you'd be wasting your time here."

"You know what else they say?" He took another swig of the little tequila bottle before handing it to me.

"What's that?"

"All good things are worth the wait," he said, leaning over to kiss my cheek. It was sweet. *He* was sweet. I just wasn't looking for sweet. Because I wasn't looking for anything. All I hoped to find in Honduras was myself. That's about all I was up for these days.

"Damn, that was a journey," Richard said, handing me the canteen full of water.

It was blisteringly hot outside today. We drove almost two hours to get here. We'd hiked out to a water pipeline for a new hygiene station we were building, and the guide led us through four miles of rough terrain to get there.

I guzzled some water and splashed a little on my face. "Yeah, that was a trek."

"I can't believe we need to hike all the way back." Jessica came up behind me and laughed.

"Right? Drink. We need to stay hydrated."

"Yes, *Dr. Moore*," Jessica said before chugging the water.

Our guide made this journey daily, as he worked on the water system out here. I had a whole new respect for him now after doing it myself. He showed us where the water source was coming from for the rural village we would be spending the next two weeks in.

We started our walk back, and I maneuvered the rocky, jagged path beneath my feet. Jessica walked in front of me beside Dean. They had something going on, and she said she liked him a lot.

"What's happening there?" Richard whispered, so only I could hear, as he hiked beside me and we trailed in the back of the group.

"They like each other. It's cute." I shrugged.

"You still talking to Cruz once a week?"

"Yep." I studied the ground beneath my feet so I didn't trip.

"So, he's sticking to your rules. Impressive. You can even tame a rock star, huh?"

I slapped his arm. "No. No one could tame Cruz. Nor would I want to. But yeah, he's sticking to the once a week deal."

"So, what happened there? Did he cheat on you?"

I came to a stop. Why was he pressing this?

"What? No. Why do you want to know?" I huffed.

He ran a hand through his hair. "Because I like you, Jade. And I haven't met anyone that I liked this much in a long time. Not since Ella, at least, who I also sort of hate."

We both laughed, and I let out a long breath. "You know I think you're great. I'm just not ready to date anyone."

"But if you were?" He wriggled his brows. It was clearly his signature move.

He really was good looking. I noticed all the girls back at the compound flirting with him, and I hoped he'd actually take interest in one of them to take the pressure off me.

"If I were? What are you asking?"

"If you were ready to date, would you date *me*?"

My cheeks heated, and I turned and started walking again. "I don't know, Richard, I honestly haven't thought about it."

"Do you find me attractive?"

"Oh my gosh. You're really going to do this?" I laughed.

"I am. We're friends, right? Answer the question. Do you find me attractive?"

I stopped again and studied him. "Obviously you're attractive."

He fist-pumped the sky, and we both started walking again.

"Do you find me intellectually stimulating?" He bumped my shoulder with his.

"Intellectually stimulating? How old are you?" I laughed. "And obviously you're very intelligent. You did get the same score as me on your MCAT."

"You saw my MCAT score?"

"Please. You laid it right in front of me. You wanted me to see it," I teased, but it was the truth.

"Okay, fine. So, you've met your match intellectually. Do you like spending time with me?"

"Richard. Oh my gosh. Yes. Obviously. We're friends," I huffed, stumbling a bit on a rock.

He caught my forearm and helped steady me. "See. We're practically dating now. We've got everything but the sex."

I stopped and gasped. "What? We've never even kissed. We're not dating. We're friends."

He leaned forward and kissed me. It was soft and sweet. I pulled away after a few seconds, just as his tongue tried to enter where it wasn't welcome.

"No. We're not doing this." I stormed ahead of him.

"Don't be like that, Jade. Are you going to try to say you didn't feel anything? Because I did. I liked it. And I think you did, too. But you're too guilt-ridden over a guy who doesn't give two shits about you."

I whipped around and he almost slammed into me. I pointed my finger in his face and hissed, "Don't you dare talk about him. You know nothing about Cruz."

I walked the rest of the way in silence. Was there truth in his words, even if he got it wrong. Was I afraid to like someone else? The kiss wasn't bad, but it wasn't anything like kissing Cruz. Nothing would ever compare.

But it was pleasant.

And pleasant wasn't awful.

And most importantly, pleasant was safe.

four

. . .

Cruz

WE FINISHED our set and I dropped down on a stool backstage after a long show. My voice was raspy, and my throat felt dry as I wiped my brow with the hem of my T-shirt.

"Nice job tonight, Cruz," Luke said.

"Thanks. I think they like the new shit we tried out." I'd written a lot of new music since coming back on tour.

Writing sober was different.

Raw.

Real.

And full of emotion.

"You've got a gift for songwriting," Lennon said before he chugged a water.

"Says my brother."

"Says someone who appreciates music," he said, wrapping his arms around Bailey's middle and resting his chin on her shoulder.

"Dude, I dig that last song," Zach said as he dropped down on the couch beside Adam.

"Yeah, Lennon killed it with the music. It came out better than I expected. I still think you should start trying to sing a few." I studied our newest member of the band. I wanted him to start singing as well, so I could transition out easier after this year. He could sing and play the electric guitar. The dude was beyond talented.

"Give me a few weeks to get my feet wet and let the crowd get used to me. I think they'd pelt me with tomatoes if I tried to step in your shoes right now," Zach said with a laugh.

"Please. They'd pelt you with bras and panties."

"Alright, we'll give it a try at the next show. Maybe we can bust one out together."

"Okay. I'm down for that," I said.

"There're a few chicks that want to meet up after the show. You want to put yourself back out there?" Zach asked. He was tame in comparison to how we'd all been when we'd first come on tour with the booze and the partying. He'd hooked up with a few chicks, but nothing like Dex.

"Nah, but thanks, dude. I'm going to chill tonight."

The truth was, I had no interest in anyone but Jade. The connection I shared with her was unlike anything I'd ever felt before. There was something linking us. Something I couldn't explain to anyone, including myself. And yeah, I'd fucked up really bad. But the one thing I could do to show her I'd changed, was to stay sober and to keep my dick in my pants. Sure, she'd told me multiple times to date. But for some reason it felt like a test. And this was one test that I wasn't going to fail.

I asked her if she'd met anyone the last time we texted, six days ago, because she seemed so insistent that I date. She told me that she kissed someone. I wanted to kill the fucker. It wasn't rational. We weren't together. She'd been very clear about it. Hell, she wouldn't communicate with me more than once a week at this point. I asked her if she wanted to date him, and she said she didn't know. She didn't know what she wanted. I couldn't wait for her to get back home so I could see her. And touch her. And show her that I had my shit together now. That what happened before would never happen again.

We all went to get a late dinner, which was more like a midnight breakfast. Our trainer, Gio, traveled with us now, which was cool. I was working out more than I ever had before and feeling good.

———

I dropped my bag on the mat and took off to run a few laps around the gym. I knew the routine, and I liked it. Lennon, Adam, and Zach were also working out with Gio, but I preferred doing one-on-one sessions with him. No distractions.

He spent the next hour and a half kicking my ass with weights and drills. My legs were heavy, arms weak, and I felt fucking good. I loved pushing my body to the brink.

"Nice, Cruz. You want to do a few rounds in the ring today? They have a guy that needs a sparring partner. Want to try out these new skills of yours on an actual person?" Gio studied my reaction.

"Yeah, sure."

He whistled over to another trainer and walked me toward the octagon. Gio was a badass. He lived by his own words and pushed himself as hard as he pushed his clients in the gym. His dark hair was short, in a buzz cut. He wore a ripped-up T-shirt with a colorful sleeve of tats decorating one arm. Oranges and reds and blues bleeding together, telling a story that only he knew. I'd admired his ink when we first met, and he said it was a reminder of where he'd been, and where he was now. I didn't push it. The dude was intense, and I liked him. There was no bullshit where he was concerned.

I sparred for the next fifteen minutes with Gio shouting out tips from beside the ring. We'd been matched well, and we each took the other down a few times.

We pounded fists at the end. The dude I sparred with studied me. His name was Simon and he was a big deal around the gym. "Nice work. You new?"

"I've been at it a few weeks, yeah."

"Fuck," he said with a laugh, and raised a brow at his trainer who stood beside Gio. "I've been at it for years. I'm probably the best fighter in this gym."

"You *are* the best fighter in this gym," his trainer interrupted with a chuckle.

"I'm not so sure, brother. This guy just held his own against me. I wasn't holding anything back." He nodded at me before climbing out of the ring.

It felt good to be focused on something. Working at something. Not controlled by booze and pills and all the other bullshit. Not a slave to something that was destroying my life. I hadn't realized how bad it had gotten until I'd stepped away. That's the thing about addiction. It sneaks up on you when you least expect it. I rubbed the pad of my thumb over Jade's fingernail marks on my forearm.

Always a reminder.

I guess in a way I was like Gio. My ink told a story too. Of a place I'd been and would never return.

"Nice job, buddy." Gio clapped my shoulder and we walked over to the mats.

"Thanks."

"How'd you like sparring?"

"It was cool. You have to be alert and on your game, that's for damn sure," I said, wiping my face with a towel.

"No kidding. But you've got natural talent. If you ever want to quit the band, you could fight for a living." He smirked.

"Nah, I like working out with you, and I don't mind sparring at all. But I like that I do it as an outlet, not as another thing I *have to do.* That's why I don't work out with the guys. This is something just for me and I don't want to share it with anyone."

I realized in that moment that so much of my life was shared. My private life had been splashed all over the tabloids and social media. Everyone knew I'd gone to rehab, and hell, I didn't give a shit. But at some point, I needed something that was just mine. What Jade and I shared—it was just ours. Sure, our relationship had been scrutinized, but she'd remained very private, and she'd always protected what we had. I hadn't realized the importance of that until now. Now that there was a gaping hole in my life that I couldn't fill.

"I get that, man. Good for you. That's how it should be." Gio handed me a bottle of water, and I downed it in one swig.

"Are you meeting the guys now?" I asked.

"Yeah. They don't last as long as you, so I'll be lucky to have them for an hour." He crossed his arms over his chest and chuckled.

"Alright. I'll catch you tomorrow," I said, and we pounded fists.

I headed back to my place and grabbed a shower. It was nice having our home base back in Chicago versus the tour bus. We didn't have long stints at home, but I'd take what I could get. We were heading out for a two-week tour of back-to-back shows. We'd agreed to a European tour in the fall, but it was half the shows we'd played last year, so it would be easier to manage. And I'd allow myself time to adapt to the time change, instead of finding ways to sleep when my body wasn't ready to. I'd learned a lot from Dr. Roberts, and we still Skyped three days a week. Leaving rehab to go on tour was not the path most doctors would recommend, but she was working with me to make this work. The truth was, Lennon didn't drink, and Adam rarely drank. But it hadn't bothered me to be around booze, which surprised everyone. I don't believe I was physically dependent on alcohol, but I believe I used alcohol to cope with the areas in my life that I didn't want to deal with. And though I didn't crave alcohol, it was something that I'd always have to watch when faced with things that made me uncomfortable.

I pulled up in front of the coffee shop and jogged inside.

Jack Moore pushed to his feet and gave me that manly half-dude-hug. He patted me on the back before we both slipped into the booth across from one another. The man supported me far more than my own father ever had.

"You're looking good, Cruz," he said.

We'd formed a friendship when Jade and I were dating, and it hadn't stopped after she and I broke up. After I'd left his daughter on the floor unconscious, he hadn't turned his back on me. He'd forgiven me, but as he reminded me many times—he'd never forget. Neither would I. And I'd forever be indebted to him. Not only for being the father of the only girl I'd ever loved, but for stepping up and taking on a fatherly role when I needed it most.

I'd asked to meet with him right before Jade left for Honduras. I wanted to apologize to him for the role I'd played in her accident and tell him that I was going to rehab. At first, he'd been cold and distant. Hell, I'd expected nothing less. Disappointing Jack was almost as bad as disappointing Jade. They were just—good people. I hated letting them down. But he'd appreciated me owning what had happened and seeking help for my addiction. Hell, by the end of our meeting, he'd been the one to give me her flight info so that I could see her before she left for three months.

"Thanks, I feel good."

The waitress approached our table and we both placed our orders.

"You look like you're all muscle. You still doing that MMA training?"

"Yep, working with a trainer five days a week. It's nice having an outlet that demands me to be coherent." I winked before pouring three packets of sugar in my black coffee.

"Jesus. Do you have enough sugar in there?" He shook his head with disbelief.

"Hot and sweet, just like I like my women," I said with a smirk.

"I don't need to know how hot you think my daughter is. But I agree, she's pretty damn sweet," he said with a laugh.

"Yep. She's the best."

"So, what's happening there? She told me you text her every week."

"She only *lets* me text her once a week," I said.

"Ah, Jade does like her rules. Just stay the course. Time has a way of healing."

"I hope you're right. I think there's some dude there that's into her. I fucking hate him," I said, taking a bite of my blueberry muffin.

Jack's laugh turned into a cough and he paused to drink his water. "I don't think it's anything serious."

She told her father about this guy? Maybe it was more serious than I thought. I didn't want to put Jack in an uncomfortable situation, as he was Jade's father, so I wouldn't grill him. Though it took everything in me not to pelt him with a multitude of questions.

"Not much I can do about it. I'm the reason we're in this position."

"This is good for you, Cruz. You're learning new ways to deal with jealousy and challenging situations. Look at you. You're sitting here eating a muffin and talking it through. That's progress, son."

When Jack Moore calls me son—it means something to me. When my father says it, it's never had any substance behind it. But with Jack, it's different.

"I hate it. And I hate him. But I won't make you tell me everything you know, because that's not fair to you. Unless you feel compelled to tell me what she told you about him?" Apparently, I wasn't as mature as I liked to believe.

He smiled. "You aren't actually asking me to betray my daughter, are you?"

"Only if you're comfortable with it," I said with a smirk.

He barked out another laugh. "*Never*. But I'll tell you this. I really don't know anything. I don't think it's anything serious. But I do think Jade wants you both to take some space, date other people— you're young, and you've been through a lot. You know what my wife always used to say?"

"What?"

"It was her mantra when we first met," he said, wiping at his eyes with nostalgia. "She'd always say, *if it's meant to be, it'll happen*. She said it when we'd apply for jobs, when we wanted to have a baby and when we struggled with making decisions. And I've come to believe it. You can't change the past, so it's out of your control right now. So, just keep working on you, just like you've been doing. Let Jade figure things out and see what happens."

"You know patience is not my thing, right?"

"You don't say?" He chuckled.

"She sounds good. I think she's where she needs to be," I said.

The place was buzzing. Loud chatter filled the space, and the door chimed every time it opened, which was often. Our waitress stopped by to refill our coffee, and I dumped in a few more packets of sugar while Jack rolled his eyes. A few people gaped when they walked past our table, but I kept my eyes trained on Jack, and they moved along.

"Yeah. So, are we still good to have that little welcome home party for her at the firehouse?" I asked.

"Yes. Plan on it. You sure you're going to be in town?"

"Positive. Lennon, Adam, and Luke want to be there too. So, Zach will be there by default." I chuckled.

"How's that going? You really think he's going to be able to replace you at the end of the year?"

"I do. He's a good guy. They can actually get by with just three dudes if they wanted to, but they may bring someone in on air guitar to keep it a four-man band."

"And you're ready to leave all that behind?"

"Yeah. I mean, I'll keep writing lyrics for Exiled. That's what I like most. But I'm ready to be in one place. I'm over the long hours and the travel. The press. The lack of anonymity."

"I hear that. And what about graduation. What's happening there?"

"I should be walking in December."

He smiled and shook his head. "That's great. I don't know many rock stars out there pursuing their education."

"Thanks."

"Are your folks going to come for the ceremony?"

I covered my laugh with a cough. "Probably not. I mean, who knows. My mom is in a different place now. Maybe she'll want to come. My dad would not attend a graduation commencement unless it was a media opportunity. But I don't give a shit about that. That's not why I did it. I did it for myself. I don't need anyone there."

"Well, I'd like to be there. Hell, I wouldn't miss it."

My chest squeezed. Being sober sucked. It made me feel all sorts of shit I wasn't used to feeling. "It's not necessary."

"I'm not going because I think it's necessary. I'm going because I'm proud of you."

I looked up to meet his dark gaze. There was no humor there. "Thanks, Jack."

"You don't need to thank me, Cruz. Regardless of what happens with you and Jade, I consider you part of the family. You know, I grew up similarly to you. I don't know if I've ever told you that?"

"Really? Your dad was a rich, asshole?"

He laughed. "No. Just an asshole. Actually, a drunk, broke, asshole.

It's why I went into firefighting versus going to college. I mean, I wanted to be a firefighter, don't get me wrong. But I also didn't have four years to attend college and figure out what I wanted to do."

"What about your mom?" I asked, sipping my coffee.

"My mom was a mess. I think my dad broke her heart. She spiraled pretty bad right around the time that I went into the fire department. She lives in Florida now with her latest boyfriend. She wasn't around much when Jade was young, and after I lost Jaqueline, all of my attention went to Jade. So, I know what it's like to have parents who don't celebrate you. Or even show up for you. But it doesn't mean you can't accomplish what you set your mind to. That's up to you."

"What happened to your father?"

"He drank himself to death. He walked out on my mom when I was really young, so I didn't really know him."

I was surprised that Jack hadn't had the perfect childhood. I guess everyone had their baggage.

"I'm sorry to hear that. But look what a good dad you turned out to be," I said, surprised at where this conversation had taken us.

"It's all part of the journey. If you get knocked down, you just need to get back up. Decide what you want and go after it."

"I can do that."

"I believe you are, son."

I do too.

And I knew exactly what I wanted.

Now I just had to figure out how to get it.

five

. . .

Jade

"YOU'RE REALLY GOING to make me wait until Friday?" Richard asked.

He sat in the aisle seat, Jessica was in the middle and I sat next to the window. Jessica kept turning around to talk to Dean who sat in the row behind us. I begged her to let me sit beside the window, claiming it would help my motion sickness. But the truth was—I needed space from Richard.

He was great—but relentless. He wanted to take me on an official date, and I'd spent the entire summer turning him down. I'd finally agreed to go to dinner with him on Friday because I had a goal that when I arrived home from Honduras, I would be more... I don't know, *over Cruz*. I feared that as soon as I saw him, I would return to old habits. And it was too soon. He'd been sober for a few months, but he was still on tour with Exiled, and he needed time.

And so did I.

I had encouraged him to date. As much as it would hurt to see him with someone else, seeing it would force me to move on. And I needed to move on. I didn't know if I could trust Cruz again. We hadn't seen one another since the airport three months ago. We hadn't even talked. We'd only texted once a week. Nothing too deep.

I'd insisted we remain friends for now. But what did that even mean? I knew he'd seen my father a few times, and I was glad they'd had one another while I was gone. Dad was picking me up from the airport, and Cruz was on tour. I probably wouldn't see him for a few weeks when he returned to Chicago.

It would be better for me to stay away from him. I was desperate to stop loving this boy, but it had proved impossible. The distance hadn't made me love him any less. Because how do you cut off half of your heart? How do you shut out the other half of your soul? You don't. But this was life or death for me. Loving Cruz Winslow nearly cost me everything. And I'd have to learn to function without him. Desperate times called for desperate measures. Keeping my distance, and forcing myself to move on, was my best chance at survival.

"We have a class together. I'll see you before Friday." I stared out the window as we prepared for landing. I thought about Ponch, and all the times I'd assisted him landing Cruz's father's plane.

I thought about Cruz.

And everything ached.

Three months later, and I still ached for him.

They say time heals, but my wounds—they were going to take even more time. Maybe a lifetime. I hadn't healed the way I'd hoped I would. But stepping away from my life for the summer allowed me to see things more clearly. I wanted to focus on school and remove outside stress from my life. I had no room for blazing fires, and miscarriages, and summers on tour with a rock band, and paparazzi, and crazy bandmates attacking me, and boyfriends I couldn't trust.

A boyfriend I couldn't trust.

That was the big deal breaker.

"You're going to miss me more than you think," Richard said.

That's what he kept telling me. And you know what? I hoped he was right. It would be easy to date Richard. No drama. He didn't party an excessive amount, he was good looking, very smart, and fun. I didn't know why I couldn't get there with him, but it wasn't for lack of effort. I'd agreed to go to dinner because I wanted to give him a chance.

"I feel like the host of the bachelor. Do you want me to give her a rose?" Jessica said, busting out in a fit of giggles.

I laughed. "I'm sure I'll miss you, Richard."

"I don't give up easily, Jade."

Clearly. I studied his handsome features. His dark hair curled on the ends, his jawline was chiseled to perfection, his angular nose made him look distinguished and his dark brown eyes topped off his look. Women stared at him everywhere we went. I wished I could see him that way. Of course, I found him attractive, but was I attracted to him? I didn't think so. We'd kissed once. And it had been enough. I told him not to try it again until I gave him a green light. Hadn't happened yet. But I'd made sure to mention the kiss to Cruz. I wanted him to know I was moving on.

But had I really?

Thankfully the flight attendant's voice came over the speaker to let us know it was time to prepare for landing.

Thank god.

I was over this flight and this conversation. I was excited to see Dad. And I couldn't wait to take a hot bath. I hadn't had a bath in three months. Only cold showers.

We went through customs and I fought Richard for my bag. "Thanks, but I've got it."

Two girls, Stacy and Remy, who were part of our brigade but had been in a different small group from ours, sauntered over.

"Hey, Richard. Happy to be home?"

Oh, hey. Don't mind me standing here beside him.

"Yes and no. Not sure I'm ready for everything to change," he said, glancing over at me.

I let out a long breath as his heated gaze made me uncomfortable. "Okay, well I'll see you guys later."

I waved at all three of them and started my trek to go find Dad. I sent him a text to let him know I was heading out of the terminal. Richard jogged up beside me.

"Hold up, Jade. Was that jealousy I detect?" he asked.

"Jealous of what? What are you talking about?" I laughed.

"Stacy and Remy, obviously." He winked at me.

"I'm just happy to be home and I'm anxious to see my dad. I like Stacy and Remy. I have no idea why they ignored me back there."

"They think we're together, and they're obviously not happy about it."

I came to a stop. "What? Why in the world would they think we're together?"

"Remy likes me. I told her I was into you. She obviously assumed the feelings were mutual." He laughed. He was so cocky and arrogant sometimes. And other times he was down to earth and humble. I didn't have a good beat on this guy. Even after three months of spending so much time together.

"*Okay*. Who's picking you up?" I asked.

"My parents are here," he said.

As we made our way to the waiting crowd, I searched for Dad. He hadn't responded to my text yet. Out of my peripheral, I saw movement and turned.

"Hey," a familiar voice said.

All the air left my lungs in a whoosh. My legs trembled and I struggled to stay upright.

Cruz Winslow.

"Hey. What are you doing here?" I asked, completely flustered.

Wow. He'd filled out. His shoulders were broad and muscular. He looked—gorgeous.

Beautiful.

Perfect.

My heart raced and I wiped my sweaty palms on my pant legs.

"I convinced your dad to let me pick you up. I'm taking you straight to the firehouse." His gaze searched mine before he reached out to pull me in for a hug.

I was wrapped in a cocoon of Cruz Winslow, and it felt damn good.

Like I was home.

I don't know when I'd dropped my bags, but I did, and my hands wrapped around his middle and I hugged him tight. I pulled back, my fingers settling on his chest, meandering over all his hardness.

Someone cleared their throat from behind me and I stepped back.

"Oh, my gosh. I'm so sorry. This is, um," I said, and I had a complete brain malfunction and forgot his name. Hell, I couldn't remember my own name right now.

He laughed before extending a hand. "I'm Richard."

Cruz studied him before slowly lifting his hand. "Do you go by *Dick*... or Richard?"

Richard smirked. "Ah, you must be the rock star. Well, if things go my way, I'm guessing you'll want to call me *Dick*. See you Friday, Jade."

He adjusted his bag over his shoulder and winked before walking away.

Awkward.

Cruz leaned down and picked up my bag and my backpack. "You ready?"

"Yes. Of course." I was still in shock that he was here. In person.

We made our way outside, and he reached for my hand and interlaced our fingers as he led me through the crosswalk. Just the simple touch of his skin against mine had my body reacting in crazy ways. I was hot. And flustered. When he pulled his hand away and tossed my bags in his car, I missed his touch already. We both slipped inside.

"Hey," he said, looking at me as he started the engine.

"Hey. So how did you get my dad to agree to this? I didn't think you were going to be in town."

"We're friends, right? Why wouldn't I come see you? I didn't think you'd mind," he said.

I studied him. Was he messing with me? "Of course, we are. I just didn't know you'd be here."

"I wanted to be here. I missed you, More Jade."

"I missed you too." The words slipped out before I could stop them.

"So, is that the guy? Are you dating him now? Did I mess things up for you?"

He tried to keep it light, but I saw the concern on his face. The tic in his jaw. But it wasn't my job to rescue Cruz right now. This was exactly what I was worried about.

Old habits die hard.

"I'm not dating him. I agreed to have dinner with him Friday."

I waited for the jealous rage. The anger. The overreaction. It never came. He seemed completely calm. Who was this boy sitting beside me? He was as confident as ever, but he appeared calmer now. More mature, maybe?

"Okay, good. I wouldn't want to mess anything up for you," he said, glancing over at me before returning his eyes to the road.

I studied his profile. He looked incredible. Healthy. Gorgeous. "Wow, that MMA fighting is really paying off for you, huh? You look really good."

"Thanks. I like it. You'll have to meet Gio, my trainer. He lives in the city, but he tours with us now."

"Are you back in Chicago for long?"

"Nope. We head out tomorrow. I moved things around so I could be here tonight. But we're doing a lot fewer shows this year. Our home base is here now, not on a tour bus. It'll be much more manageable."

I squirmed in my seat at the thought of him being around more. I couldn't breathe. And was it unusually hot in here? I fiddled with the nobs on his dashboard. "Is the heat on?"

He laughed. "Nope. The AC's on high."

I put the window all the way down and pushed my head outside for more air. Being in these close quarters with him had all my alarm bells going off. We were on the freeway and my hair was whipping all over the place. But he was too close. It was too much. And I'd just gotten here. I squeezed my eyes closed and thought about the day I woke up on the floor in the hotel room. I reminded myself that I needed to yield where Cruz was concerned. I couldn't rely on blind faith anymore.

He tugged at my hand and laughed, shouting over the wind thrashing through the interior, "Get in here. What are you doing?"

"Sorry. They didn't have a lot of wind in Honduras. I missed it."

He chuckled before pulling in front of the firehouse and turning to face me. A sexy smile spread across his face as his gaze zoned in on my chest. I looked down to see what he was staring at. And *oh my*. My body really was reacting to his nearness. Betraying me like a married man in a whore house. Let's just say someone had her headlights on—scratch that. I had my floodlights on *full beam*, and my fitted white T-shirt did nothing to help the situation. I used both hands to cover my boobs and bit down hard on my bottom lip. Jesus. I was not prepared for this.

"Did you get new nipples in Honduras?" He laughed.

I buried my face in my hands. "Friends don't talk about nipples, Winslow."

"Friends don't get hard nipples when they see one another either, More Jade."

"Don't flatter yourself. My body is adapting to a new climate."

He stepped out of the car and came around and opened my door. "Is that so?"

"It is so."

"Okay, well I'd turn the headlights off before we go inside and see your father." He stared down at me with a playful smirk.

"What? How am I supposed to turn them off?"

"Don't ask me. I'm pretty fucking sure I'm the guy who turned them on." He reached for my hand and helped me out of the car.

"You are not. *I* turned them on. And *I* can turn them off." I pulled the neck of my shirt away from my body and blew down toward my chest with a few huffs. Maybe they just needed to cool down.

"I don't think that's going to do it. They seem to like that." He zeroed in on my boobs again, and I started sweating profusely.

"Stop looking at them," I hissed.

"You want me to help you out? Maybe I could top you off or something? Get the girls to calm down?" He leaned forward, invading my space. His warm breath tickled my cheeks. His lips so close to mine I had to close my eyes in order to focus.

"No," I said, pushing him away from me.

He rested his back against the car and crossed his legs at the ankles while he stared at me with a teasing grin on his face. "Let me know if I can be of service."

I squeezed my eyes shut. "Oh my gosh. Please stop talking for a minute."

I looked down at my chest and then back at Cruz and he wriggled his brows. I shook my head. "Stop looking at me, too. Close your eyes for a minute."

He closed his beautiful honey brown eyes and chuckled. "Does *Dick* make your nipples hard when he looks at you?"

Unfortunately, no.

Dick doesn't do much for me.

"Absolutely. It's a new thing for me. They respond to *everyone*. Okay, you can open now, it's all under control."

"Sure, it is."

He grabbed my hand to lead me inside and I yanked it away. I was fairly certain that's what started this whole nipple-gate and I didn't need to walk into the firehouse with my headlights on. He just chuckled beside me and held the door open.

I walked ahead of him up the stairs and it was notably quiet at the firehouse. Hopefully they were having a slow evening. I always worried about Dad.

"Why is it dark up here?" I whispered over my shoulder.

"Surprise!" The loud booming voices startled me, and I almost lost my step. Cruz's hands were on my hips as he steadied me.

Dad rushed toward me, pulling me into a tight hug. "Welcome home, Jady bug."

"Thanks, Dad. I missed you. I can't believe you did this," I said against his ear.

"I didn't. Cruz put it together."

I shook my head with disbelief and took in the room. Everyone was there. Ari, my best friend and roommate, hurried over and hugged me so tight I was sure I'd pass out. Her boyfriend, Jace, followed before Sam lifted me off the ground and spun me around, and Cara laughed at how ridiculous he was. Sam and I had grown up together, and he'd always been like an older brother to me. He and Cara had been together for a few years now, and I adored her.

"Oh my gosh, Lennon? Is that you?" I said before Cruz's brother pulled me in and wrapped his arms around me. Next up was Cruz's best friend, Adam, his girlfriend, Tory, their manager Luke, their new bandmate, Zach, and Lennon's adorable girlfriend, Bailey. I was stunned to see them here.

My dad's girlfriend, Sara, hugged me for so long that tears pricked my eyes. I'd missed everyone so much. I would never have expected a welcome home party in a million years, and it was really good to see them. These were my people. And they were all here. Uncle Jimmy, Aunt Maria, Uncle John, Aunt Teresa and their littles, Sienna and Piper. All of Dad's fire crew passed me down the line, telling me stories of Dad watching the news like a hawk while I was gone. I spent the next few hours laughing and eating and telling all of them my tales from my time in Honduras. We were saying our goodbyes, and they were all making their way out, when I caught Cruz's gaze. He stood across the room from me. His back against the wall, feet crossed at the ankles, and head cocked to the side. My eyes locked with his honey browns and I smiled. I couldn't help it. Even if I couldn't be with him right now, it didn't mean I didn't love him. It didn't mean he wasn't my best friend. It just meant that right now we were in very different places. And first and foremost, he needed to focus on his recovery. And I needed to believe that he wouldn't return to his old ways before we could ever be anything more than friends.

He walked over to where I sat at the large table which was still covered with half eaten platters of food.

"You want me to take you home?" he asked. He almost sounded nervous, which surprised me.

"Sure. Let me say goodnight to Dad."

We both said our goodbyes and made our way outside and to his car.

And here I was again.

In a confined space with Cruz.

The boy I loved too much.

six

. . .

Cruz

JESUS. She was killing me. She sat in the passenger seat and buckled herself in. I studied her profile. She'd always been the most beautiful girl I'd ever seen—and somehow, she's managed to get even prettier during our time apart. Her hair was longer, and she wore it pulled back in a long ponytail. Her skin was golden tan, as she'd been working outside for months. She donned a simple white T-shirt that outlined her perky tits, and I won't even get started on the fact that her nipples nearly sprung from her body when they saw me. I'd had to adjust myself several times when she wasn't looking. I'd definitely need some alone time in the shower later, because my dick was having a meltdown.

"My dad told me you planned the party?"

"It wasn't a big deal," I said, pulling out on the road.

"I can't believe you did that. Thank you."

I came to a stop at a red light and glanced over at her. Her jade eyes were illuminated by the moonlight when she met my gaze.

"Of course. I'm happy you're home."

"Me too. So, you go back tomorrow? Is it challenging being on tour without drinking and, you know, everything else?"

"Not too bad. I mean, it's tough doing something you don't really want to do every day. You know I'm still leaving the band, right? Obviously, I love the guys, and it's so much better without Dex now, but I'd like to start my life sooner rather than later, you know? So yeah, there're moments that it would be nice to check out. Not deal with the bullshit. That's just the fucking truth. But I won't do it. I know you probably don't believe me yet, but I'm not going back."

I pulled in front of her house, and she sucked in a strained breath. "It's not that I don't want to believe you. I just think you need time to heal. We both do." Tears spilled from her beautiful gaze, and my chest tightened.

"I get it, Jade. It's okay to want time. I hurt you really bad, and I'm going to have to prove myself to you. And I'm willing to do that. So, for now, we're friends. I'll take what I can get," I said, using my thumb to swipe at the liquid running down her cheek.

"Best friends," she whispered.

"Honestly, you're the only person I even like, so that's a no brainer."

Her head fell back in laughter. "You're so full of it."

"So, what's happening with this Dick guy?"

"His name is Richard. He was my small group leader. We're friends right now, but he thinks we should date." She met my gaze head-on.

"And what do you think?" I tucked a loose strand of hair behind her ear.

"I think I should date and be a normal twenty-year-old, you know? Try to move on a little bit for now. We both should."

Jade had been forcing this whole dating issue since the day she left. Like she'd decided in her head that the only way to get over me was to meet someone else. It made my stomach wrench. The thought of Dick or anyone touching her. Being with her. I replayed my conversation with Dr. Roberts in my head.

What if she doesn't come back?

Then she doesn't come back.

Fuck you, Dr. Evil.

"So, I know you kissed him when you were there. Did it progress to more?"

Why was I doing this? Did I even want to know? I guess in a sick, twisted way I needed to know what I was up against. Because Jade and I were going to be together. I just needed to figure out the best way to get there.

"No. We kissed just the one time, which I told you about. But that doesn't mean it won't happen again." She studied my face as she spoke.

She wanted a reaction out of me. It would be an easy out. I'd get pissed off, she'd say this is why we can't hang out right now, and the night would end. And I didn't want it to end.

Nope. I wasn't taking that path.

"Dick clearly can't kiss for shit, or it wouldn't have only happened once." I shrugged.

She slapped my shoulder. "Shut up. That's not it. He knows that I'm still getting over you."

"Do you think there's a reason it's taking you so long?" I smirked.

Her face hardened. "Yes, Cruz. Because I love you *too much*, and it's been hell getting over you. You tore my heart out. *That's why it's taking me so long.*"

She stormed out of the car and hurried to the trunk to get her bags.

I popped the trunk and reached for her forearm, wrapping my fingers around her delicate wrist. I turned her to face me. "I'm sorry. I fucked up. And I'm working hard to make up for it. I know it's going to take time. So, if you think you need to date other people, including that douchebag, Dick—then do it. I'll be here working on me and waiting for you."

How about them fucking apples, Dr. Evil.

She blinked a few times, the streetlight shined down on her beautiful face, and she tilted her head to the side. "That's very mature of you."

This was some kind of test that I wasn't going to fail. I'd surprised her by remaining calm, and I'd even surprised myself. Chalk it up to months of therapy. Yes, I still wanted to smash Dick's face in, or any guy who looked at her. But, like Dr. Roberts loved to remind me—I was in this shit show because of my own actions. So, I'd need to be patient.

"What can I say? I'm very mature these days."

"How about you? Have you been sleeping with everything that moves?" she asked, studying my face like it hid all the answers to her questions.

"Well, Jade, this might surprise you… but no. I haven't fucked a single chick. And that's all because of you," I said, lips pursed.

She narrowed her gaze at me. Her eyebrows pinched, and her hands moved to her hips. "How is it because of me?"

"Well, if I'm being honest. You broke my dick."

Her head fell back in hysterical laughter, and damn if it wasn't the best sound I'd heard in a long ass time.

She leaned in close to me and whispered, "Like, literally? I bent it?"

I barked out a laugh. "No. It's not physically broken. I think it's *emotionally* broken, at least that's what Dr. fucking Evil thinks. Apparently, it doesn't like anyone but you. You put some sort of spell on it, and now it has no interest in other girls."

"Is that so?"

"That is so. You don't need to look so judgy, though. Your nipples were telling a story of their own earlier."

She swatted my arm again. "Shut up with that. You really expect me to believe you've gone all summer without sex?"

"It's the fucking truth. Who would willingly admit their dick was broken? And, you've practically begged me to date. Why would I lie?"

"That's a good question. Well, I still think you should date. It doesn't mean you have to sleep with anyone. Maybe play the field a little, you know? Make sure you know what you want."

"I've always known what I want. I just got lost for a little bit. And I believe right now, we're waiting for *you* to figure out what you want, right?" I said, our hands somehow linked together of their own will.

"Right," she said, running the pad of her thumb over my palm.

And damn if I wasn't already hard again. All over. Her nearness had my body reacting like a teenage boy in puberty.

"So, I leave tomorrow. How do you feel about a sleepover?"

She rolled her eyes. "No."

"I thought we were friends. I believe you even said *best friends*. You don't have sleepovers with your best friends?"

She laughed. "Please. Like you've ever had sleepovers."

"I love me a good slumber party. Facials, and chocolate, and girl talk," I said, fighting the urge to lean down and taste her sweet mouth.

She turned and faced the car again. "What would be the purpose? We're both tired. It's late. You're leaving tomorrow."

"Those are my exact arguments. We're both tired, it's late, and I'm leaving tomorrow. I'm not going to see you for a while. I always sleep better with you." I took her bags and started walking toward her front door.

"I'm not having sex with you. Nothing's going to happen."

"Jesus, More Jade. Get your mind out of the gutter. When did you become such a dirty bird?" I laughed.

"I'm not a dirty bird." She huffed and pushed inside.

Ari came out of her bedroom wearing pajamas and rubbing her eyes. "I'm so happy to have you back, roomie. I've missed you so much."

Jace sauntered out behind her wearing boxer shorts and nothing else. He fist-bumped me and reached over to hug Jade. "Thank God you're back. I can't talk about nail polish or fashion any longer."

"I'm really happy to be home."

"Okay, lunch tomorrow, right?" Ari said.

"Yes. Can't wait to hear everything that's been going on." Jade smiled at her friend and moved down the hallway to her room.

I was actually shocked that she'd agreed to let me spend the night. I figured it was a long shot. But the thought of sleeping beside her, well it would be worth all the fucking discomfort I was about to face. I'm sure I'd be awake the entire night with a raging boner, but so be it.

"So, I need to take a bath," she said, fidgeting with the promise ring I'd given her, that now hung on a chain around her neck. Hell, I was just happy she still wore it.

"Want company?" I pressed. It was an asshole thing to say. She'd made it clear where she stood right now. But when it came to Jade, I'd always take the shot.

"No, Cruz. I'll be out in a little bit."

She shut the door, and I heard the lock click behind her.

Seriously?

"I'm not going to come in uninvited," I shouted through the door.

"It's a safety precaution." She laughed, and I heard the tub water running.

I checked my phone and responded to a few emails. I jotted down a few lyrics to a song that I was feeling at the moment. Being around Jade always inspired something deep inside me.

I dropped my pants and pulled my T-shirt over my head.

"Oh my god. Look at you," she said when the bathroom door flew open.

She wore pink and white shorts and a spaghetti strap tank top. They were pajamas I'd seen many times, but I took my time perusing her body. Her hair was wet and brushed back from her face.

Fucking stunning.

"What?" I asked with confusion.

"You're so—I don't know. Ripped? Chiseled?" She laughed.

I looked down and the first thing I noticed was an embarrassing boner pointing right at her. I hadn't paid much attention to my body changing over the last few months because I'd always been fit, but I guess I'd piled on some muscle since I started working out with Gio.

"You see this." I paused and pointed down south. "And the muscles are what you notice?"

Her cheeks pinked. "Not kidding, Winslow. Nothing's going to happen. But I can't say the idea of sleeping beside you doesn't sound —*pleasant.*"

She turned out the light and climbed into bed. I did the same and rolled on my side to face her. The light from the moon shined in through her window, allowing me to make out her pretty features.

"*Pleasant*? Don't insult me."

She laughed. "Thanks for picking me up, and for planning the welcome home party."

Her voice was soft, and her warm breath tickled my cheek.

She smelled like sunshine and goodness.

"Of course. I'm glad you're home."

"Me too."

"I noticed some new ink on your forearm. What did you get?" she whispered.

I reached for her hand and traced her fingers over my latest tattoo. "I inked the nail marks you left on my arm from that night. You know, as a forever reminder of what happened. A reminder why I'll never go back to that place again."

A silence stretched between us, and two tears landed on my forearm. I didn't want to make her cry. But I wanted her to know I was never going to forget what I'd done.

She reached for my hand and placed my fingers on the back of her head. There was a scar hidden beneath her hair from where she'd hit her head.

"We both have our battle wounds, huh?"

"I'm so fucking sorry, Jade."

"I know you are. I forgive you for that night, Cruz. I'm not trying to punish you. I'm just trying to figure out what's best for me, you know?"

"I know. I love that about you. It's wise to be cautious. I get it."

"I'm really proud of you for completing the program," she said, her finger was back on my forearm, tracing the ink from the night that had marked us both forever. In more ways than just the surface.

"Thanks. I'm proud of you for going to Honduras and trying to save the world."

She chuckled, and her chest vibrated against mine.

"Thank you," she whispered.

I stroked her hair until her breathing slowed, and she dozed off. I breathed in her scent and all her fucking goodness and gave in to the best night's sleep I'd had in months.

———

Sunlight hit my face with a vengeance, and I blinked several times before opening my eyes. I was alone in bed. I adjusted myself beneath the covers. Well, me and my boner were alone in bed.

"Jade?" I called out.

She stepped out of the bathroom, dressed and ready for the day. "Did I wake you?"

"No. What are you doing?"

"I have class. Just getting ready." She moved to sit on the edge of the bed.

Damn, she was pretty. I reached up and tucked her hair behind her ear.

"Your hair is longer."

"Yeah. I need to chop some of this off," she said, studying my face.

"I like it."

Her cheeks pinked. "Thanks."

I pushed to stand and walked to the bathroom to take a piss. I caught Jade leaning against the doorframe, staring down at my package.

"Like what you see?" I teased.

"It's sort of hard to miss. And I'm fairly certain it's not broken. It poked me all night," she said as I flushed the toilet and stopped to wash my hands.

"I told you. It only works for you."

"We'll see how long that lasts," she said, moving back to the bedroom to load her backpack with school supplies.

I slipped my jeans on and pulled my T-shirt over my head. She stopped me and reached for my arm. She studied the ink again and traced the marks she'd left on me.

"I can't believe you did that," she said.

"Why? It's a forever reminder."

I reached back and rubbed the tender spot behind her head, and she wrapped her arms around my middle. "Okay. So, you're off today, right? How long are you gone for?"

She pushed back from me, like she suddenly needed distance. I ran my hands through my disheveled hair. "Three weeks. You could come visit if you want."

"No." Her voice was firm and hard. "I need to focus on school. I'm hoping I start hearing from the medical schools I applied to. I sent in all my applications while I was in Honduras. I pray I get an interview. I don't have a backup plan if I don't get in."

"You'll get in. I have no doubt."

"I have plenty of doubt for both of us. Richard doesn't think I applied to enough schools," she said, pulling her backpack over her shoulder.

"Richard's a dick. They even named him so. He doesn't know what he's talking about. How many did you apply to?"

"Six."

"How many did Dick apply to?"

"Twenty-eight."

I laughed. "That over-achieving douchebag must need more options. He's probably a shit student."

"He has the same GPA as me, the same MCAT score as mine, he's older and he's done the medical brigade multiple times."

I laughed. "His name is Dick. He's got nothing on you."

"I'm not competing with him. Not really. I hope we both get in somewhere. But it worries me that they might think I'm too young and not ready. Most people take four years and do a gap year before applying to med school."

"You've never been like most people, More Jade. Don't start now." I kissed the top of her head and wrapped my arms around her. I wanted to ease all her worries.

"Thanks. I hope you're right." She led me out of the room. "So, what's going on with your classes?"

"I just started my last course, and I'll be graduating in December."

"Wow. That's amazing," she said, her gaze searching mine as she came to a stop in the living room.

"Yeah. I think I'm going to walk in the winter commencement."

"Look at you. You're like an MMA master and you're getting

your degree. What a difference a summer makes, huh?" she said, bumping her shoulder into mine. But I knew there was more meaning behind her words. We'd both grown a lot these last few months, but it would take time to see who we'd become.

I opened the door and saw the slew of press outside. At least six camera guys were set up out front. Jesus Christ. Could I not have one night with her without this? I came to a halt and she slammed into my back before I pushed the door closed.

"Shit, did you see how many of them are out there?" I said.

"I forgot how aggressive they can be. And now they're going to think you slept here." Her tone was full of panic and distress.

"I did sleep here," I said.

"You know what I mean, Cruz. They're going to think we're back together and start stalking me again. I've removed myself from all of this. I don't want to be stared at on campus and sent hate mail from crazy ass girls. I don't want this. None of it."

She was shouting now.

Angry.

I put my hands on each of her shoulders. "Relax, Jade. I'll go out the front door. I'll say I came this morning to fix something. I do own the property after all. You can sneak out the back door and cut through a few yards, and they won't even know you were here."

She swiped at the single tear rolling down her cheek. It was the first day of her last year of undergrad, and she was dealing with my bullshit. No wonder she wanted space from me.

"Okay. I just want to focus on my classes and hopefully getting some interviews for med school. I can't get sucked back into all of this."

I tucked the hair behind her ear. "I get it."

She pushed up and kissed my cheek. "Okay. I'm going out the back door."

I watched her leave and waited till she stepped outside before opening the front door and offering them a fabulous distraction.

"Do you guys ever get sick of following me around? Because I sure as shit get sick of it." I lit a smoke and took a drag.

One dude laughed. "Are we going to be visiting you here, again? You and Jade back together?"

"No, you must be slipping on your impressive journalism skills. I'm taking off today on tour. Just dropping off some paperwork to Jade and her roommate."

"You didn't spend the night here?" another one called out.

"Are you serious? Do you think I'd use the front door if I did?" It was the best I could come up with, and they seemed to buy it for now. I put out my cigarette and drove toward campus to make sure Jade made it without anyone bothering her. I paused at a stop sign and saw her up ahead. She wasn't alone.

Dick was walking beside her.

And I still wanted to smash his face in.

seven

. . .

Jade

SEPTEMBER 3rd

Dear Journal,

Well, let's just say it's been a crappy day. Jack and I had a big fight last night. He's been drinking a lot with all his new friends at the firehouse. I went to pick him up from a bar because I was worried about him and he told me to "stop nagging him." I kid you not. I left the library to have him call me a NAG? He proceeded to tell me that I don't make time for him and that I'm too caught up in school. I told him that he could find himself another girlfriend, because this NAG wasn't going to stick around and be insulted.

I mean, stereotype much? I'm picking his drunk ass up at a bar and he calls me a nag? Not happening. I dropped him at his house and refused to take his calls after I got home. I'm so mad at him. And then I woke up and got my period. It's like the gods are frowning on me today. I have a big zit on my cheek and I'm tired. The only good thing—they are going to do a screening with me at the studio today. Let me play out my fantasy a little about being in front of the camera. I'm not letting my fight with Jack or my oversized zit derail me. Onward and upward. I am woman, hear me roar. LOL. Just getting myself pumped up. Need to go charge the tundra.

Ciao for now,

J.E.

Mom's journal always made me laugh. Obviously, her fight with Dad didn't last long, because they clearly ended up together. But she was such a strong woman, even at a young age, and I admired her. I tucked her journal in my nightstand and checked my makeup before I left to meet Richard for dinner. On my way out the door, my phone vibrated.

CRUZ

Hey. It's Friday. Don't do anything I wouldn't do.

I rolled my eyes. We were no longer sticking to the once a week texts since he'd spent the night here, but I was still trying to keep some distance between us. It scared me how easily I found my way back to him. The night we'd spent together proved that I wasn't over him. Obviously, we didn't have sex. We hadn't even kissed. But we didn't need to. That was the thing with me and Cruz. We were connected in every way. He was a part of me and being near him made me feel complete. And whole. And I hated it as much as I loved it. My feelings for Cruz were a curse and a blessing. I knew he needed time in his recovery. And I needed time to heal from everything that happened. But why was it so damn hard to stay away from him?

Well, that leaves my options pretty wide open. (winky face emoji)

CRUZ

Never trust a guy named Dick. There's a reason he has that name.

I let out a long breath.

Why are you texting me right now? Just to mess with my head.

CRUZ

Probably, yes. Is it working?

I laughed.

Nope. I'm still going.

CRUZ

Fine. Don't be afraid to use that rape whistle I
gave you.

It's a date. I'm not wandering through a
deserted alley.

CRUZ

Have you not heard of acquaintance rape?
Nearly 50% of violent acts are caused by
people the victim knows. I kid you not, More
Jade.

I was done texting this ridiculousness, so I dialed his number. It was the first time we were speaking since I'd seen him.

"Hey, this is a surprise," he purred through the line.

"Stop it. You're being an asshole."

"That's the kind of anger I want to see if Dick tries anything."

"Cruz," I whined. "Please stop. I'm really trying."

"Trying what, Jade? Trying to pretend you like someone?"

"How do you know I don't like him? He's actually pretty perfect for me," I said, walking toward Third Street where I was meeting Richard.

"Perfect is fucking boring."

I sighed. "Do you want to ruin this for me?"

"I think I do."

"You have a show tonight, don't you?" I asked, trying to change the subject.

"You keeping tabs on me, More Jade?"

"Hardly. You told me you had a show when you texted me this morning. Remember? You said you had a show, and then you listed a dozen reasons why I should cancel my date."

"I'm trying to be a friend here. I just don't see the fucking point in going out with this guy," he said, and he didn't hide his irritation.

"I think we should go back to texting once a week. We're talking too much. All the lines are getting jumbled."

"No. I'll stop. Have fun with Dick."

I laughed. "Not sure how genuine that was but thank you."

"Alright, I've got to get out on stage. I wrote some new shit, and I can't wait for you to hear it," he said.

"Send me the lyrics. You know I love your songs." I stood in front of the restaurant, with one hand clutched to my chest.

"Alright. I can do that. I'll talk to you soon."

I needed to go, but I didn't want to end the call. "Hey, Cruz?"

"Yeah?"

"I wrote a song, I um, I don't know if it's actually a song. I wrote it when I was in Honduras. It might be more of a poem. But I'll show it to you after I clean it up, okay?"

"Can't wait, More Jade. I'll see you in a couple weeks. Go have fun tonight. You deserve it."

A single tear rolled down my cheek and I wiped it away. Why was this so hard? "Okay. I'll talk to you later."

The phone went dead, and I shook it off. I stepped inside and Richard stood in the entryway. His dark wavy hair was a bit over-grown and shaggy. He wore dark jeans and a button-up.

"I was afraid you'd changed your mind," he said.

There was humor in his tone, but I'm sure there was some truth to his words. Richard wasn't hurting for female attention. The hostess was currently shooting daggers at me. He was gorgeous, as well as being a really good guy. His only negative was that he wasn't Cruz Winslow.

"Don't be silly. I'm glad I'm here." The hostess led us to our table, and Richard and I dropped in the chairs across from one another.

He ordered a bottle of wine and an appetizer while we perused the menu. I reached for my phone to turn my ringer off so I wouldn't be distracted during dinner, and I noticed a new email. The waiter was busy opening our wine and having Richard sample it, so I decided to take a quick peek.

"Oh my gosh, Richard." I gasped.

"What happened?"

"I got an interview," I squealed. I literally squealed. I never squeal. But I was overcome with excitement.

"Amazing. Where?"

I bit down on my bottom lip. I needed a minute to process. "NYU."

"Shit, Jade. That's amazing. That's your top choice, right?"

"It is."

"Things are happening. I can feel it. I guess now I won't be an asshole telling you I heard from Harvard. I'm flying out in three weeks for my interview."

I picked up my wine glass and held it out to him. "Cheers to us."

"Cheers to us."

We clanked glasses and I dropped my phone in my purse. This is what all the hard work was for.

"Thanks for coming tonight. So, are you and the rock star still friends? He didn't seem too crazy about me at the airport."

I laughed and reached for a piece of bread. "He's protective. We're good friends."

"You know, I know a little bit about what happened before you left for Honduras." He held his hands up in apology. "Jessica told Dean about your accident, and he told me. It's not going anywhere. No one is gossiping to be cruel. But I care about you," he said.

I was annoyed with Jessica, but there was nothing mean spirited about her. She was just chatty. She also didn't know much, only that I'd been caught in an argument with one of the bandmates in Exiled and Cruz hadn't been there. She didn't know about him being practically unconscious from Ambien or any of the details of our breakup. I was thankful that the only ones who knew what happened were Dad, Sara, Sam, and Ari. And I trusted them one hundred percent.

"Well, thank you for caring. But I'm doing well." I smiled.

We placed our order, and I sipped my wine.

"You just got your first interview to medical school. It's impressive."

"Thank you. You should be very proud too," I said.

"I am. But I'm equally excited that you finally agreed to go out with me. I know it's hard after you've been with someone for a long time. But just because you feel a connection to someone, doesn't necessarily mean they're good for you. Take it from me. I learned the hard way."

"So, what happened with you and your girlfriend?" I asked, setting my glass down and scanning the room. The dim lighting gave the place an elegant feel. There were white tablecloths and candles on every table. I'd never been to this particular steakhouse, but I was glad I came. Today had been a good day.

"Well, let's see. We dated all through high school. So, we had a history. Our families were very close. I was pretty certain she was *the girl*, you know?"

"Oh wow. It was very serious then."

"Yep."

"And she cheated on you? Had there been other problems in the relationship?"

"I guess. Hindsight is twenty-twenty, right? I thought we were happy. I mean, I loved her. I thought that's what mattered most. But Demi didn't think I gave her enough time or attention. You know, our major requires a lot out of us. She just couldn't understand how much time I had to commit to my studies. So, we argued occasionally over that kind of stuff," he said, popping a piece of bread in his mouth and I laughed at how casually he said it.

"I guess you're okay with everything now?"

He smiled and nodded. "It took me a good year. Time has a way of healing. But I was pissed for a long time. Hell, I lost the two closest people in my life. It still stings when I think about it. But I'd rather know now, then find out later who they really are."

"Wow. That's brutal. Did you walk in on them?"

"Nope. Demi isn't an evil person. She made a mistake. She owned up to it. She told me that she and Owen had gotten really drunk and he'd confessed that he'd been in love with her for years. So yeah, there's that...he and I never got past it. She and I tried to, but the trust was gone, you know?"

I thought about Cruz. He didn't cheat on me, but he'd broken my trust in a different way. He'd been nearly unconscious after he'd promised me that he'd stopped taking pills. I'd needed him. I'd been terrified. And he was right there, but he couldn't help me.

"That's so tough. She must have felt terrible for what she did to you. Owen too."

"Yeah. That's the shitty thing. It was all for nothing. It's not like they ended up dating after. They didn't. She was guilt ridden, and he tucked tail and ran."

"Are your families still close?" I asked as the waiter set our plates down. I hadn't had a steak in months, and it smelled delicious.

"Yes and no. I mean, they had us married off in their heads, so it caused a bit of tension. But we're definitely all friendly. There aren't any hard feelings anymore. At least not from me. My mom's a different story." He laughed and took a sip of wine.

"Ah, a mama's boy, huh?"

"Yeah. She's pretty awesome. She went into mama bear mode when it first happened."

"That's sweet."

"Yep. So, I know breakups are tough. It took me a long time to get back out there. Well, I'm lying. I banged everything that moved for the first couple weeks." He chuckled. "But you're the first girl I actually wanted to take out."

I studied him. "Well, banging me isn't really an option."

"You've made that very clear. Can't say I'm not disappointed."

I choked a bit on my wine as it tried to make its way down my throat and set my glass down. "Well, that was honest."

"I like you. It's no secret. And I know you're hung up on your ex. Trust me, I get it. But just because you love him, doesn't mean he's the best guy for you. So, all I'm asking, is that you keep an open mind."

When he called Cruz my 'ex' it was like a knife to the heart. But wasn't he my ex? We weren't together, per my insistence, yet hearing those words cut me deep. This was all part of trying to move forward, right?

"I can do that."

The rest of the night was spent learning about Richard's family back east. I told him all about Dad and growing up in Bucktown.

We'd spent the summer together, but we'd never gone very deep. Tonight had been fun. He grilled me on possible interview questions as he walked me home.

"Really, Jade? You're going to say that your weakness is that you're too organized?" He laughed and wrapped an arm around my shoulder, and I didn't cringe.

"What? Ask anyone who knows me. It's a problem."

"It's the same as saying my biggest weakness is my big ol' brain. I'm just too intelligent."

"It is not." I smacked his chest and laughed.

"What's your weakness, then?"

"I'd probably say that staying focused is my weakness. I get distracted. I like to go out and have fun, you know. So, staying the course. Keeping my head down."

"Damn, yours is so much better than mine."

"Dig deep. What else you got?"

"Well, I can be anti-social when I get too focused."

"Jesus. They actually prefer that. Come on. You've got to have something. A secret porn problem. You like to sleep with a blow dryer in your bed. Duct tape your feet together, maybe."

"What?" I came to a stop and laughed.

"You're too good, Jade," he said.

He leaned down and kissed me. It was brief. But it wasn't terrible.

I pulled away, my heart racing. And not for the right reasons. Not because I was excited, but because it felt wrong. "Far from too good. Trust me."

"I'll have to take your word on that." He wrapped an arm around me again and walked me the rest of the way.

When we got to my door, I paused. "Well, thank you so much for dinner. It was fun."

He leaned down and kissed me. A little longer this time. I tried to get lost in it. His tongue slipped in and I tangled my fingers in his hair. But alarm bells went off in my head, and I pressed my hands against his chest.

"I can't. I'm sorry. It just feels wrong," I said, shaking my head.

He clutched his heart and laughed. "That's the first time anyone's ever said that after I kissed them."

"I'm sorry. I just want to be honest with you."

"Just give it a chance, Jade."

"Okay."

He leaned over and kissed my cheek, and I stepped inside.

Maybe that's all I needed to do.

Just give him a chance.

eight

· · ·

Cruz

"WE HAVE something new for you tonight," I purred into the microphone, and the crowd went crazy. They loved when I teased them with new shit.

I looked over at Zach and he nodded, and he played a few strings. Lennon wrote the music to "Spread Those Wings," and I wrote the lyrics.

Confined and chained, perception whacked,
breaking free, the chrysalis cracks.
Spread those wings and find the light,
Beautiful jade and always bright.
No more numbness, joy and pain,
Clouding over all the shame.
Hurt the one I loved the most,
I'd follow her to every coast.
Like an angel guiding me,
To feel, to live—and just to be.
It's all your goodness that I miss,
The softest lips I long to kiss.
No longer a slave to pills and booze,
Always you I'm going to choose.

No more numbness, joy and pain,
Clouding over all the shame.
Hurt the one I loved the most,
I'd follow her to every coast.

After I sing the last chorus, the crowd joins in too and the cheers were deafening and the lights blinding. Another successful show down. I walked backstage after and grabbed a bottle of water, and we all made our way into the back room. Tia was in the corner with Zach talking a mile a minute, Bailey was sitting on Lennon's lap, Adam was in a political debate with Luke, and I took it all in.

I'd been clean and sober for over three months. Had I mastered sobriety? Hell no. Far from it. But I'd come to realize a few things since I'd stop numbing myself from every discomfort life threw at me. Yeah, the prescription pills had been a new addition to my arsenal once we'd gone on tour, but I'd been drinking since I was fourteen years old. Every single family interaction I'd encountered over the last several years—I'd been plastered. Numb. And what I'd learned was that the shit waited for you to sober up. So, I'd just been buying time, chasing something I wasn't going to find by avoiding all the bullshit in my life. That's probably why I'd added in the prescription drugs. The booze hadn't been enough anymore. But nothing would have been enough. Because it's always there waiting for you when you sober up. One big bitch slap of reality. And now that I'd stopped running from it, faced my shit head on—it wasn't that bad. My dad was a sack of shit. Me being drunk or sober didn't change that. And the plus side to being forced to deal with your shit? You got to feel the other things too…the things that weren't bad. There were more good things in my life than I'd ever realized.

Watching my brother find happiness was one of the best things I'd ever experienced. Lennon was going to be okay, happy even. Seeing Jade after months of her being gone, as much as it tore me apart to give her the space she needed right now, it also felt good. Seeing her kick ass and find her way did something to me. It inspired me to push myself.

I was writing music I was fucking proud of. My lyrics were raw and real. And the execs at AF records were impressed, and fuck if that didn't feel good. To do more than just show up because you're good looking as fuck and faking your way through life was a high in its own.

"You ready, bro?" Lennon asked with Bailey standing beside him. The two were joined at the hip.

"Yeah. Let's go. Cars outside."

We were heading to Utah for two days to see Mom and I had an in-person session scheduled with Dr. Roberts. I looked forward to seeing her this time. I'd made progress. I hadn't flown to Chicago to crash Jade's date with *Dick* like I normally would. Nope. I'd stayed in New York and given her the space she asked for. Did I beat the shit out of my sparring partner who'd volunteered to step in the cage the next morning because I hadn't heard from her that night? Sure.

Rome wasn't built in a fucking day.

And he was a willing participant, and I gave him free tickets to our show, so he was well compensated. The point is, I was making progress.

———

"Obviously, I don't condone acts of violence, Cruz, but you've found a positive outlet, and I'm all for that. You used restraint and heard what Jade asked you for."

"It sucked ass knowing she was on a date with that Dick. Did I tell you his name was *Dick*?" I moved to the window, as it always calmed me down when I felt confined.

"You may have mentioned it a couple dozen times," Dr. Roberts said.

"He's an asshole. A real boy scout wannabe."

"You don't know him. Let's talk about why you really dislike him."

I rolled my eyes. "Why I dislike him? It's not rocket science, doc. He wants my girl. I fucking hate him."

She barked out a laugh. "So, he's not an, er, asshole, or a boy scout. You don't like him because he's a threat to you, correct?"

I dropped back down in my seat and faced her. My jaw ticked at her words and I took a minute before I responded. "He's not a threat to me. Jade loves *me*. I don't doubt that."

"Then what's the problem?"

"I don't like the idea of him pawing all over her, and I don't have a fucking clue what's going on," I said.

"But she was up front about going out with him. She even suggested you do the same. And she told you how the date went after, correct? Sounds pretty upfront."

I ran a hand over my face. "When you put it that way."

"There's no other way to put it, Cruz. She's being honest with you. She's not ready to dive back into anything with you yet. I will say, the fact that she let you spend the night and is talking to you almost daily, is a good sign for you. But right now, she's asking you to be her friend. So be the best friend you can be. Friendship is a big part of any positive relationship."

"Yeah. But hearing about other dudes, sucks. She told me he kissed her again. I wanted to smash the phone. I haven't kissed her in, hell, I can't even remember the last time I kissed her. It was the last time I was with her before everything went to shit," I said, leaning my head back and closing my eyes. These were the times that I didn't like feeling everything. The weight of my actions. My fucking girl was out with some douchebag named Dick because I'd failed her.

And I'd failed myself.

"Good. It's important for you to see that consequences follow actions. No one got seriously injured, and you're lucky. You're getting a second chance. And considering the fact you're the lead singer of a band currently on tour, you're being harassed by your father who's a powerful man in his own right, and you're trying to pick up the pieces with Jade—you impress me, Cruz. You're stronger than you think you are. And the key here is…you didn't smash the phone. You didn't take your anger out on her. You listened. You did exactly what she needed you to do."

"How long do I have to do this for?" I said with a moan. I was still a spoiled prick most of the time, I just masked it better by being sober.

"As long as she needs you to."

"Well, what the hell am I here for then if you can't tell me anything?" I cocked a brow at her.

"I'm proud of you. You're growing. I see it every time we meet. I would like to suggest that you and Jade discuss what happened that night with Dex, and the morning after when you found her. I think it's going to be pivotal for you both to move forward."

"She hasn't wanted to talk about it, but I know we need to."

"Yes. It will be an important piece of the puzzle. Wait until she's ready, and then lay it all out there. It'll feel good to clear the air, and both share your feelings about it."

"Alright. I can do that."

"Great. So, what's happening with your father?"

"Speaking of *dicks*, yes, let's discuss dear old dad. He called on our way to the show. Lennon and I agreed to unblock him because he just started calling from other phones. The dude's definitely tracking us because he called on the way to the hanger to ask if we were going to see Mom. Although, it is his plane, so I guess he could have found out we booked a flight to see her. But he seems to know our every move."

"Is he still trying to negotiate a way to get Dex back in the band?" she asked.

"He mentioned it again, but he's more consumed with me leaving at the end of the year. This happened the last time I tried to leave Exiled. He's a rich ass man with his production company. I don't understand his obsession with the band."

"I'm guessing it has as much to do with control as it does with money. Your father is used to having control over everything in his life, and right now he's alone, and he's completely lost control of his family," she said.

"Because of his own doing," I argued.

"Right, Cruz. But unlike you who made a conscious choice to make a change in your life, own your actions and accept your consequences, your father is doubling down. He's an out of control addict, he has unlimited resources, and now that your mother is gone, I'm afraid he has no one to answer to. He's going to go down in flames and he's not worried about who he hurts on his way down."

"He's such an arrogant prick. I know you still meet with my mom weekly, and I'm sure she's told you about the restraining order. I just hope she can keep it together with all this stress. He's a relentless asshole, and he's not going to make their divorce easy."

"Your mom is prepared for a battle. She has the best attorneys money can buy."

"Yeah. It is what it is, you know."

"That's true, Cruz. There are things in life that are out of our control. So, you just focus on yourself, and what you can contribute."

"I have a question for you actually," I said, rubbing my hand over the back of my neck.

"Shoot."

"Jade got an interview at NYU medical school. It's her dream school. I'm fairly certain she only applied to six schools because of money, and I want to help her. I offered her the use of our plane for the interview and invited her to stay at our apartment, but she turned me down. What am I missing? She doesn't have the money, we have a shit ton of money, and I want to help her. Do I push it, or back off?"

She chuckled, which annoyed me because I didn't find it funny. I truly didn't understand Jade sometimes. She was being stubborn.

"You offered, and she turned you down. What don't you understand," she said with one raised brow.

"But, why? She doesn't have the money, and Jack can't afford to fly her to New York for a one-day interview. Why not take me up on it? I mean, at the very least, we're friends, right?"

"I'm guessing Jade wants to do this on her own. She's fighting for her independence right now, and you need to choose your battles. She's asked for space, and you gave it. And she's slowly been coming around. You offered her the plane and the apartment, and she turned you down. She may feel like there would be strings attached. You also have to keep in mind that your father doesn't want you with Jade, and she's aware of that. He's even publicly tried to hurt her in the past. Offering her a place to stay alone, that he has access to, may not be in anyone's best interest."

"Shit. Good point. Hadn't thought of that. Dad rarely goes to New York. And I wouldn't show up if she didn't want me there."

"Interviewing for medical school is a high stress situation. She has a lot riding on it."

I nodded. "Thanks, Doc. You know, you're not as fucking bad as I first thought you were."

She smiled. "You aren't as bad as I first thought you were either. Keep working on *you* and everything else will fall into place. She's asking you to be her friend, so focus on that."

"I will. You're right. I've been approaching this all wrong. I'm going to be the best fucking friend Jade's ever had."

We both laughed.

I made my way out to my waiting car.

"Are we heading over to your mother's home, Mr. Winslow?" Dave, my driver, asked.

I thought it over for a minute, still processing Dr. Roberts' words about working on myself.

"Let's make a stop at the Museum of Fine Arts first."

"You got it."

I'd already beaten the shit out of someone this week in the cage—perhaps it was time to broaden my horizons. I'd been drawing on scraps of paper these last few weeks. I enjoyed creating kickass images. As a kid, I used to have the typical Crayola box and I'd spend hours making cool designs, but that was years ago. Then the rat race began with my father's shit and I've felt like I've always had to be prepared—for what, who the fuck knows. But creativity had always been a part of me. The calmer side of me, and I'm going to get it back.

And who better to share the new me with than my best friend.

nine

. . .

Jade

ARI and I walked along the sidewalk, making the trek home from the library.

"Is Jace coming over tonight?" I asked.

"He's watching Monday night football with his friends, and I thought I'd just chill at home and we could catch up on This Is Us. We're an episode behind."

I laughed. "Sounds good."

"What's happening with Richard?" she asked.

"We had class together today. I like him. He's a good guy."

"But…"

"But, what?"

"But, he's not Cruz, right?" she said as we walked up the steps to our house.

"Right. But that doesn't have to be a bad thing."

"Jade, you're in love with someone else. You're the only one that seems to feel the need to torture yourself over it." Ari unlocked the door and we walked inside, dropping our bags in the kitchen and each grabbing a water from the refrigerator.

"I know. But that doesn't mean he's good for me. I really *want* to like Richard. That has to count for something. Cruz and I are friends right now, and that's how I want to keep it."

She laughed. "I know you do. But you can't make yourself like someone because you think they're a safe bet. You already fell for a rock star, bad boy." She wriggled her brows.

"Whatever. I believe in learning from my mistakes." I chuckled.

The doorbell rang and Ari ran to answer it. She came back with a package in hand. "It's for you."

"Really? I haven't ordered anything."

"Open it." She shook the box in front of my face before handing it to me and hopping to sit on the counter.

I cut the box open and pulled out another box inside. When I removed the top, there was a black suit inside. A pencil skirt and suit jacket, along with a cream-colored shell.

"Oh, wow. Is there a note?" she asked.

I fiddled around in the tissue paper and pulled out the card and read it aloud. "A little something to wish you luck on your interview. No one deserves it more than you, Jade. Go kick ass. Love you more, your best friend, Cruz." I barked out a laugh.

"Your rock star, bad boy, sure is thoughtful," Ari said, pulling the suit from the box. "This is gorgeous, and a size four. The bad boy sure knows you."

"Yeah." I played with the ring that hung from my necklace.

"And you turned down his offer to fly you to New York and stay at their swanky apartment. You're really sticking to your guns, girl." She hopped back up on the counter and faced me.

It wasn't about sticking to my guns. It was about being careful. What I'd come to realize was that there were different types of heartache. And I'd already experienced my fair share. Losing my mom at a young age was brutal. Unfair, even. But it wasn't in my control. It wasn't in anyone's control. But getting my heart broken by Cruz Winslow a second time—that was in my control. And I wasn't going to let it just happen. And I was going to do everything I could to make sure it didn't happen again.

Cruz was the other half of my soul. There were times that I actually felt like my heart might stop beating when I wasn't with him.

But when I think back to that day and waking up in the hospital—it's a reminder that Cruz lied to me. That he had a problem that I couldn't fix. Something bigger than the both of us. I thought about all we'd been through—the miscarriage, the fire, and Dex, and I wanted to push it all away and protect myself.

Protect my heart.

"I can't go to my interview with Cruz on my brain. And what if his father showed up? What then? No. This is something I need to do on my own. That's why they invented this thing called credit cards," I said, admiring the suit she held in her hands.

"I get it. But he sure is trying to show you that he's changed."

"I agree. And maybe he actually has. But that doesn't mean he won't hurt me again," I admitted.

"Well, no one can guarantee they won't hurt you, Jade. Even Mr. Perfect, Richard. He's capable of hurting you too."

But he wasn't. My heart wasn't Richard's to break. Only Cruz could do that, because he still had it. I just wouldn't give him the rest of me.

"Go try it on. It's so much better than the cheap one you showed me online." Ari laughed as I put a frozen lasagna in the oven for dinner.

"Alright. I'll come show you in a little bit. Dinner will be ready in forty-five minutes."

"Ah...I love when you slave over the stove for me." Ari laughed as she hopped off the counter.

I walked to my room and reached for my phone and texted Cruz. This was the first time I was initiating the conversation.

> Hey. I just got the suit. Thank you. That was beyond thoughtful.

CRUZ

> No problem. You're going to kill it. I'm going to be in town later in the week and I'd like to see you.

I twirled the ring on my necklace.

> Of course I want to see you too.

CRUZ

Cool. I'll text you when I get in and we'll
figure it out then.

> Okay. Sounds good.

He was playing it cool, and that surprised me. He'd backed off asking about Richard, and he'd stopped pushing about us getting back together lately. As if he were completely respecting my wishes. So why didn't I feel happy about that?

———

"So, big interview next week for both of us," Richard said as we walked to class.

The weather was starting to cool down, as fall approached. He had his Harvard interview and I had my interview at NYU. We'd both been invited to interview at Northwestern next month, which was very exciting.

"Right? I'm sure I'll be nervous when I get there. Right now, I'm just excited to go," I said.

"Jade?" a familiar voice called out and I turned around.

Cruz Winslow sauntered my way, and my head wasn't the only one to turn in his direction. Two girls in front of me whipped around and gaped. He wore dark jeans, a T-shirt, and an army green-colored sports coat. His hair was styled to perfection, overgrown and sexy. He took my breath away. His honey-colored gaze locked with mine.

"What are you doing here? I thought you were getting in tonight?" I hoped he and Richard missed the tremble in my voice.

His fingers intertwined with mine and he leaned forward and kissed my cheek. "Yeah, I flew in early. I was in touch with the university about graduation, and they asked if I'd consider speaking to Professor Watt's creative writing class about writing lyrics this morning. I was going to call you after to see if you want to meet up for dinner. You know, just to catch up."

I was dumbfounded, and I'm sure I didn't hide it well. Richard cleared his throat beside me, and I pulled my hand away from Cruz, missing the contact the moment I did so.

"Yeah. I can do that."

He smiled and then moved his gaze to the boy beside me. "Oh hey, *Dick.*"

Richard chuckled. "Hey. What's up?"

"The sun, the sky, my career, *your luck at the moment.* That's a loaded question, Dick."

I shook my head and laughed. I couldn't help it. "You know you're ridiculous, right?"

"I do. I better run. I'll text you about dinner."

I didn't want him to go. I wanted to wrap myself around him and keep him here. I bit down on my bottom lip and nodded. "Yeah. Sounds good."

He leaned down once again and kissed my cheek. His hand grazed my chest as it skimmed the front of my shirt and my body started reacting in all sorts of ways. He laughed and tossed me a wink. "See you soon, bestie."

He glared at Richard before turning on his heels and walking away.

People turned to stare at him as he moved past them. He was gorgeous, and today he looked part rock star, part sexy professor. It worked for him.

"Well, that was awkward." Richard said.

"I know. I'm sorry."

"Look, Jade. This thing between you two is clearly not finished. Not by a long shot. Hell, I wanted to grab some popcorn and watch the fireworks myself just now," Richard said.

I shook my head and sighed. "We're not together. But you're right. I'm connected to him in a way I can't explain."

He smiled. "I get it. It's obvious. And he's not walking away without a fight."

"I'm sorry. I don't even know what it is. I can't be with him right now. But I can't be with anyone else either, if that makes sense?"

"It does. And you've been honest about it. I'm the one that pushed things because I thought I'd wear you down. But now that I see what I'm up against, I don't think that's going to happen." He chuckled. "At least not yet."

"I'm sorry."

We walked in the building and down the hall, before taking our seats. "Don't be sorry. I get it. And if you want to make him think we're dating to keep some distance, feel free. The dude clearly hates me anyway."

I nodded. That wasn't a bad idea. "I may take you up on that. Thanks. I think I need to be alone right now. Focus on my interviews and school."

"Sounds like a wise plan."

Class started, and Richard and I took notes and shifted into work mode. He was a good guy. I was glad to finally clear the air. Things weren't finished with Cruz, but I also wasn't about to jump back in blindly. But the idea of seeing him again tonight had my belly fluttering.

I finished class, went to research for a few hours, and ran home to change before dinner. Cruz knocked on the door at six P.M. sharp. He looked good, per usual. It was effortless for him, as he wore a plain white tee and dark jeans.

"You look good, More Jade." He kissed my cheek and we made our way out to the car. Ari wasn't home and being alone at the house with him was a bad idea right now. I was feeling all sorts of things at the moment and being in a public place would be a better choice. He opened the passenger door for me. For a broody rock star, the boy always had impeccable manners.

"How were classes today?" he asked when he climbed in the driver's seat and buckled up.

"Good. How did it go for you? Were you nervous?"

"Nah. I'm used to singing in front of pretty big crowds, so that shit doesn't get to me."

"I don't know how you do it. I hate public speaking," I said, studying his profile, his eyes trained on the road.

"You get used to it. How does Italian food sound?"

"Great."

When we got to the restaurant, we were seated at a little table in the back. The place was buzzing with chatter and the smell of garlic and warm bread filled the space around me.

"So…" he said, reaching for a piece of bread.

"So."

"I wanted to talk to you about something." He paused when the waiter approached, and we placed our order.

"Go on. What do you want to talk about?"

"Your interview in New York. You didn't want to use the plane or the apartment. Is it because you're afraid I'll show up?"

When Cruz Winslow was vulnerable, it did something to me. Always had. It was rare for him to show his vulnerability, and it was so sincere it made my heart heavy.

I laughed. "I'm not afraid you'll show up."

He studied me. "So, then why? Don't friends help one another?"

I let out a long sigh. "Your dad is not my friend, Cruz. He doesn't like me, for whatever reason, and the thought of him showing up at *his* apartment or joining me on the plane. I can't risk that. This is the most important interview of my life. I need to focus. But I appreciate the offer more than you know."

"You know his reasons for not liking you have nothing to do with you, right? Hell, he doesn't even know why he dislikes you. You're a threat to him. And he doesn't like that. But it's not about you, it's about him. He's got serious issues."

"A threat to him how?" I asked curiously, reaching for my iced tea when the waiter set it down.

"Because he knows how much you mean to me."

"Ah, okay, I guess. I mean, there's nothing I can do about that," I said.

"So, what's going on with you and Dick? He seemed very possessive when I ran into you this morning," Cruz said, and he didn't hide his dislike for Richard in any way, shape, or form.

"He wasn't being possessive at all. That's in your head. You were the one who grabbed my hand, and possibly grazed my boob on purpose," I said with a laugh, quirking a brow at him.

A wicked grin spread across his face. "Ah, you noticed that, did you. It was a little test."

"What kind of test?" I asked as the waiter set our plates down and my stomach growled.

"Well, I've seen those new over-active nipples of yours, since your trip to Honduras. Let's just say the headlights weren't on when I approached you and *Dick*. But one little graze with *my* finger, and they were on high alert." He smirked. So cocky and arrogant.

I rolled my eyes. "Well, he wasn't touching them. Of course, you just helped yourself and got a reaction."

"Don't talk about Richard touching your tits, Jade. We may be friends, but I'm not going there with you," he hissed.

I couldn't help but laugh at how ridiculous he was. "No one is touching anything. Relax. Not that it's up to you."

"Good to know. But he sure wants to, so keep an eye on that. I don't like him at all."

I shook my head. "You don't know him."

Why were we even talking about Richard? He wasn't a factor. But I wasn't about to tell Cruz that. If he thought I was wavering, he'd pounce. And I wasn't ready for that. He needed more time and so did I. He'd just gone back on the road, and he needed to focus on his sobriety.

"I know enough. He looks at you like he's picturing you naked. I fucking hate him."

My head fell back in a fit of giggles. He was beyond ridiculous, and I loved it.

"You don't say?"

"I do say."

"So, how's your little problem downstairs?" I wriggled my brows and smiled.

"Are you referring to my broken dick, Jade? Is this a joke to you? Do you know what it's like to go months without sex? With the worst case of blue-balls of your life?"

I covered my mouth with my hand to muffle my laughter. "I know what it's like to go months without sex, yes."

"Ah, good to know I'm not the only one suffering." Although he attempted to be serious, the grin he was trying to contain snuck out.

"I don't know. I don't think it's a bad thing to be by yourself for a while. You know, while you figure out who you are and what you want. I'm sure you can handle your blue-balls issue *in other ways*," I whisper.

"Are you asking me if I take care of business?" He cocked his head to the side, and his honey-brown gaze locked on mine.

"What? No. I wasn't asking that. I was just making a suggestion. You know, so you aren't suffering."

"Oh, I'm suffering, Jade. And hell yes, I take care of business. Several times a day. In the shower. Before bed. First thing in the morning," he said before forking a bite of lasagna and popping it in his mouth.

I stared at him, my jaw probably hanging on the ground. My face heated and I reached for my water. Jesus. Was it hot in here?

"Wow. That's a commitment."

"And do you know what I think about every single fucking time?"

"Um, no. I'm good. I think we're crossing some friendship boundaries," I said, wiping my sweaty palms on my jeans beneath the table.

"Come on. You and Ari don't share your bedroom antics? Bullshit. You just don't like hearing about it from me because it turns you on."

My eyes bulged out of my head and I looked around the room to see if anyone heard him. "Keep your voice down. People will hear you."

"I don't give a shit if the whole world knows I slap my oversized sausage multiple times a day thinking of your naked body and those perfect tits," he said, like we were discussing the weather.

I gulped down some water and waved the waiter over for a refill.

"Okay. That was a lot of information."

He shook his head and smiled. "I love that you still get shy with me. Does that embarrass you that you have that effect on me?"

"No. I mean, not really." Are you kidding? I wanted to jump up from my chair and dance around the room that I had any effect on this beautiful boy. But I wouldn't tell him that.

"So, back to Dick. How much time do you spend with him?"

"Oh, we're back to that, are we?"

"What? This is normal friendship conversation, right? I mean, I'm not one for small talk with anyone but you, so I don't have a fucking clue."

I turned the spaghetti noodles in circles, gathering them around my fork. "We have several classes together, so I see him a lot."

I took a large bite of noodles and closed my eyes as the flavors exploded in my mouth.

"Do you love him?" His tone was serious and his gaze even more intense. Did he really think I was in love with Richard? Wow. I was a better actress than I thought.

I coughed as I swallowed my food. "What? No. I'm not in love with Richard."

"Good. So, was he fine with you coming to dinner with me?"

He thought my non-existent relationship was a lot more serious than it ever even ventured.

"He was fine with it. He's not an insecure guy." That was partly true. Richard was a confident guy. We just weren't together.

"I guess he'd have to be with a name like Dick."

I laughed. "You know you're ridiculous, right? And no one calls him Dick, but you."

"Most people just don't have the balls to call him on it."

I rolled my eyes and smiled. God, I'd missed him.

"Thank you so much for the suit. It's absolutely perfect. You didn't need to do that. But I love it, so thank you," I said.

"Of course. I wish I could have helped more. I know how important this interview is to you. Because it is to me too, Jade. You know I want you to achieve your goals."

Oh god. When he says this kind of stuff, I find it hard to hold back. I have to ignore it, or I'll feel too much right now. "Yeah. I'm so excited about it."

"You're going to kick ass. I'm really proud of you," he said, reaching across the table and locking his pinky finger around mine.

I sucked in a long, slow breath at the contact. "I'm proud of you, too."

And I meant it. Cruz had been sober for a few months and he'd found a positive outlet in his MMA training. He was on tour with Exiled, and probably facing every temptation on the planet, yet here he was. Sitting across the table from me, telling me he was proud of me.

This was progress.

ten

. . .

Cruz

I WAS PLAYING ALL my fucking cards tonight, and I'd flustered her. Seeing her with Dick today had pissed me off, but I thought about what Dr. Roberts said, and kept my cool. I couldn't control what Jade did, but I could control how I reacted to it. And I was determined to be her friend until she came to her senses. Hopefully it happened sooner rather than later.

We sat in the car in front of her house. We'd shut the restaurant down talking about her upcoming interviews, and she wanted to know all about my training with Gio.

"Do you think you'll ever fight?" she asked with concern.

"I mean, I'd like to beat Dick up, but I doubt he'd get in the octagon with me."

"Stop. Richard plays soccer, he's not a fighter, and he really is a nice guy."

"Well, there's no one else I want to fight, so no. I've sparred with a few guys, but I'm not looking for another obligation. It's just something I'm doing for me," I said, as we faced one another in the front seat of my Audi. The streetlight shined down on her, illuminating her gorgeous face. I wanted to kiss her so bad, I tried to focus on anything but her mouth.

"I get that. I'd love to see you doing your thing," she said, biting down on her bottom lip.

"Come with me tomorrow. You can get in a little workout. Wouldn't hurt for you to know a few self-defense moves."

"Really? Yeah, that sounds fun. I have class all day, but I'm done at around three P.M."

"Perfect. I'll pick you up at three-thirty," I said, happy that she'd agreed to see me tomorrow. My plan was working.

"Okay. When do you fly out?"

"Tomorrow night around eight. So maybe we can just grab a pizza after the workout?" I said. Because pizza and workouts were something friends did. Didn't matter that I was already fantasizing about seeing Jade in her workout tights all sweaty and tired.

Focus.

"Sounds good. So, um, are you just sleeping at your place tonight?" She fidgeted with the ring that still hung on a chain around her neck and stared down at her hands when she asked.

I leaned forward and tipped her chin up to meet my gaze. I was taking a different approach this time. If Jade wanted to put me in the friend-zone I was going to have to put her there as well.

"Are you asking me to have a sleepover again?"

"What? No. I mean, I hadn't thought about it," she whispered, avoiding my gaze.

Bullshit. It was all either of us were thinking about.

"I think another sleepover might be dangerous," I said, waiting for her jade greens to lock with mine.

"You do?"

"I do."

"Why?" she asked, holding her chin up high now, like it was a shield against what I might say.

"Because the next time I'm in bed with you, I won't be there as your friend. I'll be there because you want me as much as I want you. And you'll be mine in every way."

"Oh," she said, her eyes doubled in size as they took me in.

"Do you remember what we were like together? The way we made one another feel?" I asked.

"Yeah. Of course." Her voice was just above a whisper.

"Good." I leaned forward and kissed her cheek. My fingers found her trembling hand in her lap.

She didn't move. She stayed completely still. She just held my hand and her breaths came hard and fast. Fuck me. I used my other hand to adjust myself from where I sat. The last thing I wanted was to get out of the car with a raging boner.

My lips hovered right beside her ear. "Okay, let's get you inside."

I pulled back and she shook her head, wiping her palms on her jeans. "Yeah, yeah. Let's go."

I smiled as I got out of the car, knowing how I was affecting her. I walked her to the front door.

"Alright. See you tomorrow afternoon?" I asked.

"Yep. Sounds good. Thanks for dinner."

"See you tomorrow, More Jade," I said, walking backward to my car.

She waved and tripped over her own feet when she stepped inside, and I heard her laughter fill the air around me. And I fucking loved it.

When I got back to my place, I pulled out the sketchbook I'd purchased at the art gallery a few weeks ago and flipped through the pages. Drawings of Jade filled my book. Writing music was an outlet for me, but it was something I shared with the world. Even my MMA fighting was something I did with Gio. But, drawing, sketching—that was mine. No one saw these but me. And I liked it. I didn't hold back. At some point I'd share them with my girl. But she wasn't ready yet.

I flipped to a clean page and pulled out my charcoals and got to work. It cleared my head. I poured my feelings onto the paper. I liked the imperfection that came with using charcoals—a reflection of life. Some of the most beautiful things were imperfect. And you could blend all those imperfections together on paper, just as you could in life.

And Jade Moore—well, she was perfection on and off the paper.

———

"Good, Jade, keep your arms up and protect your face," Gio said, as Jade bounced around on the mat beside me.

This was by far my favorite workout yet. Jade wore black leggings and a white tank with a pink sports bra beneath it. Her dark hair was pulled back in a long ponytail that trailed down her back. Jade was small, but she had more muscle now. Her arms were defined and cut. Obviously, she'd worked hard this summer.

"Like this?" she asked.

"Yes," Gio said, glancing over his shoulder at me. "Go take a few laps, Cruz."

That fucker. I was enjoying the show.

I finished up my third lap and Gio walked over to me as Jade did push-ups on the mat. "You want to spar with Simon again? He's got a fight coming up and he said you challenged him more than any of the sparring guys they have lined up for him."

I ran a hand over my chin. "Yeah, let me make sure Jade has time to hang out for a bit."

"Yeah, you probably need to spar. You didn't get in much of a workout aside from the one your eyes got staring at her ass the whole time," he said with a laugh.

I flipped him the bird and jogged over to Jade. "Hey, do you mind if I spar with this dude real quick? It won't take long. And then we can go grab a bite and I'll take you home."

She wiped her forehead with a towel and turned to face me. Her face was glistening, her cheeks pink and her hair sweaty. And damn if I didn't fight the urge to pull her against me and kiss her hard.

"You're going to fight someone?" She didn't hide the anxiety in her voice as her brows pinched together with concern.

"We're going to spar. He has a fight coming up and needs someone to practice with."

She blew out a long breath. "I don't like the idea of someone hitting you."

"Well, then I'll try not to get hit too much." I laughed and reached for her hand, leading her over to the octagon.

Her hand fit in mine like it belonged there. Because it fucking did.

Simon's trainer nodded. "Thanks for doing this, Cruz."

"Yeah, no problem," I said, turning to Jade. "Stay next to Gio."

"Jesus, is he always this crazy around you. I've never seen this side of his moody ass," Gio said to Jade with a laugh.

I flipped him off again and Jade laughed.

Simon bumped fists with me. "Don't go easy on me. I'm about to face my toughest opponent yet. I need to get pushed."

I nodded. "Alright."

We both moved around the mat and I let him make the first move and set the pace. He came at me with a cross punch, and it barely skimmed my shoulder. Jade gasped in the background, but I tuned her out.

I was focused. When his front kick came at my head I ducked and moved, and he wobbled a bit allowing me an opening for a leg kick, causing his left leg to come out from under him as he stumbled and I pounced. His trainer called time and I moved to my feet and helped him up.

"Damn dude. You sure you don't want to start fighting? You've got a knack for this," Simon said before moving to get a drink of water.

"I'm sure," I said, walking over to grab a bottle from Gio.

"Those were some good moves, brother," my trainer said.

I looked over at Jade. She was studying me, and her gaze was intense.

"You okay?" I asked before wiping my face with a towel.

"Yeah. Just fighting the urge to jump in and be your backup," she said, and Gio barked out a laugh.

"Please do not jump in there. He's got this handled just fine."

I smiled. I got it. I was the same way with her. No way in hell would I ever stand by and watch someone fight her.

"Two more rounds and we're out of here, okay?"

"Yeah." She licked her lips, and I leaned over the ropes and kissed her cheek. I wanted to do a lot more, but we weren't there yet.

"Alright lover boy, let's go," Gio said.

The second round moved just like the first. We each got a take-down and wrestled around on the mat. The third round intensified, as we both tried out a few jabs and sidekicks. Simon had me in a chokehold until I broke free and I heard Gio arguing with Jade.

I scrambled back to my feet, and Simon shook his head. I chuckled and dove at him one last time and took him down. We wrestled around, going back and forth for the last few seconds. We were well matched, and he'd pushed me hard.

"Nice job, man. I couldn't keep you down today, which is probably a good thing because I think your girl was about to jump in and go spider monkey on my ass," Simon said, chugging some water and winking at Jade.

"Turns out he didn't need backup," she teased, and he fist bumped her.

"Damn. She's a keeper, dude. Any girl who's got your back like that," he said.

It didn't matter what Jade and I were right now. She always had my back, and I'd always have hers.

We said our goodbyes and walked out to the car. "You hungry?"

"Yeah, always," she said, buckling herself up.

Jade and I were definitely making progress, and I knew she'd been all spun up last night when I said goodbye to her. I wasn't going to see her for a few weeks, so I wanted to make sure I left her thinking about me after today. Dick would have full access to her while I was at back-to-back shows over the next few weeks.

"Let's grab a pizza and go out to Oak Street Beach," I said, knowing it was her favorite thing to do. Jade had brought me there when we first met, and it would forever be a special place for us.

"Okay. I haven't been there since the last time we were there together," she said, as she gazed out the window.

It was a gloomy day in Chicago. The sky was gray, and fall was around the corner.

"You don't take Dick there?" I pressed, because I needed to know.

She turned to look at me and rolled her eyes. "No. I haven't taken *Richard* there."

"Interesting," I said.

"You're overthinking it. We just haven't gone yet."

"Or you don't think much of him."

She laughed but didn't respond. We stopped to grab a pizza before we parked at the beach, pulled the blanket from my trunk, and made our way down to the water.

"You going to sing me a rendition?" I said, reminding her of the time she sang me Shining Star in this same spot. I knew I loved her that day, but I was too chickenshit to admit it back then.

"How about you sing me something new. You said you wrote me something." Jade leaned back on her elbows and stretched out her legs.

"I thought *you* wrote something, too? You never showed me."

"Yeah, well, you're the professional singer. I say you go first, and maybe I'll email mine to you," she said.

"Alright. That's fair. It's not going to sound as good without music."

"I don't care. I'm more interested in the lyrics," she said, reaching up to adjust the elastic in her hair. A few strands had fallen out from her ponytail and they framed around her pretty face.

"Okay. Well, I have something new I've been working on." I took my phone from my back pocket and pulled up my notes.

"Can't wait to hear what's going through that head of yours," she said with a smile that made my chest squeeze.

Darkness comes, and pulls me in,
Surrounding me like a second skin.
And then it happens, takes you away,
Haunted by sins from that day.
I realize it's all on me,
This is not who I want to be.
Feeling better, found my way,
A little more light with each passing day.
Like a magnet, drawn to you,
So much love, you know it's true.
Forgive my sins, and follow me,
You're the air I want to breathe.
An inner strength and pounding fists,
Life has thrown so many twists.

When you're with me, I am whole,
You have my heart—you are my soul.
Don't fly away, don't go too far.
Stay with me beneath the stars.
Need your laughter, need your love,
Need your light that shines above.
Like a magnet, I'm drawn to you,
So much love, don't know what to do.
Forgive my sins, and follow me,
You're the air I want to breathe.
Forgive my sins and follow me.
You're the air I want to breathe.

I set my phone down and looked up to meet her gaze. Two tears trailed down her cheeks, and I leaned forward and swiped them away with the pad of my thumb. I wanted to pull her to me, but Jade had a wall up right now and I needed to respect that and be patient.

"I didn't mean to make you cry," I said as I reached for the tips of her fingers and pulled them to my lips.

She moved closer to me. She wasn't climbing in my lap, but she wasn't pushing me away either.

"No, it was beautiful. Just hit me with all the feels, you know?"

"Good, can't ask for more than that," I said. I studied her, wanting to capture the emotions I stirred in her.

"Can I ask you something?"

"Anything."

"Tell me what happened that morning. You know, when you found me. I've never really known any of the details about what happened, because, well, I didn't want to know at first. But now I do," she said. Her face hardened a bit as she spoke, as if she were reliving it.

I sat up a little straighter and let out a long breath. Jade was entitled to know everything that went on that morning, no matter how uncomfortable it was to revisit it.

"Adam woke me up shouting my name and I stumbled out of my bedroom. I was stunned to see you on the floor. Jesus, Jade. I lost my shit. I fell apart. I grabbed you and tried to wake you up, and Adam called 911."

"I was near the hotel room door, right?"

"Yes. And you were in and out of consciousness. It was so fucking scary." I shook my head, still in disbelief about what happened. Dex had hit her, and her head came down on the entry table and she fell to the ground. She'd lain there for hours.

"And you hadn't known I was coming to see you, so you were probably very confused to see me there."

"Yeah, and the fact that I'd taken two Ambiens and washed them down with whiskey, well that didn't help much either. I'd gone from being completely sedated to being sober as shit and terrified that I'd lost you."

"And Dex was gone, right? He'd left after it happened?"

"He said he didn't realize you were knocked out, and he panicked. Fucking piece of shit just left you there," I said.

"Yeah. He was angry that night."

"Are you ready to tell me what happened? He was there with a girl when you arrived, right?" I asked.

"Yeah. They had a big pile of cocaine on the table, and I walked in. She wanted to leave, but he didn't. I ran in your room and tried to wake you, but you were—I don't know. I couldn't wake you. He said we were going to talk about why I didn't like him. He dragged me back to the front room, and it went from bad to worse pretty quickly. I pushed him off me and he knocked all his cocaine on the floor and got angry. He pinned me to the couch, and I fought him off. I ran for the door, and he caught me by my hair or shirt collar, I don't remember."

I stroked her hand with mine and fisted my other hand beside me. My rage for Dex was unexplainable. I'd beaten the shit out of him, and it still wasn't enough.

"I'm so fucking sorry, Jade. I fucking hate him."

She looked up at me. Her jade green gaze filled with emotion. "I don't. Not anymore. He was out of his mind, Cruz. He has a serious drug problem. And I can't waste my energy hating him."

"I don't mind wasting energy hating him."

She laughed and wiped at her falling tears.

"Life is about forgiveness, right? But it's also about learning from past mistakes, and that's what I'm trying to do now," she said, squeezing my hand. "I'm not trying to punish you, I'm really not. I just don't want to get hurt again."

I couldn't stop myself if I tried. I reached for Jade and pulled her on my lap and wrapped my arms around her. "I get it, and I'm so fucking sorry for hurting you."

She looked up at me and placed her hand on my cheek. "I know you are."

"I love you, More Jade."

"I love you too. But it's just not our time right now. You need to focus on your sobriety, and I need to focus on my life."

I touched my forehead to hers, and we sat like that for a few minutes. Neither of us saying a word. The only audible sound was our breaths coming hard and fast, as we acknowledged all the pain and all the hurt.

But most importantly—all the love that was still there.

eleven

. . .

Jade

THE ALARM on my phone went off, but I was already awake. Today was a big day. I'd dreamed of attending NYU medical school for as long as I could remember. I made my way into the bathroom and washed my face and straightened my hair. I thought of Cruz as I pulled my new suit on and looked in the mirror. We'd made progress after our talk at the beach. It actually felt good to talk about what had happened last year, and I was glad we'd finally done it. It was a step in the right direction.

My phone vibrated.

> CRUZ
>
> Thinking of you. Good luck today. I'm proud of you. Kick ass. Love you.

My chest squeezed. I loved him too. But it was too soon after everything that had happened. We were both still healing.

> Thank you! Wearing my new swanky suit. Feeling very sophisticated. Love you more.

Cruz thought I was still dating Richard, and I'd be smart to keep it that way.

One more text came through. There was a photo attached of Dad and Sara both holding a thumb up. Ridiculously cute.

DAD

Proud of you, Jady bug. Just be yourself.

Thanks guys. Love you both.

I made my way downstairs and Ubered over to the university. I tried to eat a protein bar, but my stomach was in knots. I tucked it in my purse, closed my eyes, and concentrated on getting my breathing under control.

NYU offered free tuition to the students they admitted to their medical school. It also happened to be in my second favorite city. The idea of living in New York and attending medical school thrilled me. I was lucky just to get this interview. Getting in would be even more of a longshot. But I was all about long shots these days. I didn't think Cruz and I could ever get back to where we were this quickly. We were the best of friends now. Four months ago, we were barely speaking.

Yep. All about the long shots.

I made my way to the lobby where we were scheduled to meet. There was a group of students there, dressed similarly to me, so I walked over that way.

"Hi, I'm Siera," a girl with blonde hair slicked back in a bun said.

"Hey, I'm Jade. Nice to meet you."

Three more people introduced themselves, Jonah, Kylie, and Brad. They were all here for the interview.

"Where do you go to school, Jade?" Jonah asked. His voice echoed a bit in the large lobby. The marble floors were gleaming in the light coming in from above.

"I go to Northwestern."

"Ah, great school. Kylie and I go to Columbia. Brad attends Stanford, and Siera goes to Duke."

"That's great. Is this your first interview?" I asked, forcing myself to look up as I spoke. I fought the urge to go all introvert and focus on the interview.

Kylie chuckled. It sounded a bit condescending, but I was also on edge, and could just be reading into it.

"God, no. This is my, what?" she said to Jonah, throwing her hands in the air in dramatic fashion.

He rolled his eyes. *"It's your third."*

"Right. It is my third. I can't keep it all straight. I interviewed at Columbia and Harvard already," Kylie said. Her red hair was swept into some sort of fancy knot at the nape of her neck. She was tall and lean, and screamed confidence, but not in the good way—in the, *I'm-better-than-you*-way.

"Oh, wow. That's amazing. Congratulations."

"Well, this is my first interview and I'm so freaking nervous," Siera said, and I smiled at her.

"Me too."

"Aren't you two adorable. Don't worry at all, girls. It's a piece of cake. I just go in knowing that they should be so lucky to be interviewing someone of my caliber."

Brad stood beside me and chuckled but covered it with a cough. He was tall with dark hair and clad in a navy fitted suit. "I guess it's good to be confident. Have you heard back yet from Columbia or Harvard?"

Kylie cocked her head and took her time perusing him from head to toe, as if she were assessing his value. "I haven't' heard anything yet. But that's normal. They said we probably wouldn't hear anything until December."

"This is my first one too, and it's definitely my top choice," Jonah said.

"The best advice I can give you all is to just be yourself," Kylie said, like she ran the place.

Siera's gaze locked with mine and we both smiled. Clearly Kylie was annoying everyone, which only added to the fact that we were all nervous.

A few more people walked up and joined our group, before a woman, Dr. Devore stepped out and introduced herself as the dean of admissions. She took us on a brief tour and told us what to expect today. We'd be interviewing with two different people, and we'd also have the opportunity to sit in on a class in between our interviews.

Relax. Enjoy this. You've worked hard to be here.

I said the silent mantra on repeat in my head as we walked over to see the lab. The equipment was top of the line and attending this medical school would be an honor. I took in the high-tech x-ray machine, and Dr. Devore talked to us about the global opportunities that would be available to us. I thought of my time in Honduras and the impact that the experience had made on my life. My belly fluttered when I thought about the future.

We toured the campus and then took a short break to use the restroom and get a snack. We all headed over to a little coffee shop and I ordered a hot tea. My hands were cold as it was still early in the morning and the sun had yet to come out.

"I don't know guys. I think I might like Harvard better," Kylie said, her whiney voice grating on my nerves.

"Well, good. Hopefully you go there and don't take a spot that one of us would like to have," Jonah said with a wink. I couldn't quite tell if they were friends, or just happened to attend the same undergrad.

"Trust me. If Harvard wants Kylie, Harvard gets Kylie," she said, speaking in third person which was a huge pet peeve of mine.

"Well, I love it here. This is definitely my top choice," I said, sipping my tea.

"Aww…that's so sweet. Are you on a gap year or are you a senior, because you look young," Kylie said, her gaze moved around my face like she was deciding what to make of me.

"Um, I'm still in school."

"I'm not surprised. How old are you?" Kylie asked, and I saw Sierra roll her eyes at the annoying girl.

"I'm twenty. Turning twenty-one in a few months," I said.

"Oh my gosh, *you're a baby*," she said, clasping her hands as if she were praying for me.

What the hell.

"How old are you?" Blake asked her.

"I'm twenty-four. They prefer older candidates. I've taken two gap years so that I can put my best foot forward, because why not?" Kylie said with a chuckle.

I'll tell you why not. Because we don't all have the luxury of waiting longer to start in the workforce.

Thankfully it was time to go, and we were led over to another building for our interviews. I waited for my name to be called, pushing back all the nerves that had gathered in my stomach. When I stepped in the large office, I took in all the dark wood and traditional décor.

"You must be Jade. I'm Professor Bloomington. Take a seat and let's get to know one another," he said. He was tall, with gray hair and kind eyes.

"Okay, thank you."

I spent the next hour and a half talking with this brilliant man and sharing my thoughts on the future of medicine and my reasons for pursuing this path as a career. He shared the school's philosophies and his own personal journey to becoming a physician and teaching future doctors as well. I was absolutely certain this was the school I was meant to go to. I just hoped they'd want me as much as I wanted to come here.

———

"Thanks for picking me up from the airport," I said to Dad as we took our seats at our favorite Italian restaurant in the city. His girlfriend Sara had to work, or she would have joined us as well.

"Are you kidding? I'm so proud of you, Jady bug. So, tell me how it went."

"Well, Dr. Bloomington is brilliant, and then I interviewed with a student and she was amazing as well. I loved the campus, the people, the energy, you know? Their students all get amazing residencies and it's just an incredible opportunity if I were to get in. They offer so many global opportunities, too. Really, Dad, it's just such a cool school. And the fact that they offer free tuition. Can you imagine if I graduated from medical school with no debt?" I was talking a mile a minute, but I'd been dying to fill him in on the interview.

"They'd be foolish not to take you."

"Says my father. Oh my gosh, you're totally reminding me of this girl at the interview. She was pretty full of herself. She thought I was a baby and made sure to mention it throughout the day." I rolled my eyes at the memory. "But trust me. Lots of qualified applicants don't get in."

"You worry too much, kiddo. I have faith in you."

"I know you do. Thank you," I said with a laugh. I loved this man so much it was painful at times.

"So, what's going on with this Richard kid?"

"Nothing. I haven't even told you about him since Honduras. Why are you bringing him up?" I asked, and we paused to place our orders.

"Cruz might have mentioned it when I spoke to him last. He said he's really trying to give you space, and then he hissed something about your boyfriend's nickname being Dick?" Dad said with a shrug.

"Oh my gosh, how often do you talk to him? He's ridiculous because A. his name is Richard; B. he's not my boyfriend; C. it's none of Cruz's business."

Dad barked out a laugh. "I think Cruz would beg to differ."

I rolled my eyes. "Well, I did go out with Richard once, but there just wasn't anything there. I haven't told Cruz that it's over because right now I think we both need time, and it keeps a little distance there until I figure things out. He needs to focus on his recovery, and I need to focus on school. I think it's good for me to be on my own right now."

Dad studied me before he spoke. "Have you forgiven him for what happened?"

"Yes. I mean, it wasn't his fault. At least not the part about Dex attacking me. But I need to know that I can trust him again before I jump back in," I said, reaching for my water and taking a long sip. "Because honestly, when we begin dating again—*if* we begin dating again—there's going to have to be an understanding that this is it, this is forever."

"I get that, and trust is important in any relationships. I had a hard time moving on after Mom passed, you know that. But we can't always protect ourselves from everything, or we wouldn't be living." Dad tore off a large piece of bread and smothered it in butter.

"I know, but you can take precautions to protect yourself from getting hurt, and that's what I'm doing," I said.

"To an extent, Jade. You were very guarded for a long time after Mom passed, always a cautious kid about who you let in. And that's why it was so nice to see you so happy with Cruz. I worried that you might not ever get there. I worried that what happened to Mom had scared you so much you wouldn't let people in. And what happened to you with Dex was terrifying. Hell, I'd still like to hurt that little shit. And Cruz, well, he messed up really bad. But he's human, and he's working hard to right his wrongs, and I commend that."

"I do too. And I know I can't control everything that life throws at me. Mom's death was out of everyone's control. So, that was a hurt that I couldn't avoid. But letting Cruz hurt me again—that's in *my* control."

"You can't protect your heart from everything, or you won't be living. Cruz didn't die—he made a mistake. And people mess up. It's part of life. You can't avoid that. Now if you tell me that you just don't love him anymore, well that's part of life too. And he'll have to understand that."

I gasped. "No. Of course not. I love him so much it hurts most of the time," I said, swiping at the two tears that ran down my cheek. "That's why he has the power to hurt me so much. Love isn't always enough."

Dad reached across the table and grabbed my hand. "Loving someone doesn't mean that you'll never get hurt, Jady bug. But it means that you love one another enough to get over the hurdles that life throws at you. And trust me, it doesn't matter who you're with, life will challenge you at times. So, be with the person that you love the most, and make it work. And right now, if you want to be alone, and figure things out—this is the time to do that. I was terrified for you to go on your own to New York for that interview."

I squeezed his hand and laughed. "Well, it wasn't for lack of effort. You sure tried to weasel your way in."

Dad's head fell back, and he smiled. "It's hard for me to let you go sometimes. It nearly killed me when you decided to spend the summer in Honduras. But I'm proud as hell of you for doing it."

"I know. I love you, Dad."

"Love you too, Jady bug. Okay, enough of the mushy stuff. Tell me more about this interview."

We spent the next few hours talking and laughing, and I told him all about the lab at NYU and the anatomy class that I sat in on. Spending time with my dad was exactly what I needed.

The next morning, I was up early for class. The last few hours of my day were spent in Elaine's office doing research. I'd been her research assistant for more than a year now, and we'd grown so close. She was a brilliant emergency room doctor, and I looked up to her immensely.

"Well, kiddo. How does it feel? Your work is going to be published in one of the most prestigious medical journals by the end of this year," Elaine said.

"It feels really good." I stacked up the papers I had spread out on her desk and started loading things into my backpack.

"Good. It should. And you feel good about the interview at NYU?"

"Yeah. I mean, everyone there was brilliant, so that's a little intimidating. But I think it went well," I said, pulling my backpack onto my shoulder.

"Trust me. They like humble candidates. Not the self-proclaimed superstars." She laughed. "What about Northwestern? You're interviewing there next week?"

"Yes. I'm looking forward to it."

"Good. Those are two really great options. Alright, you get out of here and get some rest. You work too hard," she said with a chuckle.

"Glass houses," I teased.

"Touche. I'll see you tomorrow."

I made my way outside and was surprised at the drop in temperature. The wind was blowing, and the sky was gray and dreary. Something caused me to turn around and I don't know what it was, but what I saw had me moving faster. I glanced back over my shoulder, as I thought I might be imagining things. A tall kid wearing a hoodie was watching me. I couldn't make him out from this distance, but I could swear it was Dex. My walk turned into a jog and I looked back once more before I turned the corner. He wasn't there anymore. Maybe I'd imagined the whole thing? Maybe it was just some kid in a hoodie who happened to be tall and thin. It didn't mean it was Dex. Last I heard, he was living in Los Angeles with his mother.

My phone rang and I nearly jumped out of my skin. It was Cruz. FaceTiming me.

"Hey," I said, glancing back once more to make sure no one was following me.

"Hey yourself, More Jade. What's up?"

"Not much. Just leaving research."

"It's getting dark. I don't like you walking alone," he said.

"Dad? Is that you?"

"Such a smart ass. I'm sure Jack wouldn't approve of you walking alone at night either," he said, and I studied his handsome features. He was sitting on his bed in his hotel room, his hair was sweaty and disheveled, he didn't have a shirt on, and his honey-brown gaze locked with mine.

"It's five o'clock in the evening, you fool. Are you telling me you wouldn't walk alone at this time of day?"

"I've got mad skills, More Jade. No one is going to mess with me."

"I can see that ol' shirtless one. You showing off your big muscles?" I teased.

"I don't know. Are you looking?"

I rolled my eyes. "So, what are you up to tonight?"

"Just finished my workout and thought I'd give you a call. You know, being the reliable best friend that I am. How's the dating world?"

I laughed. I couldn't help it. The dating world was non-existent, but he didn't know that.

"All good."

"Yeah? You got another hot date with Dick?"

"You're an awfully nosy bestie. You tell me first. Any hot chicks on your horizon?" I asked.

"Only one."

I smiled. "Hey, do you guys still hear from Dex?"

Cruz's posture stiffened. "No. Why?"

"I just wondered if he was still pushing to get back in the band?"

"Yeah. I mean, he and my dad can try all they want, it's never going to happen," he said, picking up a water bottle and tipping his head back as he chugged it.

"Good. And he moved, right? He lives in California?"

He studied me before he responded. "Yeah. Why? He didn't reach out to you, did he?"

"No. No. Nothing like that. I was just thinking about everything and wondered where he ended up."

"Last I heard he moved to California. I know he's gotten together with my dad out there too," he said rolling his eyes. "I'll check with Luke and make sure he's still out there."

"Oh no. No worries. I just wondered."

"So... what are you doing tonight? You going out?" he asked, and his shoulders tensed a bit as he waited for an answer.

"Nah. It's a bubble bath, studying kind of night," I admitted.

"Damn. I wish I was there."

I laughed and rolled my eyes. But I wasn't really annoyed at all.

I wished he were here too.

twelve

. . .

Cruz

"SO, how often do you see Dex?" I asked my father over the phone.

I got a weird vibe from Jade and wanted to make sure nothing was up. Luke checked in to see what was going on with Dex and was told that he was still in Los Angeles. But, if anyone knew what was going on with him, it was my father. Just like with everyone else, Dex was controlled by daddy dearest. The drugs, women, money, career, my father had a way of making you dependent and if you weren't strong enough to see that he'd take you down with him. That's what Lennon and I—and Mom now, were trying to break free from.

"I haven't seen him in a while. I think he's actually cleaning his act up. Heard he'd checked into a program out in Los Angeles. But I bet he still wants back in Exiled."

"That's not happening. You do understand that, right? He was a train wreck to begin with, but he went out with a big bang when he hit my girlfriend and left her lying on the ground unconscious. You do see that there's no coming back from that, correct?" I said, dropping to sit at the desk in my hotel room.

"I don't believe anyone is ever at a point where redemption isn't an option. Hell, if that was the case, I may as well throw in the towel with your mother."

"Yeah. I'm not getting in the middle of that, but I can tell you this. Mom is doing well. She's never been better. She's sober and healthy and she seems really happy. You're still partying twenty-four, seven. You've made no effort to clean yourself up," I hissed. He was grating on my nerves and I regretted taking his call.

"Why fix what isn't broken. Just because Mom couldn't handle herself does not mean I have a problem. Do you know if she's dating anyone? She won't even take my calls."

"Well, you did have an affair with a teenage girl, and she nearly took her own life over it. I'm guessing she isn't going to be taking your calls anytime soon."

"That's where you come in. You need to help me. Tell her I'm doing better. She listens to you," he said.

"Yeah, I can't do that."

"Why?"

"Because it isn't true. You aren't doing better," I said, scrubbing a hand over my face and wondering why the fuck I agreed to open myself up to this man again. Dr. Roberts claimed forgiveness was a two-way street. It was one of her favorite sayings. *If you want it, you also have to extend it to others.* But this man just might be the exception.

"You judgmental little fucker. So now you're drinking the Kool-Aid too?" he snapped, and I could feel his rage through the phone. He wasn't used to things not going his way and now he was having a temper tantrum like a child.

"I'm not judging you. I'm calling it as I see it. I'm not lying to Mom for you."

"But you'll spend my money, right?"

"For fuck's sake, get over yourself. I make a shit ton of money on my own from Exiled. I have a trust fund from grandfather. And as far as you constantly dangling your airplane over mine and Lennon's heads—Mom reminded us that she owns half of every-thing, and those planes are just as much hers as they are yours. And seeing as you're holding up the divorce, I don't think you have a leg to stand on here," I said.

"So, this is how it's going to be. You and Lennon are siding with your mother."

"There're no sides, Dad. You fucked up. You cheated. This is your battle. I'm just telling you how it is. I took your call, didn't I?" I wanted to throw this arrogant fucker a bone. Because for whatever reason, a part of me still wondered if he could redeem himself.

"Well, I own a big stake in Exiled. So technically, I'm your boss."

I laughed. He was grasping at straws. "Alright. If you say so. I'm not even going to be in this band in a few months," I said.

"We'll see about that, Cruz. There are all sorts of loopholes when it comes to signing a contract, son. And as far as I can see, I own your ass."

"Why the fuck do you even care? Exiled will be successful with or without me," I hissed.

"Because whether you like it or not, you're the star of the show. I know you want to believe it's Lennon or Adam, but you're wrong. And everyone knows it. No one gives a shit about those two. They care about you. And this band brings me in a shit ton of revenue, and unlike you, I don't walk away from profitable endeavors."

"Well, I'm okay with being different," I said, knowing he was about to blow. I just didn't care.

"We're not as different as you think, Cruz."

There is nothing he could say that I'd find more offensive than insisting we were alike.

It was my worst fear.

"I need to go. I have a test to take."

"Still pushing this whole school concept, huh?" he said with a laugh.

"Yeah. I'm actually graduating in December, not that it means anything to you."

"I don't see the point of wasting time and energy on something that serves no purpose. You have a career as a musician. People would kill to be *you*. Yet you spend your time on something useless.

What are you going to do with a degree? Nothing that will make you as much money as this does."

"So, I take it you won't be attending the ceremony?" My tone dripped sarcasm.

"You'd be correct. I'm not supporting a decision that I don't agree with."

"You mean you aren't supporting a decision that doesn't make you money," I said.

"However you want to look at it, *son*."

"Alright. I need to go. Make sure Dex knows he's not coming back, so you both need to stop pursuing it. He needs to drop it, or we will expose him."

"No, you won't. Because you don't want anyone to know what happened to Jade. I'm not stupid. You could have destroyed him. But she obviously doesn't want what happened to go public, so you've kept it under wraps."

"Just give him the fucking message," I said, ending the call, before getting up and kicking the trash can across the room.

I picked up my phone and sent a text to Gio.

I need to work out NOW.

GIO

Meet me downstairs in five.

I needed to hit something or someone, and I needed to do it now.

———

I'd insisted that we never had a show on Halloween when we signed with AF records, and it was something they'd respected. Not my best negotiating once I realized we'd have a show the day before and the day after, but regardless, I could be there for Jade on a day that was difficult for her.

Jade's mother passed away on Halloween when she was only five years old, and this day had continued to be filled with darkness for her ever since. Though we weren't technically together right now, I'd made a promise to always be there for her and it was one I intended to keep.

"Does Jade know you're here?" Lennon asked as we stepped off the plane in Chicago.

"She told me not to come because she had class today, and she claimed she was going to dinner with *Dick*, but I knew I needed to be here. I'm still not sure why *you're* here though," I said with a laugh. I lit up a smoke and inhaled. My brother had insisted on coming with me tonight. I was only able to be here until tomorrow morning, but it was worth it to me to make sure Jade was okay.

"Because you told me she had plans with another dude, and I just want to be here for backup. You know. Just in case you need me."

I stopped abruptly and put out my cigarette as we approached our waiting car and turned to look at my brother. "Holy shit. You're worried I'm going to slip up? My how times have changed." I chuckled.

"I'm not worried you're going to drink or anything. I'm worried you're going to beat the shit out of someone and make things worse with Jade," he said, sliding in the car beside me.

"Listen. I know Jade. And I know when she needs me. And she needs me today. No one is beating the shit out of anyone. If I get there and she's actually with the dude, I'll leave."

"Bullshit. If you saw her with someone else you wouldn't leave." He laughed and grabbed a water from his backpack and chugged it.

"I keep my fights in the gym. Plus, *Dick* is not her type. Trust me."

"Then why is she dating him?" Lennon rolled his eyes.

"She's not. She's trying to convince herself that she likes him. It's a Jade thing. Don't try to figure it out."

His head fell back, and he laughed. "Alright, brother. I'm going to have to trust you. So where are we going first?"

"You're going to *our* house, and I'm going to *her* house," I said, quirking a brow at him.

He studied me. "Will you call me if there's a problem?"

"There's not going to be a problem."

"Okay, if you say so," he said when we pulled up in front of Jade's house.

"I say so. I'll see you later. Go do something. You're too young to sit around worrying."

I heard him chuckle as I stepped out of the car. Was I worried that Jade would be with Dick? Not really. For some reason, my bat senses told me there wasn't anything there. But my girl had decided we couldn't be together right now, and whatever she needed to do to prove it to me, I'd have to go along with. At the moment, she wanted me to be her friend, so that's what I'd be. Because I'd fucked up and this was where we were.

I knocked on the door and Ari stood on the other side when she flung it open. "I knew you'd come."

"Well, I came uninvited, so we'll see if she lets me stay. Is *Dick* here?" I asked, keeping my voice down.

She rolled her eyes and laughed. "What? No. Richard's not here. Between you and I, I've never even met the guy," she whispered. "She's been in bed since she got home from school. She didn't even go to research. Says she's sick. It actually breaks my heart, because I don't know what to do to help her."

"Alright. I'll take it from here." I rumpled her hair and made my way to the back bedroom.

The room was dark, and just a bit of light streamed in where her curtains gapped open. I sat on the side of her bed and pushed the hair back from her face. Her eyes sprung open, and she took me in. She didn't speak. She used her hands to cover her mouth to muffle the sob that broke free. I kicked off my shoes and stretched out to lie beside her and pulled her onto my chest.

"Shhhhh," is all I said, as I stroked her hair.

She broke down in full sobs now, and I just held her close. We stayed like this for a good hour. Her sobs subsided, and her breathing settled.

"You okay?" I asked.

"Yeah. I just hate Halloween."

We both chuckled because this had nothing to do with

Halloween. She was grieving for her mother and this day would always be tough for her.

"I can't believe you came," she whispered.

"Did you really doubt I'd show up?"

"Yes. I told you I had a date," she said, tilting her head back to look up at me.

"Ah, yes. Where is *Dick*?"

"Well." She fiddled with the ring that she still wore on a chain around her neck. "I don't think that's going to work out."

"You don't say."

"I do say." She forced a smile.

"You're not dating him anymore?"

"I think saying we were dating is a bit of a stretch."

"So how serious was it?"

"It was a lot more serious in your head, than it actually ever was."

"And why is that?" I said, my tone teasing.

"Maybe I wanted you to think it was more. Just to keep you at arm's length. But I really did want to try to date him. I thought it would help me get over you. But I just couldn't do it."

"Ah, so you were trying to make me jealous?"

"No. You did that on your own," she said, and I chuckled.

"Well, I hate *Dick*."

"You don't even know him." She hugged me tighter.

"I don't need to."

"I think I should be by myself right now. Focus on school and my interviews."

"I get that." Jade was so determined to be strong, and get through things on her own, and right now I needed to let her figure it out.

"How about you? Have you dated at all?"

"Nope."

"How come?"

"Been there done that," I said, tracing my finger along the lines of her face. Her cheeks, her nose, her eyes.

"You don't want to play the field a little? There's no guarantee that we're going to get back together."

Who was she trying to convince? Me or her?

"I'll take my chances."

"I love you, Cruz. Even if we can't be together right now," she whispered.

"I know you do. I love you more."

We both dozed off, and when my alarm went off in the morning, I kissed the top of Jade's head before shifting her onto the pillow so I could get up.

"Hey," she said, peeking one eye open and watching me.

"Hey. I have to get going. We head out on the European tour today. You going to be okay?"

She propped up on one elbow. The sun was just coming up, and orange and pink hues illuminated her pretty face. Her eyes were puffy, her lips were chapped, and she was the most beautiful girl I'd ever seen. Always had been.

"Yeah, of course. Thanks for coming."

I dropped to sit beside her on the edge of the bed and tucked her hair behind her ear. "I'll always be here for you."

I pushed to stand, and she reached for my hand. "Hey. I'm ready to show you those lyrics I wrote. They were written for you, really. I wasn't ready to show you before, but I am now. I'll email them to you soon, okay?"

"Can't wait to see what's going on in there," I said with a laugh and kissed her forehead.

When I got to the door, I turned back to look at her. "Love you."

"Love you, more," she whispered.

thirteen

. . .

Jade

"SHE COMES OUT FROM HER CAVE," Ari said, as I made my way into the kitchen.

"Yeah. I feel better today."

"I'll bet you do." She wriggled her brows at me.

"Please. Nothing happened. It was sweet of him to come, huh?"

Ari hopped up to sit on the counter. "Sure was. But he always shows up, doesn't he?"

"Yeah. He does," I said quietly.

"What are you so afraid of? Why can't you forgive him?"

"I do forgive him. I'm just being cautious. I want to make sure he doesn't get caught back up in that whole rock star lifestyle, you know?"

"I get that you want to protect your heart, I really do. But he went to rehab, it's been almost six months. He's on tour and he's keeping it all together and still making you his priority."

"Damn, he's even charmed you I see," I said, pouring us each a cup of coffee, and handing her the mug that said, *Good Morning, Asshole.*

She laughed. "Ah, my favorite saying ever. He didn't charm me, just calling it as I see it. When everything went down last year, I was so pissed at him, trust me. But he beat himself up over what happened, and he actually did something about it. And he's proved himself over and over. On top of that, let's call a spade a spade. You're miserable without him."

"Yeah, but I know how caught up I get when I'm with him. I'm so afraid to cross the line and get hurt again. I don't think I could take it a second time around. I have so much going on with school and research and interviews. There's no room for drama. And Cruz's lifestyle, well, it's not an easy one."

"No one ever said love was easy, kid." Ari cocked her head to the side, her blonde shoulder-length hair bounced around and she laughed.

"Thanks, Mom."

"Life's messy. We all have our fair share of drama. But I promise you, you're going to miss out if you hide from everything good, just because you're afraid of getting hurt," she said.

"Are you sure you don't want to study psychology? You've got a gift."

"Nah, the classes are too hard. I wouldn't have any *me-time*," she said after we dropped our mugs in the sink and walked out the door, making our way to class.

I thought about what she said. I hated that I was afraid to go all in with Cruz again. And that's what it really came down to—*fear*. And I didn't know how to get past it.

———

I had my Northwestern interview today, and I was ready with an hour to spare. Not a lot of sleeping goes on the night before a medical school interview. I slipped into my black suit and glanced in the mirror letting out a long breath. I dropped down at my desk and pulled out Mom's journal and opened to today's date.

November 5th
  Dear Journal,

The network talked to me about increasing my hours. I really feel like I'm making a name for myself. I want to get hired on here after I graduate, so I'm going to just keep my head down and work hard. Jack and I are better than ever. He's stopped going out after work so much. I think he's trying to impress the older guys at the firehouse. But he's finding balance, and I can't ask for more than that.

Last night, we had THE TALK. You know... the one about the future. About what we both want. He told me he sees us married with children, and as much as that topic used to scare me off, it didn't this time. I believe everyone has one person. One perfect match. Jack Moore is mine. He's not perfect, and he makes me mad sometimes. But he's perfect for me. I don't know how, and I don't know why. But I do know that I can't imagine my life without him. I do know that when he talks about the future, I like it. I didn't even gag when he brought up marriage. I never thought I'd be that girl. But the thought of marrying this boy, well, it gives me all sorts of butterflies. We're going to keep that little confession right here in this book.

The thing is—Jack encourages me to pursue my dreams. I can go after everything I want with him by my side. I love that about him. So, you heard it here first. Someday I'm going to marry that boy.

I used to think you had to choose. You know, between a career and a relationship. As much as I love my mom, I want more out of life. Mom is content being a wife and a mother. I never saw that as my path. I've always wanted to make a name for myself. Accomplish things. Impact the world. But I realize now that I can have both. I can do all of those things and be a wife and a mom. Who knew? LOL. Okay, off to work. I have places to be, and people to impress. Oh, and a hot fireman who is taking me to dinner tonight. Does it get any better than this life that I'm living? I don't think so.

Ciao for now,

J.E.

I laughed as I closed Mom's journal and tucked it back in my desk drawer. Even though she wasn't here with me, she was always teaching me about life through her words. And she was right. Life was filled with gray areas. I had always been a black and white type of girl, and I was learning that gray areas weren't the worst thing in the world. You couldn't control who you loved, or the curve balls life threw at you. And there was no hard and fast rule on forgiveness. And I needed to remember that.

My phone vibrated beside me.

CRUZ

Good luck today, rock star. You're going to kick ass. You never sent me the lyrics you wrote. I'm dying here, More Jade. Give me something.

I laughed. It had been a few days and I was still holding back.

Turns out, Cruz Winslow was my gray area.

I pulled up the lyrics on my laptop before sending them to him. I didn't really know if they were actual lyrics, or just my thoughts. But I'd been working on this since I left for Honduras. I wanted him to know how I felt about him. I'd tried so hard to make him believe that I'd moved on and was dating other people, but the reality was—I hadn't moved on at all. I'd just kept him at a distance. That's why I didn't share this with him before now. I'd been punishing him for what happened, and it was time to let it go. To forgive. To remember that we're all human and imperfect. I'd been holding on to anger and it was time to make peace with it. I didn't include a message with the email. I just sent what I'd written, because I knew he'd understand.

I'm so alone and lost right now,
Want to forget but don't know how.
This broken heart beats just for you,
How to move forward—don't have a clue.
You woke me up, you made me whole,
My trust, my heart, you all but stole.
But broken hearts take time to mend,
Don't want to lose my closest friend.
You showed me life in a new light,
Bright and shiny and worth the fight.
Losing you, means losing me,
Don't know how to act or who to be.
I want you back but it's too soon,
My everything—my sun, my moon.

Loving someone beyond the norm,
Means allowing your heart to be ripped and torn.
My safe cocoon tucked deep inside,
Protect my heart and try to hide.
You're such a force, so hard to fight,
My painful cries haunt me at night.
There's no one else I'll ever love,
Not another soul to the sky above.
My one and only, that is you,
My only love, you know it's true.
I dream that you are holding me,
On the beach and running free.
Sing me songs deep from your soul,
I am yours, and finally whole.
Don't give up on me, time will tell,
To heal and love and not to dwell.
Clinging hard to my safe place,
Scared to see your beautiful face.
Those honeyed eyes see right through me,
They know just who I want to be.
I miss you more than I can say,
My love for you grows every day.
My heart beats slow when not with you,
My only love, my only Cruz.

A weight lifted off my shoulders once I hit send. I'd finally said everything I needed to, and I was ready to move forward. Whatever that meant. Cruz would be gone for the next month on his European tour, so we had time to figure things out. I needed to be on my own right now, but I was ready to let go of all this anger and fear. I closed my laptop and grabbed my bag and started my trek over to the medical school. The future was bright, and I was ready.

For all of it.

Several hours later, after interviewing with a doctor, a professor and a student, I was done. I was hit with an overwhelming sense of relief. I felt like it went well, and I didn't let my nerves get the best of me.

"How'd it go?" Richard asked as we walked out together. We'd both interviewed on the same day.

"I think it went well. I feel good," I said, reaching in my purse to turn on my phone. I promised Dad, Cruz and Ari I'd text them right after.

"Long day, huh?" he said. We'd arrived at the interview first thing this morning, and six hours later we were finally heading home.

"Yes. I'm glad to be done." I laughed and waved goodbye when it was time to veer off to my house. "See you later."

"Yeah, see ya, Jade."

I was glad Richard and I could remain friends. When I walked through the door, I dropped down on the couch and saw a text from Cruz.

CRUZ

Powerful words, baby. You gutted me—but in the best way. Best lyrics I've ever read. Straight from the heart. Can't wait to discuss when I see you. Boarding the plane now for London. Let me know how the interview went. Love you more.

I was happy he was impressed by what I'd written. I shot everyone a quick group text to let them know I was done, and it went well. Ari came bounding through the front door.

"We're celebrating tonight. I'm so proud of you and I'm not taking no for an answer," she said, dropping down on the couch beside me.

I laughed. I actually wanted to go out and celebrate, and I hadn't felt like that in a long time. "I'm totally down."

"Holy hell. Who are you and what have you done with my best friend?"

I rolled my eyes. "I'm trying to be a normal college kid, remember?"

"You've never been normal, but that's what I love about you." She wrapped her arms around me and laughed. "Yay. Everyone is going out tonight. Beer shots on me."

I had learned my freshman year in college that me and tequila did not get along. So, I stuck to beer. I'd occasionally take shots of beer, so it looked like I was joining in on the fun. My best friend had taken a liking to my little invention as well.

"Who's going?"

"Jace, Brayden, Sage, Cam, Lucas, Mila, you, and me," she said, tugging me by the hand toward her room. "Let's find you something cute to wear."

An hour later, Ari and I were cleaned up and heading out the door. We were all meeting for dinner at our favorite Mexican restaurant not far from campus. Viva Mercado's was a local hotspot, especially for college kids as we could load up on rice and beans which came free with your meal. The place was small with dim lighting, oversized booths, and the best chips and salsa I'd ever had.

"Oooh girl, look at you," Mila said, as she slid beside me in the booth. "Congrats. Two interviews down, right? When will you hear back?"

Mila and Lucas had been dating since my freshman year, and I'd met them through Ari. I loved this group and it felt good to be out and having fun.

"Thank you. I don't think I'll hear anything until after the holidays. But it's good to have them behind me."

"Okay, we've got eight shot glasses and eight beers. Here's to Jade," Ari said, handing everyone a Corona and a shot glass.

"Oh my gosh. You guys don't need to drink beer shots on my account." I laughed.

"We're proud of you. Just go with it, girl. Remember, this is all part of being a normal college kid," she whispered in my ear as everyone raised their glass.

I laughed and held up my little shot glass filled with beer to meet theirs.

"To Jade, who's as much a rock star as the boy she claims she's not dating, but he somehow always seems to be in Chicago these days," Mila said, and everyone chuckled. "Our very own rock star friend who is one step closer to going to medical school."

I smiled. It felt good.

"To the most humble and hard-working girl I know," Ari said, and we all clinked glasses.

I felt my cheeks heat. "Thank you so much."

We ordered dinner and finished off our one beer by pouring it into our shot glasses until we finished it. I didn't want to get too crazy because I had a ton of homework that I wanted to get started on tonight. But I was glad that I came to celebrate, and I was starting to feel like myself again.

"So, was it brutal?" Brayden asked, as he sat across from me and everyone broke out in their own little conversations.

"It wasn't too bad. Everyone was super nice, and I think attending undergrad at Northwestern made it easier because I was familiar with the campus, and I knew a few people in the group," I said.

Brayden had decided to take a gap year after graduation, and he'd accepted a scribe position with a well-known surgeon during that time.

"Okay, good to know. And your NYU interview went well?" he asked before taking an oversized bite of his enchilada.

"I think so. I mean, it's hard to know. It's so competitive, and you just hope you stand out in some way," I said, reaching for another chip.

"Yeah, I'm not looking forward to that stress," Brayden said with a laugh. "But I'm sure you killed it."

"Thank you. We'll see what happens."

"Enough shop talk, bud," Ari said, rolling her eyes at Brayden. "Hey, you guys know that song currently going viral on iTunes, '*Spread Those Wings*,' by Exiled?"

"Yes. I love that song," Sage shouted. "I played it on repeat this morning."

"Well, Cruz wrote that song for our girl, here." She beamed at me.

I shook my head and smiled. She was really on one tonight.

"Ugh. Why can't you be a singer?" Mila said to Lucas and we all laughed.

"Sorry. I don't have a musical bone in my body." Lucas leaned forward and kissed her.

"That's pretty cool, Jade. Does he send you the lyrics when he writes songs for you?" Sage asked as she leaned against Brayden's arm.

"Yeah, usually. He's a really talented songwriter." I bit down on my bottom lip. Thinking of Cruz made my stomach flutter.

"So, he writes you songs, he comes to town to see you, but you're not dating?" Cam, one of Jace's best friends asked.

"Great question," Ari and Jace said in unison and smiled.

"You know, he's on tour, and right now we're just really good friends and we'll see what the future holds," I said. It was the truth.

But what I left out was the fact that I wanted a future with Cruz.

I couldn't see a future without him.

It didn't exist.

fourteen

. . .

Cruz

IT WAS Thanksgiving back in the states, and we were performing in Australia tonight. We were all chilling in our suite before we went to the venue. We'd been here for a week, and this was our last show here.

"It's weird to have a show on Thanksgiving, right?" Bailey asked, smiling at my brother like the sun set on his ass.

"Well, I'd rather be on stage than stuffing my face with turkey. And technically, it's the next day here, so," Tia said to her sister.

"Well, it's Thanksgiving for Mom and Dad *right now*, so…" Bailey rolled her eyes at her sister.

"How about you? Is it weird for you being here?" Shayna asked, turning her full attention to me. Tia's best friend had joined us this past week on tour, and she was a cool chick, but I wasn't looking for new friends.

"It's fine. It's not forever," I said because we were still keeping my departure under wraps for now, but everyone in this room knew it was coming. I assumed that Tia told her best friend everything as the chick couldn't keep her mouth shut for more than a minute.

"That's true. How do you normally celebrate Thanksgiving?" she asked me.

The girl had been giving me a shit ton of attention, and I'd tried to make it clear that nothing was going to happen, but she kept at it. Maybe she was just a friendly chick, who knows. I'd assume Tia would have filled her in that I wasn't going to bite, especially since she'd dubbed me "the rock star monk" the last couple weeks.

"With my girl," I said, no hesitation.

Her face dropped. "Oh. I didn't know you had a girlfriend."

Lennon laughed and shook his head as he glared at Tia. "It's complicated. But he's definitely unavailable."

"Hey, I know the dude is a monk these days, but I didn't think he and Jade were back together." Tia held her hands up as if she were defending herself. "Thanks for the four-one-one."

"It's none of your fucking business," I hissed.

Yeah, I was sexually frustrated for sure. But I was going to stay the course. Jade and I weren't dating, but we were together in every sense of the word. She was mine and I was hers. It was just understood. And I was giving her the time she needed, and I sure as shit wasn't about to fuck that up with a meaningless romp.

Shayna glared at her best friend as if this was the most devastating news. I hadn't given her even the slightest hint of interest, so she should have been able to piece this shit together.

"Well, I'm fairly certain he hasn't been laid in months, so I guess I just thought maybe he'd want to have some fun," Tia said, and everyone turned to look at her. "What? Come on, we're on tour together. I'd know if he were hooking up."

"Don't you have your own shit to worry about? Why are you always in my fucking business?" I snarled.

"You know the quickest way to fix that moody attitude of yours, don't you?" She wriggled her brows and Zach laughed. He and Tia had something going on, but it didn't stop her from being nosy as shit with everyone else.

I gave her the bird when my phone vibrated, and I saw a FaceTime call from Jade flash across the screen. I moved to my bedroom and shut the door. Too many people were in my business lately, and there was only one person I actually wanted to talk to. This was a good sign. She was reaching out on her own now. It had been me initiating things these past few months. This was progress. Though I was doing the math in my head and wondering why she was calling at four A.M. We hadn't talked all that much over the last few weeks, as I was trying to respect that she wanted to be on her own right now, not to mention the time change while we were here.

"Hey," I said, settling on the bed, and propping my back against the headboard. "Everything okay? It's early there."

"Yeah, I fell asleep right after dinner last night, so I'm wide awake now and thought I'd try you. Happy Thanksgiving. Are you getting ready for your show?" she asked, propping herself up on her bed at her dad's place in Bucktown.

"Yep. Last show. How's it going there? What time is everyone coming over?"

Jade and her father had a tight group of friends that came to their house every Thanksgiving. I'd spent the last two years with them, and I was definitely missing it today. The normalcy. The comfort.

Jade.

"Everyone's coming around three o'clock."

"I'm glad you called. We still haven't gotten to talk about those lyrics you wrote." We'd texted about it and the few times we'd spoken had been pretty rushed and I'd wanted to hear about her interview.

"Oh. Well, I'm no songwriter. But it was how I felt."

"How you felt or how you feel?" I asked.

Her cheeks pinked, and she smiled. "Obviously, it's how I feel."

"So, you're not dating anyone new?" My tone was all tease, but I wanted to see where we stood.

She rolled her eyes. "No. I told you I was just going to be on my own for a while."

"How's that going for you?"

"You know, it hasn't been that bad," she said with a laugh.

"You're not missing me as much as I miss you?"

Her face softened and she whispered, "I'm missing you a lot."

"Yeah?"

"Yeah."

"Me too. I can't wait to see you," I said.

"I'm excited for your graduation. Only two more weeks. Will you be home for long?"

"Just two days. But things slow down after Christmas. Can I spend those two days with you when I'm home?"

"Yeah, of course. I was hoping I'd get to see you a lot when you're here."

"Me too, More Jade. Hey, can I ask you something?" I said.

"Of course."

"Did you do those silly questions again this year?" I asked, making fun of the questions Jade put under everyone's plate on Thanksgiving every year. It was my favorite of her wacky traditions.

"They aren't silly, and yes. Why?"

"Choose one for me. It'll make me feel like I'm there, having a normal holiday."

She studied my gaze and tilted her head to the side. "I knew it. You love the questions too."

I laughed. "Whatever. Hit me with it."

She set the phone down and I heard her shuffling around her room before she returned with a bowl. She shook it in front of the phone and dipped her hand in. "Okay, let's see what we've got here. Ah… *what do you think is your best quality*? I can't wait to hear this one."

"Best quality? Well, I could go on and on." I laughed. "I'd say my best quality is my ability to know when I've found something good, and not to give up on it even when I'm incredibly uncomfortable and tortured."

Her head tipped back with a laugh. "How do you do that?"

"Do what?"

"Make me laugh even when you're probably serious."

"I'm totally serious. Remember when we first met and you told me your dad believed there was one perfect match for each person," I said, pushing to my feet and changing T-shirts as I heard Luke outside my door calling everyone to get on the bus.

"Yeah."

"Well, I believe it too. And you're mine. And I'm not giving up." I pushed my fingers through my hair and slipped on my combat boots.

"Okay, rock star. You better get going. Have a good show, and I'll see you soon."

"Happy Thanksgiving, Jade."

"Happy Thanksgiving." She paused and bit down on her bottom lip. "I love you, Cruz."

"Love you, more."

She was coming around. I ended the call and met the guys out in our suite, and we made our way to the venue. I was ready to get back to the states and see Jade. But for now, I'd focus on our show.

Gio and I found a gym not far from the hotel, and we stepped outside and waited for our ride. I'd had a late night last night, as our show ran long, and I needed to blow off some steam today.

We stood on the sidewalk outside our hotel and I lit up a smoke. Gio rolled his eyes every time I did it because it completely contradicted the whole working out thing, but I'd never been one to follow the rules. I wasn't ready to give cigarettes up completely yet. I'd cut way back, but for whatever reason, I was on edge today. Maybe it was the call from my father telling me once again that I wasn't going to walk away from Exiled without a fight. The dude needed a new hobby.

"Cruz, is there any truth to Farah Clearwater's statement?" Some dude yelled out from behind me.

What the actual fuck? I turned to face him. He wore jeans, a button-up and a sports coat and looked far too put together to be sinking this low.

I hadn't heard Farah Clearwater's name in months, so maybe this was just old tabloid news being revisited. It wouldn't be the first time they dredged up a bullshit story.

"Dude, beat it. We're not interested in gossip." Gio snarled at the guy.

"According to Ms. Clearwater, you two have been secretly seeing each other for a few weeks. Her claims don't sound like gossip," he said, stepping toward me with his bulky camera.

I let out a long exhale of smoke in his face. "Back the fuck up. I don't know Farrah fucking Clearwater and I don't know you. So, get the fuck out of my face, or we're going to have a problem." I dropped my smoke and snubbed it out.

"Just giving you a chance to tell your side of the story, brother."

"I'm not your brother, and there are no sides to this story. I've never met the chick," I said, and our car pulled up to the curb.

"You heard the man, now step the fuck off," Gio said, squaring his shoulders as he faced the dude.

I laughed. "Come on. Don't feed it. That only encourages them more." I climbed in the car and he slid in beside me.

"Jesus. How the fuck do you deal with that?" Gio said, shaking his head.

"I go to the gym and beat the shit out of the bag," I said, taking a swig of water.

"Who's this Farrah chick?"

"The fuck if I know. Dex banged her a while back and for some reason, she's fixated on telling the world she and I are together."

"You think Dex is behind this shit? Maybe it's a way to get back in if he thinks he's got you by the balls."

I nodded. "Probably. Let me shoot Jade a text," I said. I needed her to be aware that Dex was not to be trusted. He was most likely behind this, as he had the most to gain from it right now. We'd kicked him out of Exiled and this was probably a stunt that he thought he could use against me to get back in. I sure as shit didn't want him near Jade. Ever since she'd asked about him, I'd had an unsettled feeling. And, for all I knew my father and Dex were in this together again. Nothing would surprise me where either were concerned.

> Hey. Farah fucking Clearwater is back in the news selling her bullshit story. I think Dex is behind it, so just be aware.

MORE JADE

I heard about that online. There was a guy parked outside my door this morning asking if I was okay with you moving on. LOL. These people are so annoying. Don't worry about me. I've got my handy dandy pepper spray, rape whistle, and my ninja moves.

Not fucking around, Jade. You need to take this shit serious. You want me to have Luke get someone out to your house to take care of any reporters that might be hanging around?

MORE JADE

NO!! It's not a big deal. Please don't do anything like that. I promise, I'm fine.

Alright. Sorry you have to deal with my shit.

MORE JADE

I'm sorry YOU have to deal with your shit.

Not for much longer. I'm done with Exiled in June.

MORE JADE

No more Farah Clearwater. No more Dex. And even your dad won't have anything to bother you about.

I laughed. She just got me, and I fucking loved it.

See you in a few days.

MORE JADE

Yep. You're graduating, rock star. Miss you.

Miss you more.

"What's the deal with you two? She forgiven you yet?" Gio

asked. He and I had grown close, and he knew a little bit about why Jade and I weren't together at the moment.

"She's getting there."

"Good. You impress me, man," he said.

"Why's that?"

"You deal with a lot of bullshit being the lead singer of Exiled. You have, quite possibly, the most fucked up father I've ever met, and you remain sober. And you're a kickass fighter, who could turn that into a career if you wanted to," he said, with a smirk.

"Not happening. And, thanks for saying that. Now, enough of the soft shit. How about you find me a sparring partner. I need to beat the shit out of someone who is willing."

He laughed. "Let me see what I can come up with when we get there."

"Sounds good."

I googled Farah Clearwater's name to see what I was up against. No one would believe her after she cried wolf last time, but I should at least be prepared for the shit storm that was most likely coming my way.

I read through a few articles that sounded like complete bullshit, even if I was an outsider who didn't know we'd never met, I'd find this shit hard to believe. She'd basically said that we'd been on and off since last year, yet when asked, the only picture she could produce was a photo of Jade and I that had been taken by the press, and Farah had clearly photoshopped her face onto it. Even the press called out the photo and said that it looked an awful lot like the one of me and Jade that had gone viral. She had yet to come up with anything else. Red fucking flag. I found it fascinating that this chick could take this story this far when we hadn't actually ever met. I mean, where was she getting her information?

Fucking Dex. The dude was an asshole. Always had been. Always would be.

So much for his sobriety. The guy wasn't fixing shit. He was stirring the pot.

But I was done playing his games.

fifteen

. . .

Jade

"CRUZ CHRISTIAN WINSLOW," the dean of the art school called out over the speaker.

Our group was on their feet, screaming and cheering as he walked across the stage. I fought back the tears that threatened. For some reason I was overcome with the fact that he'd surprised everyone by graduating while being on tour with Exiled. The truth was, he'd surprised me. I'd always believed in Cruz, but after all we'd gone through last year, a part of me had lost hope that he would be able to survive all the pressure and all the temptation that came with being the lead singer of Exiled. He'd fought hard for his sobriety, balanced all the drama going on with his family, and he'd lost his anonymity—but he'd taken it all in stride. And he'd come out the other end stronger than ever. I was so freaking proud of him. And in six months he would walk away from Exiled. Maybe this really was our time. Maybe Cruz and I could have our happily ever after.

Dad squeezed my shoulder and smiled down at me. Sara stood on the other side of him, and I was thankful they'd come out to support him. Adam, Tory, Lennon, and Bailey were all sitting in our row. Cruz's mother had flown out last night so she could be here to support her son. No sign of Steven Winslow, but no one was surprised. I know it bothered Cruz, even if he wouldn't say so.

I hadn't been alone with Cruz yet, as he got in late last night, and had to be here at the commencement first thing this morning. I was anxious to see him. Had been all week. What did it mean? I didn't have a clue. But I knew I missed him. I knew I loved him. And I knew I was proud of him. Would I still proceed cautiously, especially with all this Farah Clearwater gossip making its way through the media? Yes. Did I believe any of it? No.

But it was a reminder of the life Cruz was still living.

I hurried to the side and snapped a few pictures of him as he walked back to his seat. Instead of turning in his row, he walked straight for me. He ducked under the flagged off area and crashed into me with a hug. Why did it surprise me that he wasn't following the rules? He never had. He'd always marched to the beat of his own drum, and that's one of the things I loved most about him.

He spun me around and I heard Dad and Lennon laugh behind me. I buried my face in his neck and took in his masculine scent.

My beautiful rock star.

"Congrats," I said against his ear.

"Thanks for being here." He set me down on my feet.

"Don't you have to go back to your seat?" I asked, looking around nervously as we stood off to the side.

"No. I'm only here until tomorrow. I'm not spending three hours in a chair."

I laughed and shook my head. "Okay then. Let's get out of here."

His mom came over and hugged him, and my father pulled him into a hug and whispered something in his ear. Cruz's face lit up, and I was thankful for the bond they shared. Sara, Lennon and the rest of the group took turns congratulating him, but each time I looked up his gaze locked with mine.

"So, I was hoping I could take everyone to brunch," Cruz's mom, Juliette said.

"Do we have to?" Cruz whispered in my ear, and I slapped at his chest.

"Yes. They're all here for you," I said so only he could hear.

"Sounds great, Mom."

He grasped my hand, and I intertwined my fingers with his. I didn't know what we were, and honestly, I didn't care. I wanted to hold his hand and celebrate him. And that's exactly what I was going to do.

Brunch dragged on for two hours, and Cruz shot me a look across the table multiple times to let me know he was ready to go.

So impatient.

We all said our goodbyes, and Lennon and Bailey headed out to Cruz's childhood home to spend time with Juliette.

"You want to go to the beach?" he asked me once we were alone.

"Yeah."

We walked back to my house so I could change, and he left his cap and gown with me. Of course, he hadn't worn a suit beneath his gown. He wore black joggers and a T-shirt with tennis shoes.

Always the rebel.

We took his car out to our favorite spot at Oak Street Beach and spent the next few hours talking and laughing.

"So, no more *Dick*, huh?" he asked.

"I don't know why you insist on calling him that. But no, I told you, that was over. Richard and I are friends."

He nodded. "But you still need to be on your own?"

I laughed. He was the least patient human being I'd ever met.

"I'm feeling really good. I've been focused on school and working with Elaine, and it's been a pretty drama-free semester. But I'd be lying if I said I didn't miss you, because I do. All the time."

"Fuck. I can't promise you drama-free, Jade. Not yet," he said.

I moved closer to him as we sat on the blanket. The sun was just going down and the sky was covered in pinks and oranges. Peaceful and serene.

"Trust me, I know. Nothing about you is drama-free. And it's not your fault, I get it. It's out of your control."

He reached for me and pulled me on his lap, wrapping his arms around me. He buried his face in my neck. "What if we just take it really slow?"

I laughed as his scruff tickled against my skin. "You only have one speed, Cruz Winslow."

"Not true. Look how patient I've been these last few months."

"That's true. You have surprised the hell out of me," I said.

He pulled back to look at me. My gaze locked onto his honey browns. "Yeah? So, let me see. You aren't dating anyone else. I'm not dating anyone else. You miss me, and I miss you. So…"

My head fell back in laughter. "Point taken. Fine. *Slow.* I don't want this to be news, not with all this Farah Clearwater drama. It will only become a media frenzy. I just want to spend time with you when I can. Just you and me."

"I like the sound of that. Is kissing you part of this new plan? It's hard to keep up with all the rules," he said.

His hair was a mess, his face chiseled and gorgeous, and his full lips teasing me with every word he spoke. I licked my lips and tried to calm my breathing. It had been a minute since I'd kissed this boy, and my need for him was equal parts powerful and terrifying.

"I suppose a kiss wouldn't hurt. But that's it, Winslow. We're taking this slow."

He flipped me on my back in one fluid movement and propped himself above me, his breaths coming fast and hard. "Slow is my least favorite word."

I smiled up at him because he was ridiculously beautiful. I didn't speak. Couldn't find my words, and my pounding heartbeat was the only audible sound. His mouth came over mine. Slow and gentle. We took our time tasting and exploring. My need for this boy was so strong. So, overpowering. All-consuming. I found it difficult to contain my desire. My fingers tangled in his hair, urging him closer. A growl escaped his throat as he tipped my head back for better access.

Oh. My. God.

This was so much more than a kiss.

So.

Much.

More.

My body ground against his, moving on its own volition. An

ambulance siren in the distance startled me, and I pulled back. A wide grin spread across his handsome face as he looked down at me. The heat in his gaze polarizing.

"Missed you," he said, his voice gruff.

"Missed you more," I whispered before pushing him back and moving to sit.

"That was some kiss, More Jade."

"It sure was. Let's just sit with this for a while, okay?" I said.

I was caught in a riptide—the turbulent water pulling me out to sea. The current so strong, I couldn't fight it anymore. I didn't want to. I moved to sit on his lap. I wanted to be blanketed in his warmth. Surrounded by Cruz Winslow. My all-consuming rock star.

"I love you," I whispered against his ear.

"Love you more."

———

"Do you like it?" I asked my father when he held up the black sweater he'd just unwrapped from me.

"It's perfect, Jady bug."

"Last one," I said, handing a package to Sara. She loved the hat and scarf she'd opened a few minutes ago, but this one was my favorite.

She tore open the package and studied the picture in the frame. It was a candid I'd taken of her and Dad at Thanksgiving. Sara was looking at me with a big grin, and Dad was looking down at her with so much adoration. The picture spoke a thousand words, and I was happy that I'd captured it.

"I love this," Sara said, eyes glassy.

Dad looked over her shoulder and shrugged. "I'm not even looking at the camera. Next time give me a heads up you're taking a picture, huh?"

Sara and I laughed. He didn't get it, but that was okay. They were in love and that was big progress for my father.

"Okay, one more for you. This one is actually your birthday

gift," Dad said, handing me a package. It was weird having your birthday on Christmas, but Dad always insisted on separating the two.

I'd already opened a new pair of tennis shoes, two sweaters, and a pair of jeans. "This is from Sara and I. Hell, who am I kidding. She picked it out."

We all laughed as I opened the small square box and pulled out the most gorgeous gold charm bracelet. There were four charms dangling from the dainty chain. A stethoscope, a Northwestern Wildcat, the Chicago skyline, and a music note which I assumed represented Cruz.

"I love it." I beamed as I turned my wrist over and had Sara help fasten it on.

The doorbell rang and Dad moved to the door, mumbling something about people having some nerve to show up on Christmas.

In walked three men carrying large boxes filled with floral arrangements. Peonies and hydrangeas. I knew immediately who they were from and fell back in a fit of laughter at the over the top display of affection.

It was so Cruz.

"Oh my gosh." I moved toward the counter as they pulled out each arrangement.

"Twenty-one arrangements for a Miss Jade Moore's twenty-first birthday," one of the men said matter-of-factly.

"He doesn't do anything in moderation, does he?" My father laughed, as Sara and I helped them unload the boxes.

Dad handed them a twenty-dollar bill. "Thank you for coming out on Christmas."

"We can't accept that, Sir. We've been very well compensated for making this delivery on Christmas morning." He smiled, and Dad shook his head with a laugh.

"Of course, you have. Well, thank you for coming out. Merry Christmas."

I reached for the card on one of the displays.

This is my favorite day of the year because it's the

day you were born. Baby Jesus has nothing on you, More Jade. I love you, more. Cruz.
 P.S. Are we still taking it slow?

I looked up to see my father's smirk and Sara's starry-eyed gaze.

"Have you forgiven this kid yet?" Dad asked.

I laughed. "Yes. We're taking it slow."

Dad glanced around the apartment covered in beautiful pink and white arrangements. "If this is slow, I don't want to see him at full speed."

I laughed and walked to my bedroom to call him. Cruz performed last night in New York at a Christmas Eve concert to raise money for military families. Exiled would be recording in the studio today. Yes, on Christmas day. These boys worked hard, and not many people knew that the life of rock stars was not all fun and games.

Cruz and I were pretty much back together. I'd tossed my life jacket aside and jumped back in with both feet. Well, almost all in. We'd made-out last time we'd been together. And to say there were fireworks was an understatement. I was like a drowning woman who'd come up for air. We'd decided not to take things further, as my mind was set on taking it slow.

Why did I insist on that again?

But Cruz had spent the night with me again, and we'd kissed for hours. All night, really. There'd been no sleeping, and I didn't care at all. I was on a cloud for days after. We talked multiple times a day since he'd left, and I was happy.

Really happy.

The next few weeks passed by in a blur. School and research were keeping me busy, and Cruz and I talked multiple times a day. I walked out of class and pulled the collar up on my coat. The sun was out, but February in Chicago was still chilly.

"See ya, Jade," Richard said as we parted ways.

I waved goodbye and reached for my phone. I wanted to catch Cruz before he left for his show tonight.

When my phone powered on, my stomach dropped to see that there were fourteen missed calls. I opened the first text from Sara, and I came to an abrupt halt in the middle of the sidewalk.

SARA

I know you're in class. We were called to a bad fire and I didn't want you to hear about it on the news. Call me when you can.

My hands shook as I dialed Sara's number. My brain was trained to think the worst. I hated that insecurity about myself but obviously it was an instilled reaction after Mom's death.

"Jade," she said, and it sounded more like a croak which immediately put me on edge.

"What's happening. Where's Dad?"

"He's missing right now. Part of the apartment building came down and Jack ran back in because a woman said her child was inside." Sara was unable to hide the panic from her voice. I was moving while we spoke, as I'd hit the Uber app on my phone and saw a car up ahead.

"What does that mean? He's not talking to anyone? They can't hear him?" The firefighters have walkie-talkies just for this reason. Dad has told me stories about how thick smoke can get in these buildings, making it difficult to find a way out.

"No. We lost him." Her voice broke on a sob and I struggled to run toward the waiting car. My legs trembled, my heart raced, and I felt like I was having an out-of-body experience.

"Send me your location. I'll be right there," I shouted when I stepped into the car.

I waited for Sara's text and gave it to the driver.

I sat in silence for a moment, processing what I just heard. Sara wasn't dramatic. Ever. Hearing her fall apart was terrifying.

I picked up the phone and did the only thing that came to me.

I dialed Cruz.

"Hey, how was class. Why aren't we FaceTiming?" he said.

I couldn't speak. Fear clawed its way through me, and I couldn't get the words out.

"Jade? What's going on?" He sounded panicked.

"My dad ran back in a burning apartment building to find a child and he hasn't come out," I croaked.

"What?"

"*I need you.*" Those were the only words I could get out. I covered my mouth with my hand as the sobs broke free.

"I'm on my way," he said.

No more words came from me. I couldn't speak. I couldn't think. I couldn't fathom a world that my father wasn't in. The car pulled in front of the apartment building, or what was left of it, and when my feet hit the ground, I took off sprinting. I ran toward the chaotic scene playing out before me. The building was a tall highrise structure, much larger than I'd expected. It looked like half of the building was still on fire. Fire trucks. Paramedics. Police cars. Everyone was there. Adults and children were wrapped in blankets and crying. I saw firefighters attacking the flames billowing from the tall structure with hoses, and Sara slumped against the fire truck with a paramedic. Police officers were trying to control the area, but I ran right past them. The sky was clouded with smoke, and I pulled my hoodie over my mouth and nose to keep the smoke out.

"Sara," I said, but it came out hoarse and gravelly when she looked up and wrapped her arms around me.

"They are in there now looking for him." She sobbed.

"He'll be okay. He has to be." I tightened my hold on Sara as the realization settled in.

Dad might not be okay.

And I wouldn't be okay without him.

sixteen

. . .

Cruz

I STEPPED off the plane and checked my phone. The last words Jade had said to me were barely audible. I'd jumped on a plane, and luckily, I was only an hour away as we'd performed in Wisconsin last night. I'd do whatever the fuck it took to be there for her.

I had a car waiting and saw a text from Jade telling me to meet her at the hospital. She said they'd found her father, but she didn't say what condition he was in. My girl wouldn't survive this if anything happened to Jack. He was her—everything. Hell, I loved the dude as if he were my own father. You didn't get any better than Jack Moore.

When I arrived at the hospital, I saw Sam and Sara and a few firefighters in the waiting area.

"What happened?" I asked as I approached.

"Dude, glad you're here. He's going to be fine. They are just giving him some oxygen now. He'll be released in a while," Sam said.

"He walked out in one piece. And he saved the four-year-old boy who'd been left inside. He's a hero." Sara covered her face with her hands and her voice broke on a sob.

"He sure as hell is a hero. And he's going to be fine because he's a badass." Sam wrapped an arm around Sara and laughed.

I shook my head. The man was a beast. "Where's Jade?"

"We were with Jack, but the doctor booted us out so he could finish up. Jade was shook. She went to the bathroom a while ago and hasn't come back. You know how she gets when she's scared. She likes to be left alone." Sam shrugged. He and Jade had grown up together, and he knew her well.

"Which way did she go?"

Sara pointed in the direction of the bathroom. "Head that way and turn left at the end."

I walked that way and paused at the ladies' restroom. A woman walked out and I stopped her. "Could you possibly check and see if there's a girl with dark hair in there?"

She stared for a minute before she clapped her hands together. "Are you Cruz Winslow?"

"I am." I was anxious as hell to find Jade, and I didn't hide it.

"Okay, just one quick selfie, and I promise I'll check."

I nodded, and she snapped the picture before hurrying in the restroom.

"Nope. No one's there," she said. "Thanks for the photo."

"Yep. Thanks for checking."

I scanned the area. At the end of the corridor, I saw someone sitting on the floor. That was my girl. Always trying to handle things on her own.

I moved her way and her head came up just as I bent down in front of her.

When her jade gaze locked with mine, my chest split down the middle. I dropped to sit beside her and pulled her on my lap.

"It's okay. I'm here," I said against her hair.

Sobs racked her body. I wrapped my arms around her and held her close.

"He could have died, Cruz."

"He's going to be okay, baby." I rocked her back and forth.

Her green eyes were clouded with despair. Her tear-streaked cheeks red and puffy.

She wrapped her arms around me and buried her face in my

chest. "If I lost him, I'd have no family. I'd be all alone. I'd have no one."

Her words destroyed me. I held her tighter and tried to comfort her. "You're not alone, baby. I'll always be here for you. You're never going to be alone."

Jade fell apart in my arms and I'd never seen her unravel like this. And I swore to Christ right then that I'd do everything in my power to make sure this girl never hurt again.

"It felt like he was in that building forever, and I started to think he'd never walk out. And I don't know what I'd do if I lost him."

"I know it was scary, but he's going to be okay," I said.

And we sat there in silence. I rocked her back and forth as she lay limp against my body, as the fear of losing Jack had overtaken her.

Her cries subsided, and she pushed back to look at me. "Thank god he's okay."

"He saved that kid's life. He's a hero."

She swiped at her eyes and pushed to her feet. She wobbled a bit before she steadied, and we walked back toward the waiting room. Jack was just walking out when we got there. Jade studied her father and he pulled her in for a hug.

"Everything's fine, Jady bug. You need to go home and get some rest, kiddo," Jack said as he covered his mouth and let a loud, husky cough escape.

"I think you should take your own advice," Jade said, staring at her father.

"Yeah, yeah. We're heading out now. Sorry I worried you."

"Don't be sorry, Dad. You just need to be safe," she said, reaching for her dad and hugging him tight once again.

Jack pulled back and looked at his daughter. Her puffy eyes were a dead giveaway that she'd been crying. "You worry too much. I'm fine."

Sara laughed and shook her head. "You scared us, Jack. You did run back into a burning building after all."

"I had to find that kid. I didn't mean to scare you."

Jade and Sara both rolled their eyes and shook their heads at the same time.

"Of course you did," Sara said.

"Thanks for taking care of our girl," Jack said, giving me a half hug.

A lump formed in my throat, because it was the first time he'd ever called her *our girl*. She'd always been his girl, and I hadn't even been offended by it.

"Always," I nodded.

"Okay, call me when you guys get home," Jade said.

I led Jade over to my car and turned to face her before I pulled out of the parking lot. "Hey."

"Hey." She smiled.

"You hungry?"

"You know I can always eat. But I also desperately need a shower, so maybe we could just pick something up?" she said. She seemed lighter now. More relaxed. Jack was going to be okay. She'd worked through all those fears and emotions that had swallowed her whole today.

"Let's grab some Chinese food on the way home. I know a place that stays open late." I pulled out on to the road. The wind rattled against the windows.

"Oh my god. You had a show tonight, right? I'm sorry for asking you to come," she said as if the realization of the day was hitting her.

"Yeah. It's fine. Shit happens."

"Meaning?"

"Meaning Zach was forced to perform. Trust me, the dude is as good as me if not better," I said.

"I highly doubt that. I'm sure there will be some angry fans."

"Don't worry about it. If they complain, they can have a refund. Life happens. This is where I needed to be, and everyone understood that. Now that Jack's okay, I'll fly out tomorrow and make it in time for the next show."

She covered my hand that rested in my lap with hers. Of course, my over-achieving erection sprung to life. "I can't thank you enough for coming. When it happened—I don't know. I just wanted you with me."

"That's where I want to be."

"I was just so scared that he wouldn't walk out of there, you know?" she said.

"Yeah. And of course, he came out holding a kid in his arms. It's so your dad to do that, right? He's a fucking hero."

"You know jumping on a plane and rushing here isn't exactly taking it slow." She smirked.

"Yeah. Well, I've told you that taking it slow isn't exactly my thing. Are we moving too fast for you?"

"No. I'm the one who asked you to come. I think I've been trying to protect myself in a way. I was so consumed with you for such a long time, and after everything happened, I just felt like I needed to be more guarded and cautious. And then the thought of getting hurt again terrified me."

I parked in front of the restaurant and reached over and pulled her to sit on my lap. Her tiny frame molded against me as I wrapped my arms around her. Jade fit perfectly there. She fit perfectly everywhere. She was my other half. And I wasn't complete without her. My lips grazed hers, and the thought of tasting her sweet mouth had me on edge.

"I won't hurt you like that again, Jade. I can't promise I'll never fuck up, because we both know that isn't realistic. But I can promise that I won't go back to that dark place. Not ever again."

Her lips teased mine and she tangled her fingers in my hair. "God, I missed you."

"Missed you more, baby." My mouth crashed into hers, and I couldn't get enough. My tongue dipped inside, and I took my sweet time kissing her as her body ground against mine.

"Cruz," she moaned into my mouth.

I pulled her back, because if I didn't do something, I was going to strip her naked right here in the parking lot, which though it sounded tempting was a bad idea. Jack had survived a fire today. We didn't need to risk some dirtbag paparazzi catching a picture of me and my girl making up for lost time in my car.

"Chinese food doesn't sound that good anymore, does it?" I laughed as I took in her swollen lips and heated gaze.

"No. I lost my appetite. At least for food."

I laughed, and she climbed back over to the passenger seat. I tore out of there and made it to her place in record time. She stepped out of the car and I rushed her. I threw her over my shoulder and ran her into the house.

"Ari," she shouted through her laughter, checking to see if her roommate was home as I hurried her down the hall.

"Looks like we're alone." I tossed her on the bed and her hair fell all around her as she smiled up at me.

"Looks like we are," she said, propping herself up on her elbows.

I kicked the door closed and locked it. I glanced down at my phone before setting it on the nightstand. "I've got twelve hours before I have to leave, and I don't plan on leaving this room."

"Don't make promises you can't keep." She wriggled her brows.

"You missin' me, baby?" I asked, yanking my T-shirt over my head.

"Yeah."

Jade sat forward and reached for my jeans, unbuttoning them slowly as she looked up at me with those big green eyes and licked her lips. Christ. I'd never wanted anyone or anything more in my life. She pushed my briefs down along with my jeans and there was no denying how badly I wanted her. She ran her fingers down my chest.

"Looks like you missed me too?" She teased when her eyes landed on my raging hard-on. "And I can't get over how chiseled you are."

"You know all that training means I can last even longer now."

"You've never had a problem in that area," she said, as I reached for the hem of her shirt and pulled it over her head.

I tipped her back and she arched up so I could peel her leggings from her body.

"Well, I've got twelve hours to familiarize myself with your beautiful body. I'm going to make you feel so good you'll still be thinking about me after I leave," I said as I settled above her.

"Oh yeah? How are you going to do that?" Her voice was gruff and breathy as she writhed beneath my touch.

"By kissing you here." I kissed her neck and reached back to unsnap her white lacey bra, tossing it to the side, before cupping her perfect tits in my hands. Slowly. Tasting and savoring her with every kiss.

"Oh my god," she whispered.

"And here," I said, moving my mouth down her body and stopping at her breasts. I took my time with each one until she was panting.

"Please, Cruz." Her words were barely audible.

"You made me wait and now I'm going to take my time with you. Enjoy every inch of this beautiful body," I said, gripping her hips and holding her still as she squirmed beneath me.

"You're punishing me?" she whined, and I laughed.

"I'm rewarding you. Trust me."

I slipped my fingers beneath her panties and slowly pulled them down her legs. I made my way back up, kissing her inner thighs as I moved closer to where I knew she wanted me. I paused to look at her one last time. Her face flushed, eyes heated and full of need, and her lips parted just enough to allow her little pants to release with each breath. I buried my face between her legs, teasing and taunting until she wrapped her fingers in my hair and tugged me closer and I gave her what she needed. She cried out my name, and I savored her sweetness.

Damn, I'd missed her.

This.

Being with her.

I was done taking my time. I pushed up on my knees and reached in my wallet for a condom.

"Someone was feeling confident, huh?" she said, laughing at my secret stash as she pushed up on her elbows.

"Ready and willing, baby. I mean, you said we were taking it slow last month, so I was hopeful things would progress." I covered myself before leaning over her and kissing her hard. She whimpered and I nearly exploded.

Because it was all worth the wait.

Right here.

Right now.

seventeen

. . .

Jade

MY BACK RESTED against Cruz's chest as we settled in the hot bath. The water absorbing us both like a safe little cocoon where no one else existed but us. I was physically and emotionally drained from this day. I'd thought I'd lost my father, and I'd stopped fighting my need to keep Cruz at a distance.

And wow, had I opened the floodgates.

We'd just spent the last two hours in bed, making up for lost time.

And now, I was all consumed.

Just like that.

Had I ever really stopped? It didn't feel like it now, as he enveloped me in his arms.

"I missed you," he whispered, his lips grazing my ear.

I flipped over on my stomach, resting my elbows on his chest. "Missed you more."

He reached for the necklace hanging around my neck where the promise ring he gave me hung.

"Can we put this back on your finger?" The vulnerability in his eyes nearly broke me.

"Yes," I said, reaching behind me for the clasp. He held out his hand and caught the chain in his palm. I slipped the ring off and slid it down my finger. Exactly where it belonged. Cruz reached up and dropped the chain on the counter beside the tub before looking down at my finger and smiling.

"That's where it should be."

"Yeah. I like looking at it, so this makes it easier." I laughed.

He pulled back to look at me. "So, anything I need to know about your time with *Dick*?"

"No. It was nothing."

"Well, you did kiss the asshole. Nothing more happened?"

I shook my head. "I kissed him twice, and I told you both times. Anything you need to tell me about our time apart?"

"No. I told you. I had the whole broken dick thing going on." He brushed the hair back from my face, and I rested my cheek beneath his neck.

"It sure seems to be working just fine now." I laughed, and my body vibrated beneath the water.

"Oh, you think that's funny, do you?"

"A little bit."

"Well, it only works for you. We've established that now. So how do you feel about your dad?"

"I think he's going to be okay. That was scary though," I said, as I traced over the script on his arm with my finger.

"It was. He's fucking tough."

"Yeah. Thanks for being there. You know—for me and for Dad."

"Always. You know that."

"So, what happens now?"

"Meaning?"

"With us?" I pushed up to meet his honey-brown gaze.

"Nothing's really changed, has it? I mean aside from you pretending to have a fake boyfriend when you got back from Honduras, and then insisting we take it slow these last few weeks. I've been all in the whole time."

"I guess I mean with you back on tour and me swamped with school. I can't travel as often as I did last year."

"We'll make it work. My schedule is a lot better than it used to be, and I can come home more often now. You'll come out when you can. We only have a few months left. We've got this," he said.

"You've got it all figured out, huh?"

"I've had plenty of time to think while I waited for you to come to your senses."

"I'm glad we found our way back. Nothing felt right when we were apart," I said.

"We both did some growing during that time, and I know you needed time to forgive me for what happened. Now we can move forward."

"I like the sound of that. How's Zach doing? Do you really think the label will let him take over when you leave?"

"Yes. I'm officially done touring shortly after you graduate in June. Luke gave them a few options. I'll stay on writing music for them, and Zach will do vocals. They may bring on a fourth dude to keep it a four-man band, or the three of them will be fine. Either way, I'm out. Physically speaking. I mean, I'll still be writing for them, so I'll have my hands in it a bit, but I won't have to travel anymore."

"That's going to be so nice. What's happening with your dad and Dex?"

"Haven't heard much about Dex. He's disappeared from the press, which is a relief. Although I still think he's behind the Farah Clearwater bullshit. Hell, maybe he and my father are working together. But, Luke heard Dex had gone into a program. Hell, maybe he'll get his shit together. Still not ever going to be a part of Exiled, but it doesn't mean he can't turn his life around. But if he's still messing with Farah Clearwater that's not a good sign."

"Agreed. He was in a really bad place for a long time. I don't think most people come out of rehab and transition back into life the way you did," I said. I ran my fingers over his scruff. I loved the prickly feeling against my fingertips.

"Yeah. The success rate is low. That's why I have this as a reminder," he said, lifting his forearm to show me the tattoo where I'd marked his arm. "I was lucky because I hadn't gotten involved with the hard stuff like Dex did, and I hadn't been taking those pills for all that long. The booze was a part of my life for a long time, but oddly, I don't miss it like I thought I would."

"You don't?"

"No. I realized that I only drank heavy because I was unhappy. I'm done living that way. I look at my dad and I know that's not who I want to be. Ever. So, I got out fast, and I have no intention of ever going back. You know, I never used to think about the future before I met you. But it's all I think about now."

I smiled and swiped at a tear that traveled down my cheek. "Tell me what you think about."

"You, *More Jade*. Always you."

"I don't know yet where I'm going to go to medical school, or even if I'll get in," I said, suddenly anxious about what our future held.

"You will. And it doesn't matter where. I'll go wherever you go. I can write from anywhere, and I'd be happy living in New York or Chicago. As long as I'm with you."

"So, you're really going with me? Just like that?" I asked, locking onto his honey-brown gaze.

"Just like that."

I settled my cheek back on his chest. "Okay. So, we have a plan."

He barked out a laugh. "Always the planner."

"Well, one of us needs to be."

"Can I ask you something that's been bothering me," he said, placing his finger under my chin to force me to look up at him.

"Yeah?"

"Why'd you ask me about Dex a while back?" he said.

"What? Oh. Well, I saw a guy that looked a little bit like him on campus."

Before I could react, he was pushing up and lifting both of us out of the water. He reached for two towels and handed me one, tying his around his waist.

"Fuck, Jade. Why didn't you tell me that?" He grabbed my towel back from me impatiently and wrapped it around my body, cinching it right above my chest.

He moved to the bedroom like someone just told him the house was on fire.

"What? What are you talking about? I didn't tell you because it was nothing. I saw a guy that resembled him."

His fingers moved across his phone screen as he typed out a text to someone before tossing his phone on the bed.

"You wouldn't have asked me about where he was if you didn't think it was him. Fuck. I should have trusted my instincts. I knew something was up that day." He reached for his phone again when it vibrated on the mattress and read his screen.

"You're acting insane. I don't think it was him. It was getting dark. The guy had on a hoodie. He was just tall and thin, and it made me think of Dex. But Dex is in rehab in California, so it's not him," I said, placing a hand on his forearm to calm him down.

He dropped to sit on the bed and pulled me on his lap. "And what was the guy doing? When you saw him?"

"I don't know? *Being a slacker.* That's why I noticed him. He was just standing by the Fine Arts building. He didn't look threatening or anything. He just stood out because everyone was moving around him. It was no big deal. I shouldn't have mentioned it," I said, running my fingers through his over-grown, messy hair and brushing it away from his beautiful face.

"Being a fucking slacker? Sounds like he was stalking you. Are you kidding me? Baby, you've got to be smarter than that. The dude attacked you. He doesn't get to be anywhere in your fucking vicinity."

I pushed to my feet. "Don't treat me like a child. I can take care of myself, Cruz. I spent three months in Honduras and did just fine. And I've survived plenty in my life, so don't act like I'm some fragile little girl."

He pushed to his feet and looked down at me, his face hard. "Then don't act like one. You're smarter than that."

I marched to my desk and reached for my purse, before pulling out my keychain. "Don't make me pepper spray you, you arrogant ass. I always have this on me. I can take care of myself."

He walked toward me and wrapped his long fingers around my wrist. "Put that down."

"Say you're sorry," I said, using my free hand to tighten the towel around my chest.

He reached over and tugged my towel free. It fell to the ground in a heap at my feet. "I'm sorry you're upset. I'm *not sorry* that I worry about your safety."

I huffed and reached down on the ground to pick up my towel. He knocked it out of my hand again and lifted my chin to meet his gaze.

"What?" I snarled. "I'm not talking about this while I'm naked and you're covered."

He yanked his towel free and pulled me against his body. My heart raced as his warmth heated my skin. "Drop the pepper spray, baby."

I tossed it on the desk. "Happy?"

"I'm happy when you're safe." His gaze locked with mine. "Jade, you know we have security for Exiled. You've seen what can happen when we don't. Why would I treat the most important person in my life any differently?"

I let out a long breath and wrapped my arms around his middle. "I'm ninety-nine percent sure it wasn't Dex. You're overreacting."

"Maybe. But that's not a chance I'm willing to take. The last time I let my guard down where you were concerned, I almost lost everything." He reached down and grasped my fingers and ran them along his tattoo. "Never again."

"So, you don't think I can take care of myself?"

"Not when you don't know what you're up against. No."

I rolled my eyes. "I disagree."

"Shocker." He laughed.

I pushed up on my tiptoes and kissed him. I needed to end this ridiculous conversation, and I didn't want our last few hours to be spent arguing over Dex.

"I love you, Cruz Winslow," I said as I pulled away and looked up at him.

He tossed me back on the bed and settled above me. "Love you, more."

It had been a few days since Cruz left and the press was back at it. Someone snapped a few photos of him leaving my house, and when asked about it, Cruz told him that we were very much together.

Always had been and always would be.

It was a romantic gesture, but now social media was blowing up with all sorts of talk about our relationship. There was even more interest because Farah Clearwater had just claimed to be in a relationship with Cruz. So everyone had an opinion. The people who were important to me knew the truth, and that's all that mattered. Thankfully I'd kept all my social media settings on private, and I just tried to ignore the outside noise. I'd been here before, and we didn't have much longer to deal with all of the public scrutiny.

I met Dad and Sara for dinner, as I wanted to see how he was doing after the scare.

"Hey," I said when I found them standing outside of our favorite restaurant.

Dad pulled me in for a hug and I turned to hug Sara. The hostess led us to our table, and we ordered quickly as Dad was starving, per usual.

After, we talked a bit about the fire—the little boy and his recovery and how grateful his parents had been—I mean, for real, my dad has been a hero before but holy crap! I was so proud of him and to hear him talk about it, it was as if these scenarios were just part of the job. He kills me!

"So, what's going on, kid. How's Cruz doing? He's in Florida now, right?"

"Yeah, he'll be back next week. He's doing well." I could feel my cheeks heat just at the mention of my boyfriend. My God. What was wrong with me?

"I'm glad you guys figured things out."

"Why's that?" I asked, reaching for a piece of bread from the basket.

"Because that boy is crazy about you. I don't think he'd have handled it if you didn't." He laughed.

"I'm pretty crazy about him too, even when he irritates me," I said.

"Why? Because he's worried about Dex? You'd be foolish not to be aware of that, Jade." Dad's tone was serious, and my shoulders tensed.

"Oh my gosh. He called you, didn't he?" I rolled my eyes.

"Hell, yes he did. And I'm glad, since you didn't mention seeing Dex to me."

"Because *I didn't see him*," I said, throwing my hands in the air. "I saw a guy that looked a little like him. *Not actually him.* Not even a doppelganger, for that matter. Just a tall, skinny dude, that made me inquire about where he was. It's called curiosity, Dad. This has been blown so far out of proportion."

"Well, curiosity killed the cat, kid. We're not taking any chances, and that's all I'm going to say about it."

Sara laughed. "I think she would know if she saw him."

I nodded and smiled at her. "Exactly. Thank you."

"Well, I'd rather be safe than sorry," Dad said.

I rolled my eyes again. I couldn't believe Cruz had gone to my dad about this.

Traitor.

I wanted to be angry.

But I loved them both too damn much.

eighteen

. . .

Cruz

"I CAN'T BELIEVE I let you talk me into this," Lennon said, rubbing the back of his neck.

"Dad's in town and he's been nagging me to meet. Maybe he knows something about Dex. Luke had a guy looking into Dex, and he said the dudes literally disappeared from the face of the earth. I know he's behind this Farah bullshit and I want to find out what he's after. I want to know if daddy dearest is working with him. And remember the saying, keep your enemies close. It's not a bad idea to keep communication with Dad open. Who knows what the hell he's going to pull when I part ways with Exiled this summer," I said.

"Good point. How sick is it *that we* have to stay in touch with our father, so we'll know when he's going to attack?"

I pulled the door to the steak house open where we were meeting Dad, and the hostess smiled as if she had been expecting us. "Follow me. We have a table waiting for you."

We walked toward the back of the restaurant and my father sat in an oversized booth, holding the phone to his ear. "I need to finish this later. My boys are here."

He pushed up and gave Lennon and I a half hug. This was new.

"I took the liberty to order us a nice bottle of wine," he said as he took his seat.

Lennon rolled his eyes. "We don't drink. How out of tune are you with our lives?"

"Ah. Didn't know if we were still sticking with that whole sobriety phase. Alright, I guess I can polish the bottle off on my own." He waved the waiter over. "They'd like to order something else. Maybe a Shirley Temple?"

Dad's laughter was loud, and the waiter forced a smile before turning his attention to me.

"Waters fine, extra lime please." I gave my father a hard look while Lennon ordered a Pepsi.

Dad sampled his wine when the waiter brought it out and took a hearty sip before setting his glass down.

"So, how were your holidays, boys?"

"I'm sure you're more than aware that we worked through both Thanksgiving and Christmas." Lennon kept his answers short, as his guard was up where my father was concerned.

"You know, Lennon, I'm still your father. I'm sorry if me bedding your high school girlfriend has you that traumatized. It's time to move on."

I couldn't help but chuckle at how sick and twisted the man was. Yeah, Dad had an affair with an old flame of Lennon's but that wasn't the worst part of it. He'd cheated on our mother and slept with his best friend's teenage daughter. The list was long, but he had a way of minimizing his offenses by focusing on small pieces of his depraved little world.

"I think you're missing a whole lot of offenses there, big guy," I said. I noted the veins bulging in my brother's neck, and I put a hand on his shoulder to calm him down.

Lennon leaned forward. "How about what you did to our mother? Shall we talk about that, you selfish prick."

"Your mother is a grown ass woman. She can fight her own battles. She'll get over this. Give her time," Dad said, chugging the rest of his Chardonnay and snapping his fingers for the waiter to refill his glass.

Classy.

"How about what you did to your own son? Paying some psycho bitch to claim Cruz knocked her up. Who the fuck does that?" Lennon said, his words laced with venom. My brother had found his backbone somewhere between getting a grip on his sobriety and falling in love. And I was impressed. Hell, the kid was a force to reckon with now.

"So, we're going to let some, what did you call her, *psycho bitch*, come between us?"

"She's back in the news, if you hadn't heard. You opened a shit-storm by bringing her crazy ass into our world."

"I didn't bring her in. Check with your pal, Dex. He's the one who brought her in. I just fanned the flames. I barely interacted with the girl, and I haven't talked to her since. I've apologized for the role I played in it. Now let's move on. We're family."

"You're not my family," Lennon said, and even my jaw dropped a bit. I'd never seen my brother take such a strong stance against our father. But Lennon was making his own money, and since distancing himself from Dad, he'd learned that he didn't need the man anymore. In fact, he'd come to realize that my father was at the crux of most of his problems. It was a valuable lesson we'd both learned this year.

"Is that so?" Dad chuckled. Good Christ, the man must have a heart of steel because he seemed completely unphased by Lennon's words. "Then you won't be needing my planes, and homes, or any of the other things you both feel so entitled to?"

We paused when the waiter approached, and we ordered dinner. I wondered why we were even bothering to have a meal together. Jesus, this was dysfunction at its finest.

Lennon folded his hands on the table and glanced over at me before speaking. I was letting him take the reins. Hell, the kid seemed to have a lot to say.

"Do you know that I almost died from an overdose twice? I'm twenty-one years old, Dad. That's how out of control I was, and you continued to push your drug dealer on me. You liked me that way. You know, just barely hanging by a thread, so you could use me the way you wanted to. Like I was your little puppet. Well, I'm here to tell you those days are over. And you can dangle all your fancy toys in my face but guess what? I don't give a shit. I wouldn't even be flying on the plane if Mom didn't remind me that they also belong to her. So, once the divorce goes through, I won't be using anything that belongs to you. And for the record, I can buy my own shit now. Maybe not a private plane, but I'd sit in steerage on a coach flight before I'd ever come to you for a favor."

The words hung in the air around us. Not quite where I saw tonight going, but I was proud of Lennon. He needed to get this shit off his chest. This man was toxic. And Lennon was absolutely-fucking right, Mom was a partner in everything in this fucked up marriage and especially after the divorce, maybe then some—and she's got a kick ass lawyer.

My father's face was bright red. "I don't plan on divorcing her anytime soon. She may have served me the papers, but we can drag this out for a long time."

Not much of a comeback. He was losing his edge and in denial. Maybe his lifestyle was finally catching up to him.

The waiter set our food down and Lennon and my father both started eating.

Was I the only one that found this to be awkward?

"So, have you heard anything from Dex? Where he is? What he's doing? I assume he's behind the Farah bullshit," I said. I wanted to see his reaction. I could usually tell when my father was up to something.

Dad set his fork down and wiped his mouth. "I reached out to him, but he hasn't taken my calls since he admitted himself into a program. Just what the world needs. Another fucking boy scout."

Lennon shook his head and stood. "I need to use the restroom."

"He's being a bit dramatic don't you think?" Dad asked me as soon as my brother left the table.

"Not even a little bit. That was a long time coming. But you've known where I stand on this, it's no secret."

"So, tell me. You're back with Jade? The press sure seems to think so."

"It's pretty sad that you get your information from the press. You could call and ask. You know, instead of only talking business when we speak," I said. "But yes, Jade and I are very much together."

"And she wants you out of Exiled?"

I took my time chewing my food because I could feel my temper rising. "No. I want out of Exiled. I never wanted to be in the band, if you remember."

"Bullshit. When you broke up with her, you ended up staying in the band."

"I stayed in the band because fucking Dex attacked her, and I wanted him out," I said, fisting my hands in my lap.

"Exiled is going to implode if you leave. You're not getting out without a fight," he said, his ice blue stare locked with mine.

"The label has already agreed to let me go. I'm afraid you're shit out of luck, old man."

"They aren't the only ones who have a stake in this band," he said, reaching for another full glass of wine and chugging it.

"You know, it may have helped if you fought this hard to save your marriage and your family. Why you fucking care so much about Exiled is beyond me," I said, tossing my napkin on the table.

"My wife and my family don't bring in any revenue." A wicked smile spread across his face and I pushed to my feet.

"We're done," I said, slipping my jacket on.

"Oh son. We're just getting started."

I motioned to Lennon when he returned from the restroom, and he followed me out of the restaurant.

And a sick feeling settled in my stomach.

Because Steven Winslow was ready for battle.

And that was never a good thing.

nineteen

. . .

Jade

IT WAS the end of February, but the weather hadn't let up. This year in particular was more bone chilling than usual, and the wind blustered around me. I trudged my way through campus. I didn't get much sleep last night as Cruz arrived late, and we stayed up most of the night talking, laughing, and obviously doing other things —my cheeks heated at the memory.

We were making plans for spring break, as he'd have almost the whole week off with me. We were planning a trip to Mexico, just the two of us, and I couldn't wait to soak up the sun and relax.

I left him asleep in my bed, before bundling up and heading out into this crazy winter wonderland. I tightened my scarf around my neck as I made my way through campus to my molecular genetics class. Of course, it would be the furthest building away. The walk usually didn't bother me, but with my teeth chattering I couldn't get there soon enough. The sidewalks had been shoveled, but a light layer of fresh snow still covered the surface.

"Jade," a voice called out, and my shoulders tensed at the sound of his voice. I whipped around and came face to face with Dex.

My hands trembled beneath my gloves, and I reached in my pocket for my pepper spray. My fingers wrapped around it, as I stared, dumbfounded at the guy who'd attacked me less than a year ago. I pulled out my pepper spray and aimed it at his face.

"Get away from me, or I swear to God I'll hurt you," I shouted, looking around and just now noticing that campus was pretty desolate on this dreary morning. I saw a few people off in the distance and took a step back from him.

"I'm not going to hurt you. I just want to apologize. Please. It's a part of my program," he said. He looked different. His face was fuller, and his blue eyes shined more than they used to. He was bundled in a navy jacket and a green beanie.

I didn't lower the pepper spray, but I didn't walk away either. He wanted to own up to what he did. I couldn't really fault him for it. I believed in redemption. Of course, I did.

"Well, get on with it then," I said, my tone harsh.

"I'm truly sorry for what happened, Jade. There's no excuse, obviously, and I don't expect your forgiveness, but I needed to say it. I was messed up for a long time. And I don't know why I did the things that I did. But I am sorry. I'm haunted by what I did to you," he said. His gaze full of remorse.

"Well, that makes two of us," I admitted. What Dex did to me still resided somewhere deep inside, leaving me less trusting than before.

"I wish I could turn back time and change things. I would if I could."

I lowered my arm, still clutching the pepper spray, but no longer feeling threatened. "Well, I appreciate the apology. And I do hope you continue on this path."

"Yeah, I'm just taking it one day at a time. My addiction cost me everything."

"Not everything," I said, shaking my head. "You're still here. You're young. There's plenty of time to do good things, Dex."

"Thank you. I want to apologize to Cruz, but he's blocked me. They all have."

"Time has a way of healing. Give him some time," I said. "But if you're behind this Farah Clearwater rumor, that's not helping things."

"Farah Clearwater? I haven't talked to her since Cruz asked me to reach out to her when Steven was paying her to sell that bullshit story. You might want to let him know his dad is batshit crazy. He's not going to let him walk away from Exiled without a fight. I'm staying away from that dude. He's bad news. Cruz needs to be aware."

I heard shouting in the distance and looked up to see Cruz running in my direction. This wouldn't go over well. His hatred for Dex was blinding.

"Fuck," Dex mumbled under his breath.

"Everything is fine," I yelled out, moving toward my boyfriend, leaving Dex standing behind me.

"It's not fine. What the fuck are you doing here? Stay the fuck away from her, do you hear me?" Cruz shouted and pointed his finger in Dex's face. I glanced around and noticed a few people moving our way looking for a free show.

"Relax, Winslow. I was just apologizing. I'm leaving. Just wanted to say my piece," Dex said, holding his hands up in defeat.

"You don't get to say your piece, motherfucker. You lost that right when you left her to die on that hotel room floor. Stay the fuck away from her," Cruz said, stepping in front of me and getting in Dex's face.

"Alright. I get it. I'm sorry. I'll go."

This was a side of Dex I'd never seen before. But in all reality, I'd never been around sober Dex. Not once in all the time I'd known him. This guy appeared normal. Nice even.

"Then go," Cruz snarled, and Dex turned to walk away.

He reached for my hand and led me away as people started to gather. I'd pretty much missed class now, due to my unexpected visit, so I just walked beside him, not saying a word. Anger radiated from his body, and I pulled my hand free and turned to face him once we were away from the scene.

"It's okay. I'm fine."

I expected him to yell and shout, but instead, he leaned down and rested his forehead against mine. His breath making a cloud between us. "You scared the shit out of me, baby."

"He apologized. That's all it was. He's sober now. He wants to right his wrongs," I said, pulling back to look into his honey brown gaze.

He shook his head. "You can't trust him, Jade. He's up to something."

"I don't think so. But he did say something about your dad not letting you leave the band without a fight. He also said that he hasn't spoken to Farah Clearwater since you asked him to reach out to her," I said.

"Of course he did. Dex and my father are the two most manipulative fuckers I know. This is probably part of some elaborate scheme they have going."

"How did you know he was here?" I asked, wondering why he'd come sprinting through campus.

"I got a call from Luke right after you left for class that his guy found out Dex was back in Chicago. Call it an instinct, I knew he'd come find you," he said, wrapping one arm around me as we started walking back to the house again.

"So, you rushed down here because you thought he was in the same state as me? Cruz, I don't need rescuing. I'm fine." I pulled out my pepper spray and showed him. "I have this, and I was in the middle of campus. He wasn't going to do anything in such a public place. I really think his apology was genuine."

"I don't give a shit what he says. One of the guys on our security team is on a plane heading here now. He's going to finish the rest of the school year here, in the city. With you. This has been in the works for a few days, and now I'm more certain than ever that you need it. Between my disturbing conversation with my father and now Dex showing up, I just think they're up to something," he said as if we were discussing the weather and not the fact that he'd just hired a bodyguard to follow me around.

"No. I'm not walking around with security. Are you kidding me? I accepted a board position for the honor society, and I have my research position with Elaine, can you imagine what they'd think of me if I showed up with security? Like I'm so important that I need *backup* for God's sake. No. Absolutely not."

"This isn't open for discussion, Jade."

I came to a stop. "Excuse me? You don't get to tell me what to do. Sorry *rock star*, you don't own me," I said, storming off ahead of him.

He walked behind me in silence and followed me inside the house. I marched back to my bedroom, passing Ari in the hallway on my way.

"Are you okay?" she asked.

"Not at the moment," I spewed, glaring over my shoulder at a smiling Cruz.

"Okaaaaay, I'm off to class. See you guys later." I heard her chuckle as she walked past my boyfriend.

"Is this funny to you?" I shouted and dropped to sit on my bed.

"No." He leaned his back against the wall facing me and stretched his long legs out, crossing them at the ankles.

"Then why are you smiling?" I tore the hat off my head, dropped my gloves beside me and unzipped my coat. Only then did I notice that Cruz didn't even have a coat or gloves on, and his cheeks were pink, as were his hands. He'd just run out the door like some sort of crazed stormtrooper in a T-shirt and joggers.

"Because you're fucking cute when you're pissed."

I rolled my eyes and tossed him the throw blanket on my bed. Even though he infuriated me, I didn't like the idea of him catching pneumonia. "You're being completely irrational."

He tossed the blanket aside and dropped to sit beside me. "I'm the irrational one?"

"Did I stutter?"

He chuckled. "That motherfucker attacked you. He pinned you to the couch and chased you around a room, where he eventually yanked you by the hair and hit you in the face. He left you for dead on the floor. Am I misunderstanding something?"

I rolled my eyes. "I'm not saying I'm going to start hanging out with the guy. He came to apologize. I listened. *We're not besties.* And I don't need a freaking bodyguard. I already stand out on campus as the girl who dates the famous rock star. I don't want any more attention."

"And I don't give a shit what anyone thinks. I need to know you're safe."

I let out a long sigh and fell back on the bed. "I don't need a bodyguard. That's absolutely ridiculous."

"So, you think we just take our chances? Trust that that crazy motherfucker suddenly found God and has been saved? Not happening, Jade." He fell back and turned on his side to face me.

"I survived a long time before I met you, Cruz."

"You're more at risk now," he said.

I rolled on my side and looked at him. I put my hand on his rosy cheek, needing to give him some of my warmth. Was he right? Dex did attack me after all. Had he just put on an act today? I thought back to that fight I had with him in the hotel room. It was terrifying. I couldn't fight him off. Was I just being stubborn for the sake of wanting to act brave? Wanting to be right?

"Please do this for me, baby. It's hard enough being away from you. I can't do it if I'm worrying about Dex. I have security and I barely notice them. I can tell him he has to stay out of sight and be stealthy. He'll just be around. You'll barely notice him."

Cruz was so persistent and I really wasn't sure what to think anymore. So I decided to relent since what the heck do I know. "Fine. I just prefer that he doesn't enter the buildings with me because I'd rather not have anyone know he's there. Is that fair?"

"Completely fair. Thank you." He kissed me on the nose.

"We're almost done with all of this. Soon, none of this will be an issue because we'll be together."

"Thanks for agreeing for once, ol' stubborn one," he teased before propping himself above me and tickling me.

Cruz Winslow was the master at distracting me. And when his lips trailed down my neck, I was done for.

———

Cruz and I went to visit Dad and Sara before stopping for pizza in Bucktown. I'd been going to see him more often since the fire happened. I always worried about him, but even more so now. They were both working the night shift so they couldn't join us for dinner, but I was glad I got to spend an hour with him before heading back to campus.

I glanced over at the supersized bodyguard who sat two tables away from us, and pointed two fingers at my eyes, before pointing them at him, as if to say, *I'm looking at you.*

He smirked and Cruz laughed.

"I'll just assume he's here for you today?" I said.

"You know what happens when you assume, right?"

"I do."

"Give Bernard a chance. He's a good guy," Cruz said.

"I just like giving him a hard time. He's not bad at all, and so far he has kept a low profile so I can't complain. Let's talk about Cabo. I'm so excited about our trip."

"You're going to love it. We've been a couple times. The place we're staying at is very secluded. I'll get to have you all to myself," he said, his heated gaze locked with mine.

"And then after that, we only have a couple weeks to go until you're done. You're not worried about your dad finding some legal loophole that would make you stay?"

"No. This is him having a temper tantrum because things aren't going his way. The label has agreed to let me go. They want to move forward with the band as is, and I'll write the music. Luke said there isn't anything my father can do. Aside from having a hissy fit, like he's currently doing."

My phone vibrated and I studied the screen. "Oh my gosh. It's a New York area code."

"Answer it, baby."

Cruz studied me as I spoke. "Hello."

"Hello, is this Jade Moore?"

"It is."

"Hi Jade. This is Dr. Devore. We met when you interviewed here at NYU."

"Yes, hello Dr. Devore," I said, biting down on my bottom lip as I looked at Cruz across the table.

"Well, I'm happy to let you know that we would like to invite you to attend the New York University School of Medicine," she said, pausing and allowing me to respond.

At first, no words left my mouth before I yelped. "You're serious?"

"Very," she said with a chuckle.

"Oh my gosh, thank you so much. This is the best news ever," I said, jumping to my feet.

"I'm so happy to hear that, Jade. We hope you'll be joining us in the fall, and your official letter will be emailed to you right away."

"Yes, you'll definitely see me in the fall."

"Okay, we'll be in touch soon. Congratulations, Jade. Goodbye."

"Thank you. Goodbye," I said before we ended the call.

Cruz was on his feet and pulling me into his arms the minute I set my phone down.

"I'm in," I squealed.

"Of course, you are. I'm so proud of you, baby."

He spun me around, and we both laughed.

"You ready to move to New York with me?"

"So ready. Let's run over to the firehouse and tell your dad. He's going to be really fucking proud of you."

"Yes. Let's go." I reached for his hand as he led me out of the restaurant.

"Come on, Bernard. We're on the move again," I teased, and he laughed.

I couldn't even be annoyed with him, because everything was falling into place.

And I'd never been happier.

twenty

. . .

Cruz

WHEN WE ARRIVED IN CABO, Jade took in the resort with wide eyes. This was my father's favorite hotel, so I knew it wouldn't disappoint. The man was a shit father and husband, but he had extraordinary taste when it came to the finer things in life.

"Are you serious? This is an actual house," she said, dropping her backpack on the chair as she gazed around the space.

"Technically, it's a villa." I laughed.

I wanted to do something special for her. She'd been accepted to NYU medical school. It had been her dream school and I was fucking proud of her. Anyone would be lucky to have Jade.

"We have our own pool? This can't be right?" Jade said as she moved out to the patio.

The turquoise water sparkled in the distance, and all you could see was ocean for miles. The sleek outdoor tiles were covered in plush lounge seating, a private pool, and a hot tub. The Cape hotel was known for providing privacy, and top of the line service.

I dropped down to sit in the large circular chair and pulled my girl on my lap. "Proud of you, baby."

"I'm proud of you too," she said, turning to nuzzle into my neck. "This is a dual celebration. You graduated this year too, remember?"

"Well, you got into your dream school. You're such a badass."

"I still can't believe it. It's such a relief to just know that I'm going to medical school. All that stress, and all the hard work, was all worth it now," she said, pulling back to look at me.

"No one deserves it more than you."

"Honestly, that's not true. So many people deserve it. Trust me, everyone has to work really hard to get here. I'm not alone in this journey, and I'm just really grateful that they accepted me," she said.

I loved how fucking humble she was. She really didn't think she was anything special. But I knew differently, and so did every fucking person who met her.

"You ready to live in New York? This is going to be tough on your dad, right?"

"I'm so ready. I think he'll be okay. I mean, I'll graduate from medical school debt free. He understands that it's an amazing opportunity for me," she said, running her fingers through my hair.

"You know if you wanted to go somewhere else, I'd pay for it." I'd told her this before, but Jade was hell bent on doing this her way. And when she set her mind to something it was difficult to get her to waver.

She shook her head. "I know you would, but this is my thing. And the fact that I got into one of the best medical schools in the country and I don't have to pay tuition, it's a no-brainer. The cost of living will be something I'm going to have to work around though."

"We'll get a place together. Think of all the money you'll save," I said, studying her mesmerizing jade gaze.

"I'm open to discuss it," she said, which caused my jaw to hit the ground. I'd asked Jade to live with me a couple hundred times and she'd always laughed it off.

"It's about fucking time. What changed your mind?"

She laughed. "We've been in college. You've been touring with Exiled. Things were different. But they're going to change, right? I mean, you're moving to New York with me. Can't ask for more of a commitment than that. We're finally going to be together full-time. We'd be spending the night together every night anyway, so it seems silly to pay double rent. Especially in New York City."

I pulled her down and wrapped my arms around her. "That makes me really happy. We'll find our own place."

"Yeah, it can't be too swanky, Winslow. You're going to have to work with me on what I can afford. We're going fifty-fifty," she said.

"Not happening."

She pushed up to look at me. "Why?"

"Because I have a shit ton of money. Who cares who pays? Also, the rent you and Ari have been paying this year has all been going into an account for you to use for whatever you want. So, you have a little savings stashed away."

"What? Why did you do that?" She looked distressed, and I pulled her back down to me.

"Because I can. I don't need the money, Jade." I reached down and held out her left hand and twisted the ring I'd given her around her finger. "And, you promised me forever, remember? So why wouldn't I invest in your future."

"I don't know? It's just a lot. I like to carry my own weight, you know?"

"Trust me, I know. We'll find a place together. One that you're comfortable with. But I'm not living in a shit shack so you can prove a point," I said.

She laughed. "Got it, princess."

I pushed to my feet, holding her in my arms. "Princess, huh?"

"What are you going to do about it?" she teased as I carried her into the villa and dropped her on the bed.

"You're about to find out."

"Don't threaten me with a good time, Winslow," she said, wriggling her brows as her head fell back in laughter.

"Never." My mouth came over hers and I kissed her with a ferociousness I could no longer contain. Things were finally coming together for Jade and I. And I wasn't going to let anything get in the way.

"We could change up our plans and just stay here forever. I could teach kids how to swim and you could sing for the locals. We could live a simple life on the beach in a little shack," she said, as her legs tightened around my waist as I held her out in the ocean.

"I'm down. I mean, not for the shack, but I'll take you on a beach any day of the week."

She laughed. "You're so bougie, Winslow."

"I've always had a taste for the finer things. More Jade being my favorite."

"I love you," she said, her hair wet and trailing down her back. Water droplets scattered around her face, and her jade greens glistened as the sun shone down on her. I reached for the tie on the back of her white bikini and yanked at it.

"Love you more," I said, as she squealed against my mouth when I kissed her.

She gasped and reached for her bathing suit top as the tie came loose and she struggled to keep it in place. I tugged at the tie around her neck and did the same thing.

"Oh my gosh, what are you doing?" she said, laughter clouding her words.

"What? I'm practicing for our days as kicked back beach people. No one's out here."

"This is not a topless beach," she said, pushing the hair back from my face, holding her suit up with her free hand.

"It's a private beach though." I wriggled my brows.

"Let's go inside. I want you all to myself, and I don't want to worry about who's watching us."

"You don't have to ask me twice," I said, as I tried to sprint through the water toward our room and her head fell back in hysterical laughter.

When we got back to the room, I dropped her on the bed and yanked at the bikini top barely clinging to her body. Jade's skin was tan and glistening and her long hair fell all around her on the bed.

Effortless beauty.

She had little freckles speckled around her nose from the sun.

She smiled up at me. "Thanks for bringing me here."

"Thanks for coming with me."

She reached up and wrapped her arms around my neck. "How about we shower off all this sand first?"

"Done," I said, carrying her into the shower.

Naked soapy Jade was something I'd never turn down.

———

My phone buzzed on my nightstand and I stretched my arm and reached to see who it was.

"Who is it?" Jade asked, her voice groggy from sleep. She nestled her head in my neck and the white sheet was tangled around her beautiful body.

"It's Ponch. Just reminding us that we have an hour before we need to meet him at the hanger."

"I don't want to leave," she said, wrapping her arm around me and hugging me tight.

"Me either. We'll definitely have to come back here."

"Definitely." She pushed up on her elbows and looked at me. "But for now we have to go back to our crazy routine of shows and classes."

"Crazy routine, huh? You sure you aren't missing school a little?" I teased her, flipping her on her back and settling above her.

"Not even a little."

"Hey, there's something I want to show you," I said, pushing up and moving over to my backpack in the closet.

"Ooooh, is it more lyrics?"

"Nope. Just something I've been doing for the last few months. It's no big deal. Just helps me clear my head. But unlike my lyrics, I don't have to share this with the world. But I'd like to share it with you."

Jade pushed to sit, crossing her legs, as the sheet managed to stay wrapped around her. I wanted to tear it free but resisted the urge. She looked so serious and curious that I didn't want to ruin the moment.

"I'm happy you're sharing it with me," she said, studying my face for clues.

"It's not a big deal. You're overthinking it, baby."

"Well, anything you're interested in, I'm interested in."

Wasn't that the fucking truth. This invisible line that connected us in a way neither could explain. If it meant something to me, it would mean something to her. And vice versa. Hell, I knew Jade wasn't a huge fan of MMA fighting, but she watched fights with me on TV and she asked about my workouts every day. It mattered to her because it mattered to me.

I tossed my sketchbook on the bed. "I've been drawing."

"Can I look?"

I laughed. "Of course."

She gasped at the first page when she took in the profile I'd sketched of her face. "This is incredible."

"Says my girlfriend," I said with a laugh.

She flipped through each page, taking in the sunsets, the many drawings of her face, a few buildings of different architecture that I'd seen while we traveled through Europe, and she stopped on the page of the three connected hearts. It was a cool design I'd thought up, and one I was considering inking on my arm.

"What's this one?"

"I'm thinking of getting a new tattoo. It would be small. Right here on my arm," I said pointing to my bicep.

"What does it mean?" She traced over each heart with her finger, taking in the intricate design connecting them.

"It represents us."

"And the third heart?" she asked, looking up to meet my gaze. Her eyes were glassy with emotion, because Jade fucking knew me. She knew the way I thought. The way I felt.

"It's for the baby we lost. It's sort of a symbol of what we've lost, but also what lies ahead for us. Our future. And I can keep adding hearts to this design."

"I love it. It's beautiful. You're so talented. It amazes me," she said, leaning forward and kissing me.

"I don't know about that, but I enjoy it. Dr. Evil, I mean, Dr. Roberts," I paused and we both laughed. "She encouraged me to find something that would be more therapeutic, clear my head. MMA fighting is more of a release. It's physical and competitive. And, writing music is my passion, but one I share with a lot of people. And this is just another way to express myself, you know? Put it on paper."

"I like that. I'm really impressed. Are these charcoals? How do you get it to look so textured?"

"Yep. Charcoals. I use the black and the white for shading, dimension. It gives it a different look. I like how you can change the whole appearance by going darker and lighter in certain places."

"You should teach, you know? You're so passionate about writing and drawing, and you could share that with those that are just getting started, you know?"

"Yeah, I've thought about it. I definitely want to get my masters and go a little further with my education once I'm done with Exiled. The entire time I was in college, I was in the band. That was my priority. I'm kind of looking forward to going back for me and actually looking toward the future and what I want to do."

"I love the sound of that," she said, studying each page and every detail.

"So do I." I tossed the notebook on the side and flipped her on her back.

"Hey, I wasn't done looking."

"You can look on the plane. We only have a few minutes before we need to get out of here. And right now, I want to focus on you." I kissed her hard, and she moaned against my mouth.

"You have a way of distracting me, Winslow."

"Get used to it. Because I won't ever get enough of you," I said against her sweet mouth.

And that was the fucking truth.

twenty-one

. . .

Jade

I DROPPED my books in my backpack and waved goodbye to my lab partner, Anne.

"See ya, Jade," she said.

"I'll see you tomorrow."

I stepped into the hallway outside my classroom and pulled out my phone. Bernie waited outside for me, and so far, he'd stuck to his word about not following me inside. Yes, I had a nickname for him now. The guy followed me everywhere, so go figure, he'd grown on me. He claimed he liked to stay back and survey the area for safety purposes. The guy was so serious. There'd been no sign of Dex, so Bernie was probably very bored in his current position.

The weather was finally warming up. It was April and the sun had arrived. I was still reeling from my trip to Cabo with Cruz, and we were counting down the days until my graduation and him leaving Exiled. Cruz had hired a realtor to find us a place to rent in New York, and the guy was sending us new listings every day. It was an exciting time. The sun was shining in more ways than one. I saw light at the end of this tunnel, and it felt damn good.

"Hello, Jade," someone said from behind me, and I turned to see Cruz's father there.

"Mr. Winslow, hello," I said, not hiding the surprise from my voice.

"Can we sit?" he asked, motioning to the bench at the end of the hall.

"Sure." I dropped to sit and he took the seat beside me. I glanced around to look for Bernie, but he was still outside.

"So, I hear congratulations are in order. You're going to medical school."

"Oh, thank you, have you spoken to Cruz?" I asked, because how else would he know. It was odd that Cruz hadn't mentioned it, as his last meeting with his father hadn't gone well.

"No. My son and I don't discuss you. We don't actually discuss much, if I'm being honest. I'm sure you understand that every family has their own dynamic," he said.

"Um, okay." Not really though. I didn't know any other family that had a dynamic quite like the Winslow's.

"I was filled in about your news from one of the many pairs of eyes and ears that I use these days."

I moved back on the bench just a bit because his words made me uncomfortable. *His eyes and ears?* Was he following me? And where the hell was Bernie when I needed him? I'd scolded the poor guy and insisted he wait outside because I didn't want anyone to know I had security. And now I wished he were here.

"You could have just asked. I'm sure Cruz would have told you, it's certainly not a secret."

"No, it's not is it." He ran his hand over the scruff on his chin.

"Is that what you're here to discuss? Me getting into medical school? Because I have a class to get to," I said, licking my lips because my mouth was suddenly dry.

"Give me more credit than that, Jade. This is your last class today. You don't think I've done my homework? I just came from Dean Johnson's office. I'm making a large contribution to the human biology department, and I told him I'd like you to head up the research of his choosing next year." His ice blue gaze sent a chill down my spine.

"Yeah, it doesn't work that way. First of all, I'm going to be gone next year. Secondly, I highly doubt the donor chooses who partakes in the research." I crossed my arms in front of my body.

"Very naïve mentality for such a smart girl."

I pushed to my feet. "What do you want, Mr. Winslow? I need to go."

"I'm here to make you a proposition. You've still got a long road ahead of you, and I think you should consider your options. I'm willing to make a large contribution to the human biology department here on campus in your name. You could decide how to spend the funds. I'm sure a smart girl like you has lots of ideas about how to make the world a better place," he said.

"I don't need you to make any donations in my name." I rested my hands on my hips. I resented this man and his obtuseness, like money could cure everything, assuming everything had a price. Disgusting. He should know by now that's not of interest to me.

He pushed to stand, towering over me. "Come on, Jade. It's more than a donation, I'm sure you can read between the lines. We can help one another. Nothing wrong with that, is there?"

I looked down the hall and saw Bernie enter the building. Thank God. His eyes landed on me, and he narrowed his gaze on Steven Winslow. He probably thought it was completely normal for me to be speaking to the man. Because in what other reality would this type of conversation be going on with your boyfriend's father.

"I don't need any help, Mr. Winslow, and I'm quite certain you don't need mine either," I said, looking up at him. He was tall like Cruz, and he stood a little too close to me.

"That's where you're wrong. Exiled is a business, my dear. One that brings in a lot of revenue. Now my son may believe it will survive without him, but I do not. I don't think you want to be responsible for tearing down something that those boys have worked hard to build," he said, studying my face.

I shook my head. "This has nothing to do with me. And Exiled will be fine without Cruz. He's still going to be writing music for them, and Lennon, Adam, and Zach are very talented."

"Everything alright over here?" Bernie asked as he approached.

Cruz's father looked up and stared at him, but Bernie didn't look phased. He met Steven Winslow head-on.

"Excuse yourself if you ever want to hold down a job again. Everything is fine," Steven raised a brow in challenge.

"I was speaking to the lady. I'm here for her, not you."

Go, Bernie.

I had a whole new respect for the man. And he was right. Why should we be intimidated by this guy?

I, for one, was not.

"I'm fine. Give us just a minute, and I'll be ready to go."

And I'll never give you attitude again, Bernie.

"Alright. I'll be right over here. *Watching.*" He snarled, and I almost laughed.

Steven waved his hand at him, as if he were shooing away an annoying fly on the wall.

"This has everything to do with you, Jade. Cruz was always going to be the lead singer of Exiled, before you came along. And then after you broke up with him and left for Honduras, he stayed with the band. But you come strolling back to town, and my son is willing to toss his whole life aside for you. You can't really be that naïve by claiming you don't see it? He's putting your needs before his own, and now it's time for you to do the same. His decision affects a lot of people."

Steven knew more about Cruz and I than I would have thought. They didn't speak much, so Cruz's father was definitely doing his homework. Maybe he and Dex were working together, and Dex had been following me that day as Cruz suspected.

"With all due respect, Sir. My relationship with Cruz is none of your business. I think we're done here," I said, reaching for my backpack and pulling it over my shoulder.

He stepped a little bit closer, invading my space. "What's it going to take, huh? What do you think a million dollars would do *for a girl like you?*"

"A girl like me? What does that mean?" I hissed.

"Your father can't make much of a living doing what he does. Sure, it's honorable work serving the community, but I'm sure it doesn't pay him nearly enough. What do you think a million dollars could do for a man like him? I heard he had a close call in a fire recently. Next time he might not be so lucky. But having a little nest egg like I'm offering you would allow dear old dad to take a step away from his dangerous profession, right?"

My jaw dropped. I couldn't believe my ears. My head spun and a little buzzing noise filled my ears. What was this?

"You're serious?" I said, trying to hide the tremble in my voice.

"We can do this one of two ways. I can transfer this money to your account today. No questions asked. Keep it simple. Just do the right thing, Jade and walk away. My son's worth more to me than he is to you."

My spine was stick straight now, and I squared my shoulders. "Take your money and shove it up your ass, Mr. Winslow. Cruz is worth a hell of a lot more to me than any amount of money you could ever offer me. Now I suggest you move along before I sick Bernie on your ass."

I raised a brow and waited for him to respond.

"I'm sorry you feel that way. You just made things very easy for me, but very difficult for yourself."

I shook my head. "You know what? I feel sorry for you. You have this amazing family and you've just thrown them away. Keep your nose out of my business and my father's business, am I making myself clear?"

He studied me, and a wide grin spread across his face. "Crystal. I welcome the challenge, Jade. Have a nice day."

He sauntered down the hall like we'd just had a casual conversation. What the hell was wrong with this man.

Bernie moved beside me, studying my face. "Everything okay?"

"I'm sorry for being such a jerk to you. I'm glad you're here, Bernie." I reached out and squeezed his hand.

"Shall we give Cruz a call and let him know his father paid you a visit?" he asked.

"I'll tell him later."

"You have one hour," he said as we walked to his car.

"I thought you were here for me."

"I work for him. *But I like you better.*" He winked.

When I got in the car, I closed my eyes for a minute and tried to think about what I'd say to Cruz. I was still processing what just happened. How do you tell the boy you love that his father just offered you a million dollars to break up with him? And why would he offer me such a ridiculous amount of money? Was Exiled worth that much to him? And why did he bring my father into it? I would never willingly lie to Cruz about something this big but telling him the truth about his father seemed cruel.

We pulled up in front of the house. "You know you can come sit inside."

He chuckled. "That's not how this works. But thank you. I'm glad you're not snarling at me anymore."

"Thanks, Bernie."

"You know most people call me Bernard," he said dryly.

"I'm not most people." I patted him on the shoulder before jumping out of the car.

"Jade," he said before I shut the door.

"Yeah?"

"Tell him about his father's visit. Don't make me nark on you," he said.

I sighed before sticking my tongue out at him. Was it mature? No. But this is why I didn't want a security guard following me around. He didn't know what he was asking of me. No one could begin to guess how crazy Steven Winslow could be. This was like a bad Monday night movie, all twisted and dark. But unfortunately, it was my life. And I needed to figure out how to manage this situation without devastating Cruz.

"No one likes a tattletale, Bernie."

"I've been called worse," he said with a laugh.

I waved and stepped inside just as my phone vibrated. A Face-Time call from Cruz.

Here we go.

"Hey," I said, dropping to sit on the couch.

"Did you just get in?" His voice was gruff, and I studied his handsome features as he leaned his back against the headboard in his hotel room.

"Yes, just got home from class." I dropped my backpack on the couch.

"You got out late today." He quirked a brow. How does he do that? How does he know when I'm avoiding something?

"Well, I uh, had a little visitor."

Cruz pushed to his feet and ran a hand through his hair. "Dex? Where the fuck was Bernard?"

"It wasn't Dex. And Bernie was there." I rolled my eyes and waited for him to sit back down on the bed. I haven't even told him anything yet and he's already worked up.

"Bernie?"

"What? We're friends now."

"That's impressive. It took me a lot longer to worm my way in," he teased. "So who was this visitor?"

"Your dad came to see me."

"My dad?"

"Yep. The one and only."

"What the hell was he doing there?"

There were a couple ways I could answer this, but none would be well received. So, I twisted the truth just a little bit. Just enough to spare his feelings.

"Well, apparently he had a meeting with the dean about making a contribution to the science department," I said. My stomach twisted as I tried to word things as gently as possible.

"Such a baller. Always flaunting his money. He probably needs a boost as his image has taken a hit lately. Affairs with teenagers tend to knock you down a few notches in the public eye. So, you ran into him after his meeting?"

"Yeah, I was coming out of class, and ran right into him." It was kind of true. I'd leave out the part that he was actually waiting there for me.

"Did you talk to him?"

"Yep. For a little bit."

"Jade. You're being fucking cryptic. What did he say?"

"He thinks you should stay in the band. He doesn't want you to quit," I said as I twisted my promise ring around my finger.

I'd skip the part about him threatening me.

Insinuating that my father and I could be bought.

Offering me a million dollars to end our relationship.

"It's the same old shit with him. He needs to let it go. I told you I thought he and Dex were scheming. It's not a coincidence that you ran into Dex on campus, and now you miraculously run into my father there as well. Not completely surprised he took a shot at you. He's running out of options. Was he at least friendly? Or was he nauseatingly flirty?"

Definitely not flirty.

"No. But it's no secret that he isn't my biggest fan." I laughed and tried to lighten the conversation.

"He wasn't a dick to you, was he?"

"No. He was fine."

"Where the fuck was Bernard?"

"Bernie was there. He let us talk, but he was at the end of the hallway. Your dad actually threatened to have him fired when he approached," I said.

"He's such an asshole. Glad to see you've warmed up to *Bernie* a little though." He laughed.

"Yeah, he's not so bad after all," I said, and it was the truth. I wondered how different things would have gone today if he hadn't been there. Steven Winslow had a hard time controlling his temper with Bernie standing just a few feet away. I shook off the thought.

"Good. I'm sorry you had to deal with my father, baby."

"It's fine. I miss you though," I said.

"Miss you more. I'm glad you're coming to the show in a few weeks."

"Yeah, I haven't been to a show in a while. I've never seen you perform with Zach. I'm looking forward to it."

"Alright, baby, Gio's waiting for me downstairs. Going to go get in a quick workout," he said.

"Okay. Love you."

"Love you more," he said.

Not possible.

twenty-two

. . .

Cruz

"I TAKE it you unblocked the asshole, too? How the fuck does he even know what's going on?" I asked Luke as we made our way to the hotel coffee shop.

My father had flown out to meet us in Seattle. Farah Clearwater had spent her weekend reaching out to every gossip magazine that would listen. She'd upped her game, and I had yet to respond. We'd heard from a prime time media program, The Laurel Hayes Show that they'd been approached to interview Farah about our secret relationship. They were giving us a heads up because they certainly didn't want to be slapped with a lawsuit. My father got wind of it and reached out to Luke. He said he wanted to discuss this Farah situation which he believed Dex was behind, as well as my departure from Exiled. The dude was always in our business, so I wasn't completely surprised. But I'd wondered if he and Dex were in on this together. I couldn't put much past him. But to take the time to try to help make this go away—I doubted he'd play both sides. And one thing Steven Winslow excelled at—damage control. He thrived on covering up all his dirty little secrets. The difference here was that I hadn't done anything to cover up. This was some crazy ass stalker who appeared to be obsessed with telling the world we were in a relationship. I highly doubted anyone was listening, but she continued to sell her story to anyone willing to shell out a few bucks. And taking this on The Laurel Hayes Show would be a whole new level.

"You know your father. He has his ways. He kept calling me from new phone numbers, so I eventually unblocked him. And, I do have to speak to him occasionally about Exiled, so it is what it is. Maybe this is his way of apologizing to you for his involvement with this Clearwater chick in the first place. Do I fully trust him? No. But he wants to help, and the more support we have, the better. And I'd like to hear him out regarding Dex. If he is behind any of this, I'd like to know what his end game is. Your father has a powerful legal team, so maybe they can make this Farah shit go away, or slap her and The Laurel Hayes Show with a lawsuit," Luke said, as we walked toward my father sitting at a table in the back of the coffee shop.

"Yeah. Just hard to believe he wants to help when just a few weeks ago he threatened to take legal action against me when I leave Exiled."

"Agreed. Let's just hear him out." Luke paused at the table and shook my father's hand.

I nodded and dropped in the seat across from my father. The last time we spoke hadn't ended well, so we certainly weren't on friendly terms.

"Thanks for meeting," Dad said. He almost appeared humbled, but I didn't trust this man. The only reason I took the meeting is because Exiled meant something to him, for whatever reason, and maybe he'd actually step in and help. Although that would be very out of character for the man. He thrived on control and he could no longer control me or Lennon. And he fucking hated it.

"So you have information about Dex and Farah? Is that what this is about?" Luke said, pausing so we could place our order.

"You know me, I've got eyes and ears everywhere."

I cringed. He disgusted me.

"So how is it that you think you can help?" Luke asked.

"Well, I have a powerful legal team behind me, you know that.

I've also got deep pockets, and maybe I could make the story go away."

"What are you waiting for?" I said, my disdain impossible to hide. "I don't even give a shit to be honest. Jade doesn't believe it, and I highly doubt anyone does."

"Well, you wouldn't be here if you weren't looking for a favor. And you know the saying, Cruz. I scratch your back, you scratch mine."

A venomous laugh left my mouth. He was going to blackmail me for a crime I didn't commit, to save a career I didn't even want. Did I want Farah to take this on a national program? Hell no. It would embarrass Jade, and her friends and family would see it. But would we be okay either way. Yes. I'd do what I could to stop it. I'd slap Farah's ass with a lawsuit. But I wouldn't make a deal with the devil.

"Of course, you petty motherfucker," I hissed across the table. "And what is it you want from me?"

"You stay in the band another year. I'll make this go away."

"Fuck you," I said, reaching for my orange juice and taking a swig. "I don't give a shit about Farah Clearwater." The asshole didn't even realize he'd as much admitted to this being a setup—his plan to keep me in the band. He. Made. Me. Sick.

Luke placed a hand on my shoulder and gave me a look that told me to chill the fuck out. I nodded.

"Steven, this has nothing to do with Cruz staying in the band. It's a bullshit story and we all know it. I wouldn't think you'd be okay with standing by and letting this crazy person go on The Laurel Hayes Show and slander his name."

"So, let me throw money at it. I'm sure I can make it go away. Hell, she's probably working with Dex. But nothing comes for free, son. You know that."

I shook my head. "Not happening. But for fuck's sake, why do you care if I leave Exiled? I can't figure you out."

He chuckled. "Do you not realize that my stake in Exiled has doubled my net worth. I'm on the cusp of making the Forbes richest men in the US list. Call me competitive, but I like seeing my name on top dominating everything I touch."

"This is all about a list? Are you fucking kidding me? Who gives a shit? This is my fucking life. And how do you know you won't be on it if I leave? You're insane," I said, pushing my plate away and crossing my arms over my chest.

"Bands are never the same after the lead singer leaves. It's common knowledge. And you Cruz, you've got my star power. You are the reason they've reached the success they have," my father said.

"You fucking—"

Luke cut me off before I could finish blasting him. "Steven, I disagree. Exiled is going to be fine. The fans have taken to Zach, and Cruz will still be writing the lyrics. Come on, man. Do the right thing. You're going to lose your son because you're so hell bent on controlling him. He never wanted this. We all knew it. And we stood by and let him do it anyway. Let him walk away. He's done more than anyone could have asked for so go sic your legal team on Farah Clearwater and slap them with a defamation suit. Shut her lying ass up for once and for all, and scare the shit out of Laurel Hayes. She won't want to mess with legal action."

"How do we know Farah's lying?" Dad asked.

"Fuck you." I tossed my napkin on the table.

"You sure you didn't fuck around with this girl? You wouldn't be the first good looking dude to cheat on his lady. Maybe you don't want her to take this on The Laurel Hayes Show because you know Jade will leave if she discovers the truth."

I pointed my finger in his fucking face. "I'm not you. I've never met this chick."

"Ah, that's right. Your boy Dex brought her into your circle, right? And you fucked him over by kicking him out of the band. You need to rethink your choices, son. He's probably pulling the strings now, to give you a taste of your own medicine," he said.

I tipped my head back. How long did I have to sit here and listen to this bag of shit speak? He wasn't going to help me, not unless I agreed to his terms. Which wasn't happening.

"Our guess is that Dex is behind this, yes. And if he thinks this is going to get him back in Exiled, he's deeply mistaken. You alluded to the fact that you've spoken to Dex. Did he give you any indication he was behind this?" Luke said.

"I'm quite certain he's behind it. You have an enemy in Dex, and this Clearwater woman had a relationship with him, correct?" My father sipped his coffee.

"Most likely, yes. But you also got involved with her, correct?" Luke dropped his napkin on the table, letting me know he was about done with this too.

Dad chuckled. It was a maniacal laugh that sent chills down my spine. "Been there, done that, and I owned it."

"No. You got caught," I said.

"I don't have time to mess with trash. But if Laurel Hayes interviews her, it won't fare well for you, Son."

"Laurel fucking Hayes won't interview her. There's nothing there. I've never met Farah Clearwater," I said dryly.

A grin spread across my father's face. Sadistic bastard.

"Suit yourself, Cruz. I wouldn't want to risk her taking this the whole way." He smirked.

"I'm not you. I don't have a web of lies to cover up." I pushed to my feet, and Luke followed suit. "We're done here."

And the fucker might not have realized it, but he'd just showed me his cards. The man was so hell bent on helping me. He didn't give a shit about anyone but himself. Never had. Never would.

"Cruz," he barked, and Luke and I paused to look at him. "I've given you a far easier solution. I am confident that I could make this go away for you. I can wave enormous amounts of money in a lot of faces and you can be done with this."

"Not happening, daddy dearest."

"Provided that you are telling the truth. A lot to lose if you've been fucking around, son."

"Well, you'd know a thing or two about that, wouldn't you? And on a side note, stay the fuck away from my girlfriend," I said.

He studied me with a look of surprise.

"Yeah, motherfucker, my girl tells me shit. We don't have secrets," I snarled.

He chuckled. "Doubtful, son. Everyone has secrets. Hopefully you don't have one that'll blow up in your face."

I walked away. You can't engage crazy without going crazy yourself.

"Well, that was interesting," Luke said, as we stepped on the elevator.

"What? You don't have a father who blackmails you on the daily?"

He smirked. "You're a good kid, Cruz. Don't let him get to you."

"I won't. But, I'm starting to think my father is behind this. He was far too confident that he could make it go away. He knew about The Laurel Hayes Show, and that hasn't been leaked to the press. I mean, he could have someone on our team on his payroll, but I don't think so."

I thought about what Dr. Roberts had said a few months ago about how my father was going to take down everyone around him on his way down. The man was a self-destructive addict.

"You think he'd set this whole thing up and then come to us to offer help?" Luke asked, leaning against the wall with a distraught look on his face.

"I wouldn't put anything past him. I've been so fucking focused on Dex, I may have underestimated my father. I can't stop thinking about how adamant Jade was that Dex seemed different that day she saw him on campus. Jade's not easily fooled. She's fucking smart. The dude attacked her. She should have been afraid of him—but she wasn't."

"I'm going to have Arnie dig into this immediately. And we're going to go after Farah Clearwater. It's time we find out who's behind this, and put an end to it," Luke said. Arnie was the lead guy on our legal team, and it was time to bring everyone in.

I phoned Bernard when I got back to my room and told him to keep his eye out for both my father and Dex. Someone was trying to blow up my life and no better way to get to me than to fuck with Jade. Bernard agreed to stay close and let me know if he saw anyone suspicious near Jade.

My adrenaline was still pumping since my workout with Gio. I'd been pissed off after meeting with my father, and I'd spent a few hours beating the shit out of the bag at the gym. But right now, I needed to get my game face on, as this was the largest crowd we'd ever performed for.

"How you doin' tonight, Nashville?" I shouted, and the crowd went crazy.

Nashville never disappointed.

"Zach and I are going to kick things off with a new one for you tonight."

People screamed from the crowd, chanting More of Me, the song I'd written for Jade. It was our most requested song, and everyone knew the story behind it now, as I'd done a dozen interviews over the last year answering questions about it. Someone shouted, "I want more Jade."

"Yeah, get in line, buddy. We all want more fucking Jade. You're preaching to the choir," I said, as the crowd went nuts with cheers and laughter. "I'll definitely sing More of Me before the night's over, but let's give Zach some fucking encouragement to get his ass out here and belt out a little something we're singing for the first time here in Nashville."

The screams were deafening.

Zach joined me on stage with a laugh, before grabbing his mic and talking to the crowd, "This guy definitely knows how to kick off a show, huh?"

I nodded to Adam to start the music for the edgy alternative rock song we'd been working on. A little something inspired by my father and the timing couldn't be more fitting.

"This is called, *Won't hurt at all to say goodbye*," I purred into the microphone as Adam and Lennon started the music.

Walk away, with no remorse,
You've held us down, you've run your course.
You use your power like a knife,
Wielding it throughout our life.

No more evil, no more pain,
The sun is out, there's no more rain,
Damage done, no time for more,
A broken family, no longer four.
Flaunt your power, flash your green
Dark and evil, don't need a thing.
Your shit don't work, we've risen high,
Won't hurt at all to say goodbye.
Finally free, and on our way,
What do you know, there's more to say,
Thankful you were never around,
Thought we were lost, but now we're found,
Don't need no numbing, just working through,
Learned from others about what to do.
We rose above, and found our way,
While you had nothing good to say.
You came up short, you've got no class,
Out there chasing teenage ass.
Flaunt your power, flash your green
Dark and evil, don't need a thing.
Your shit don't work, we've risen high,
Won't hurt at all to say goodbye.

The crowd roared after the last note, and it felt fucking good to get this off my chest. Words that had been burning a hole in my soul for far too long. Lennon wrote the music in one night. Like he felt the fucking song deep inside too.

We performed for another couple hours, and ended with More of Me, before saying goodnight. I was fucking beat, but I felt good.

I didn't need booze to function.

I didn't need pills to sleep.

I'd left all that darkness in my rearview.

And it felt fucking good.

twenty-three

. . .

Jade

I THANKED Ponch for flying me to Los Angeles and exited the plane. I saw the waiting car at the end of the runway and pulled my wheeled bag behind me. When Cruz exited the vehicle, I dropped everything and started running. I met him with a whoosh and nearly knocked the wind out of both of us.

"You weren't supposed to be here," I said the breathy words against his ear.

"I couldn't wait to see you."

I tangled my hands in his hair and kissed him. I swore my body burned like the sun every time he touched me.

"Thanks for coming to get me," I said, pulling away as he dropped me to my feet.

"Come on, show's starting in a little bit." His fingers intertwined with mine as he led me to the car.

"Yeah, you're cutting it close."

"It's fine. How was your last final?" he asked.

"I still can't believe I'm done. It went well. I just feel like this huge weight has been lifted off my shoulders."

"Yeah. That's got to feel good. And you graduate in a week. You did it," he said, pulling me on his lap.

I laughed as his scruff tickled against my neck.

"It feels *really good*," I smiled, because I also felt particularly good at the moment.

He chuckled against my skin. "Missed you, baby."

"Missed you more. But we did it. We made it. We'll go back for graduation and then I can travel with you for your last month. And then we move to New York. How is this our life?" I said, throwing my arms in the air.

He smiled. "We're pretty fucking lucky."

"Yeah. We sure are."

We pulled in front of the venue and several security guards waited outside. My how times had changed. Cruz would be bombarded if he tried to step out of the car alone at a show now.

"Stay right in front of me and keep your head down. Donny will lead you in."

"Got it." I gave him a quick kiss before moving to my feet.

I grabbed onto a fistful of Donny's shirt as the screams were deafening. My god. These people were out of control. I wondered if Cruz would miss all of this.

We made our way inside and Lennon charged me. "Missed you, Jade."

"I missed you too. Where's Bailey?"

Just then Lennon's girlfriend Bailey came running around the corner and hugged me. "So glad you're here. We can watch the show together."

"Yes, I'm excited."

Everyone came out and said their hellos. Adam gave me a hug and we talked about how bad we felt for Tory. She couldn't come to this show because her grandfather passed away, and she was at the funeral.

"I feel fucking bad I can't be there for her," Adam said.

"I stopped by and saw her this morning before I left. She is doing okay. She understands that you can't just leave a sold-out show. Don't stress. She'll be here soon."

"Alright, thanks," he said.

Luke walked over and gave me a hug and asked all about my

classes. He really was a good friend to Cruz, and I was thankful that he always looked out for my boyfriend.

"Hey, little mama. Glad to see you," Tia yelled as she slapped me on the butt and ran out on stage.

I don't know that I'd ever have a good read on that girl, but I liked her. Yes, I'd wanted to hate her for a brief time after she'd kissed Cruz on stage, but I knew there was nothing there and it was a publicity stunt. It sure as hell stung at the time, but now it had become a bit of a joke every time I saw her.

We moved to the side of the stage while Luke and Lennon talked, and I watched Tia perform. Cruz had his arms around my middle, his chest to my back and his chin rested on my shoulder. Bailey stood beside me watching her sister, and I saw the pride in her eyes.

"She's really come into her own, huh?" I said to Bailey. Tia was one hell of an opening act, and she'd added in a lot of dancing and acrobatic moves to her old show.

"Yeah, she's working hard."

Tia exited the stage, and Cruz kissed me hard before leading the band out to the roaring crowd. The lights flickered all around, and Cruz grabbed the mic.

I watched him move across the stage, with so much confidence and raw talent, he took my breath away. He commanded everyone's attention, and he did it with so much ease. It had been a while since I'd seen him on stage, and I was happy I'd be with him for his last leg of the tour.

"So, what do you think about this Farah Clearwater bitch," Tia said as she pulled up a stool beside me.

"Tia," Bailey said, and gave her sister a hard look.

"What? It's not a secret. Winslow tells her everything," Tia said, meeting my gaze with a raised brow.

I laughed. "It's fine. There's not much to say. I don't think the interview is going to happen." Cruz had his legal team looking into his father, Dex and meeting with both Farah Clearwater and Laurel Hayes. I didn't know how much had been shared, so I was keeping it to myself for now. But I believed Farah's two minutes of fame were up.

"I'd love to be a fly on the wall when she gets her ass served to her. And I know that asshole Dex is behind this," Tia said.

Cruz had thought the same thing. And I guess it would be like Dex to do something like this. But he did seem sober when I last spoke to him. It didn't mean he couldn't have slipped, or that he wasn't capable of doing this. But, Cruz was now suspicious of his father as well, and I wouldn't put anything past that man. I'd been tempted to tell Cruz the truth about my meeting with him, but he'd been so upset at the thought of his father stabbing him in the back again, I just couldn't do it. Not right now.

"Yeah, I just can't wait to put this behind us."

"I get that. Lennon said Cruz has handled it really well. He was not happy that their dad offered to make this go away if Cruz agreed to stay in Exiled for one more year. I mean, who blackmails their own kid?" Bailey said.

Cruz had phoned me after the meeting with his father and he'd been pretty devastated by Steven's offer, which had now left him suspicious of his involvement. Just another nail in the coffin for the man. I wasn't all that surprised. Not after he'd offered me a shit ton of money to end my relationship with his son. The man was sick and twisted. He wielded his money over everyone. I hated him for how much he hurt Cruz and Lennon. A father is supposed to protect his kids and keep them safe. Steven Winslow gave parenting a whole new name.

"Ol' Daddy Warbucks thinks he can buy his way out of every-thing. And sadly, he's probably right. It would be a hell of a lot easier to just shut this story down, rather than go to battle with the devil. But Winslow wants out, so I get it," Tia said.

I nodded, before turning when I heard my name being called out on stage.

"Oh no," I whispered.

"Did you expect anything less?" Tia laughed. "The guy's been biting at the bit for you to get here."

Cruz jogged toward me and reached for my hand. "Let me sing to you one more time, okay?"

His hair was a disheveled mess. His skin glistened with a layer of sweat, and his eyes danced with amusement. He took my breath away.

I nodded. "Okay."

Taking my hand, he led me out on the stage. I stayed behind him, gripping a handful of his cotton T-shirt in my fist. Lennon laughed when I glanced over. I don't know how they did this night after night. The crowd was loud, and my stomach wrenched with nerves.

"Look who's in Los Angeles," Cruz's voice purred through the speakers.

I could swear the stage vibrated as the cheers echoed around me. I looked out at the crowd when I took a seat on the stool that Luke brought out, and I was thankful that the lights made it difficult to see the bodies that spanned across the large auditorium.

Cruz looked at me and moved closer, standing between my legs.

The dark of the storm is all I see.

And like a dream she comes to me.

Now my world is upside down.

Makes no sense keeps spinning round.

When it stops she surrounds me.

In her light I finally see.

And she asks me…

Why would you want more of me?

She doesn't know just what I see.

Beautiful girl with eyes of jade.

Shines so bright can't find the shade.

Heart so pure even in her pain.

In the drought she is the rain.

Wasn't looking but I found her.

I'm the sickness she's the cure.

I'll drown us both in the waves.

She's the only one I want to save.

Makes no sense why she's with me.

Beautiful girl with lots of dreams.

And she asks me…

Why would you want more of me?

She doesn't know just what I see.

Beautiful girl with eyes of jade.
Shines so bright can't find the shade.
Heart so pure even in her pain.
In the drought she is the rain.

I bit down on my bottom lip and swiped at the falling tears. It happened every time he sang this song to me. A reminder of our connection. Of how much he loved me. I didn't know how I got so lucky that Cruz Winslow was mine. But I was grateful that we'd made it. Through all the ups and downs, we'd come out stronger than ever.

My arms reached for him and he lifted me off the seat, my legs came around his waist, my face buried in his neck, and he carried me off the stage.

"Thanks, baby. I love singing to you on stage and seeing you all flushed and nervous," he teased, before kissing me and jogging back out to sing more to the crowd.

I spent the next few hours just watching him do his thing.

My beautiful rock star.

———

It's surreal really, when you want something for so long and it finally happens. Some people talk about how they build something up and it's a letdown when they actually achieve their dream. Not me. Today I'm sitting in a chair waiting to be called to walk across the stage at Northwestern University. I'd dreamed of this day for a long time and being here was even better than I'd expected. I had everyone that was important to me sitting in the audience supporting me. Most importantly, my dad and Cruz. They were always there lifting me up. I thought about Mom this morning, I skipped ahead in her journal to read about the day that she gradu-ated. All the pride she felt.

I felt it all.

I felt everything.

They called my row and I moved in line beside the stage. I glanced over my shoulder. They were all there. Dad, Sara, Cruz,

Sam, Cara, Lennon, Bailey, Ari, Jace, even Juliette, Cruz's mother was seated beside her boys. Bernie was there, standing off to the side, because the man never sat down. He'd become my friend and I loved the annoying guy who'd followed me everywhere these last few weeks. There were too many Aunts and Uncles to count, sitting in the row that Dad had saved because he'd arrived so early this morning and beat the crowd. Half the Chicago Fire Department had come to support their captain. I was overcome with emotion as I looked out at all the people who had contributed to my journey. Dad and I had never been alone. It really did take a village, and these were my people.

"Jade Edington Moore." I couldn't hide the smile as I heard the ridiculous amount of cheers and screams from my family. I laughed as I shook Dean Rebarb's hand and continued my walk across the stage.

I held up my fake diploma and waved as I walked back to my seat.

I can feel you here with me, Mom.

I shouldn't be surprised. She'd always been there. Through all my ups and downs.

And today was definitely an up.

By far, one of the best days of my life.

We'd spent the day celebrating. Dad had taken everyone out for pizza and beer after the commencement. Juliette was a trooper. I don't think pizza and beer were her normal celebratory meal, but she rolled with it like a champ.

Cruz and I headed back to my house, and I was happy we finally had a minute to ourselves.

"When you walked across the stage, I was secretly picturing you naked under your gown," Cruz said when I dropped down on my bed.

"Shut up. No, you weren't." I laughed.

He jumped on the bed and propped himself above me. "I speak the truth. It's all I could think about until they called your name."

I rolled my eyes, my face sore from how much I'd smiled today. "And then what?"

"Well, then I remembered your father was sitting beside me. I mean, he whistled so loud I was pretty fucking sure I'd lose my hearing."

I smacked his chest. "You're ridiculous."

"I'm ridiculously proud of you."

He leaned down and kissed me before I pushed him back and rolled on my side to face him.

"Don't distract me. We have so much to discuss before you leave in the morning," I said.

"I wish you were coming with me." Cruz pushed the hair back from my face.

"Give me one day, and I'll get this place packed up and be on a plane to see you."

"Promise?" he teased.

"Promise."

"We should have all the Farah Clearwater bullshit behind us. My mom's attorneys are involved now as well, and they've been in meetings with Farah's people. Yes. She has people." He laughed. "And Exiled's attorneys stepped up and flew out to meet with Laurel Hayes team today. So, I'm hoping we can put this to rest after this."

"I'm proud of you."

He laughed and rolled his eyes. "For what? For having some crazy ass chick claim we're dating. Not once, but twice."

I ran my fingers along his scruff. "No. For seeing this through. Staying sober through all the stress. Not letting your father get to you. Fighting Farah's claims instead of taking the easier path. You did the right thing and you stayed calm."

"I've beat up several sparring partners over the last few weeks," he said, raising one brow in challenge.

"They went in willing. That's on them. You didn't beat up anyone who wasn't asking for it. How do you feel about your father?" I asked. Steven Winslow may be crazy, but he was still Cruz's father. I knew that it was painful for him, whether he wanted to say it or not.

"Disappointed. That about sums it up. He's an asshole and I

don't think he's going to change. I don't know that he's involved, but I won't be surprised if he is."

"Yeah. You may be right. I hate that he doesn't know how great his sons are," I said. And I meant it. Steven Winslow was missing out on having a relationship with Cruz and Lennon. Two of my favorite people on the planet. And he made no effort to fix things.

"It's alright, baby. I've accepted it, and I'm okay. I can't believe we made it. And we have our own place in New York."

Cruz and I had finally agreed on a place. It was well above what I had in mind for a budget, but my boyfriend was bougie, and we'd compromised.

"I can't wait to go see it."

"Me too. And we'll go pick out some cool furniture, and you can work your magic," he said.

"And what magic is that?"

"Your More Jade magic."

I laughed and wrapped my arms around him, burying my face in his neck.

I was ready for this next adventure.

As long as I was with Cruz.

twenty-four

. . .

Cruz

I PULLED my hoodie over my head and made my way to the waiting car. It was pouring rain in Austin, and the gray skies only added to the dreariness of the day. When I opened the door, I was surprised to see Luke and Lennon.

A sick feeling settled in my stomach.

What fucking now?

I slid into the seat beside Luke. "Is there a problem?"

"Well, we've finally got answers. Unfortunately, your father was at the center of everything," Luke said.

"Fuck. I should have fucking known." I leaned back against the seat and ran a hand through my hair. "What about Dex?"

"Dex completed a sixty-day program a while back and is living in Chicago near his family. There is nothing tracing him to this at all," Luke said.

"Farah admitted everything. Mom's attorneys met with her today. Dad's been paying her. He came up with the plan and fed her to the media. It was actually someone on his team that set up the interview with Laurel Hayes. That's why she thought it was true. Because our father fed her the story." Lennon's face was red, and he shook his head with disgust.

My phone vibrated in my pocket and I pulled it out.

"Speak of the devil." I held up my phone.

> DAD
>
> I just landed in Austin. I think I can get Laurel Hayes to cancel the interview. Let's meet and discuss.

"What did he say?" Luke asked.

"He's here. Still trying to manipulate the situation."

"We threatened a lawsuit if Farah or Laurel Haye's people spoke to your father before we did. So, I'm guessing he's coming in blind. You want me to meet with him?" Luke asked.

"No. I think Lennon and I can handle this."

> Meet me at the hotel.

> DAD
>
> See you in 30 minutes. We can figure this out, Son.

What a sick son of a bitch. He was still going to sell me this bullshit.

Lennon and I made our way to my room and waited for our father to show up.

"What a fucking asshole," Lennon spewed. "He offered you help when he was the motherfucker paying her off. Again. What is wrong with this man?"

"He's an addict with endless resources. He has no boundaries nor respect for anyone."

There was a knock on the door, and I opened it, and our father stepped inside.

"Nice. It's a two for one. That's even better," Dad said, dropping to sit on the couch in the living area of the suite. "You going to offer me a drink? I am here to save your ass."

"Nope." I pulled a chair from the dining table, and slid it in front of him, so I could face the asshole head-on.

Lennon stood, rocking back and forth on his feet.

"How are you going to save my ass, exactly?" I asked, using my hands to form a teepee as I watched the asshole spin his lies.

"I'm a powerful man, Cruz. Learn from me."

I chuckled. "No thanks."

"You don't want this to go away?"

"I know you were behind it all. What I can't figure out is why you keep meeting with me to offer to help? So you can look like the hero? Or is it so you can blackmail me to stay in Exiled? Either way, it's over. Farah will not be talking about me any longer, or she will be hit with more lawsuits than she can deal with. She turned on your ass. Showed us her bank accounts with the money you transferred. Laurel Hayes admitted you'd set the interview up. She also wants nothing to do with this bullshit, nor the lawsuits that would follow. You're done, you arrogant fuck. And I'm done with you," I said, pushing to my feet and walking toward the door.

I'd said what I needed to say. I didn't want to waste one more minute of my energy on this man.

He remained silent and didn't get up at first. I don't think he saw this coming.

"Did you hear what your son said," Lennon spewed, getting in our father's face.

"I heard him." Dad pushed to his feet. "Get fucking over it. I'm doing what's best for both of you and Exiled. If that means hurting your feelings a little, so be it."

"Hurting our feelings? You paid a psychopath to make up lies. You arranged an interview on a major network to blow up your own son. And then you offered to help him when you were the one pulling the strings. Are you that far gone that you can't see how fucked up this is?" Lennon said.

Our father pushed him back, his face bright red. "All this for a girl, huh?"

I moaned and opened the door. I couldn't have the same conversation again with this man.

"I'm done talking to you," I said.

He stopped in front of me. We were eye level. "She told you we met, huh? I bet she didn't tell you everything. Probably because she's still deciding, you dumb fuck. I offered your girl a shit ton of money. Did she tell you that? I bet she didn't, did she?"

The room spun. Nothing seemed to add up the day that Jade said she'd run into my father. But she'd never lie to me. No fucking way.

"The day you ran into her when you were meeting with the dean. Yeah, she told me you asked her to break up with me, you selfish prick. Don't fucking even say her name in my presence, do you hear me?" I was shouting now, and my hands were fisted at my sides. Lennon came to stand beside me.

"She left out quite a bit of our conversation, Cruz. You see, everyone can be bought. Everyone has a number. I didn't run into her. I was waiting for her outside her classroom. She agreed to sit down and hear me out. I offered her a million dollars to walk away. She didn't tell you that, did she? Not as honest as you thought." He paused to study me. "I didn't think so. You see, it was a test. I knew if she ran to you saying I'd offered her money, you'd come after me. But you never did. Looks like everyone has secrets. And everyone has a price. Hers is five mil. Seems I didn't go high enough in my first offer."

I launched at him, grabbed him by the collar and slammed him against the door. "You piece of shit. Why? Why are you trying to fuck up my life?"

Luke and Adam came running down the hall, as I had my father pressed up against the door.

I tightened my grasp before he finally spoke. "Because I can."

That was all he said.

Because I can.

My father was the devil. But that wasn't news to me. What was news to me was that my girlfriend had lied to me. And I couldn't wrap my head around it.

I let go of my father and stormed out of the room. Past everyone. I took the stairs and headed down to the lobby. I needed to get out of here. I called an Uber and walked out to the street. I could hear my brother right behind me, and I paused as I opened the door.

"Let me go, Lennon. I need to think. Have Zach go on stage. I can't do it tonight. I need to deal with my shit, okay?"

My brother's gaze was wet with emotion. "The man is a pathological liar. Call her. This isn't true and you know it. Don't let him win, Cruz. And, don't worry about the show. We're fine."

I nodded and got in the car and gave the driver the address. I FaceTimed Jade from the back seat. I needed to see her eyes when I asked her.

"Hey, are you getting ready for the show?" she said when she answered, dropping to sit on her bed as boxes were scattered all around her room.

"I need to ask you something."

Her face grew serious. "Of course. What's wrong?"

"That day you met with my father did you tell me the truth?"

She sucked in a long breath, and a tear ran down her cheek. "Cruz. Listen. I didn't want to upset you."

"You fucking lied to me. Why? Were you considering his offer? He offered you a million dollars, Jade. And you didn't think to mention that to me? Really? He claims you counter offered five million dollars. So what the fuck am I supposed to believe?"

Tears streamed down her face, and she frantically swiped them away. "No. No. Of course I didn't. That's insane. I told him to shove his money up his ass."

"Why didn't you tell me, Jade? This whole time you never said a word. I thought you were all about the truth. Telling the fucking truth, right? But you lied to me." I fell back against the seat.

"No. I didn't lie to you. I withheld the truth."

"Why the fuck did you do that?"

"Because I love you, Cruz. I didn't want to tell you that your father was a bigger asshole than you thought," she said through her sobs. "*You know me.* I love you."

I couldn't fucking think straight. My father had gotten in my head, and the idea that he'd offered Jade money to leave me—it was too much.

I didn't speak. I was sorting all this shit in my head.

"Cruz. Where are you? I'm coming there tomorrow. We need to talk about this."

"Don't come here. I'm leaving. I need to think," I said, running a hand through my hair.

She broke down. "I'm worried about you. Where are you going?"

"Why are you worried about me? You think I'm going to drink, don't you? I don't want a fucking drink, Jade. I want a fucking father who isn't a piece of shit. I want a fucking father who isn't paying everyone around me to fuck me over. And, I want a fucking girl-friend who tells me the fucking truth."

She gasped. "I would never do anything to hurt you. You know that, Cruz. I love you more than anything. I just didn't want to hurt you. I wanted to protect you."

"How'd that work out for you? I need to go," I said, as the guy pulled in front of the rental car company.

"Please talk to me. I love you." She covered her mouth with her hand and closed her eyes.

"I'll call you in a few hours." I ended the call. I needed to sort this shit out.

I jumped out of the car. I couldn't take the plane because my father would track me. I needed to get the fuck away from him. Away from everyone. I'd drive to Chicago. Figure out what the fuck just happened.

My phone buzzed as I stood at the counter and the girl waiting on the other side gasped. Obviously, a fan of Exiled. "You're Cruz Winslow."

"I am. I need a car. I'll drop it off in Chicago."

"Yeah, yeah, sure. We only have two cars left. Would you like a car or an SUV?" she asked, and she fanned her face with the stack of papers she pulled off her desk. "Sorry, I'm nervous."

"Don't be nervous. I'll take the car." I tossed her my credit card, answered the eight million questions she asked me, as my phone continued to blow up.

Missed calls from Jade, Lennon, Luke, and my father.

Why the fuck was he calling? Hadn't he done enough?

I turned my phone off. A long drive by myself would be just what I needed.

The girl tossed me the keys and walked me outside. "Alright. Drive safely."

"Thanks," I mumbled.

I checked out the map on the nav system. I'd be driving through a lot of rural areas, and I actually looked forward to it. To the quiet. I stopped and grabbed a pack of smokes and a bottle of water, because damn if I didn't need a cigarette right now.

I got on the road and drove for a few hours. I thought about Jade. I was pissed she hadn't told me, but I'd be lying if I didn't admit I understood why she didn't. Who the fuck would want to tell the person they love that their father offered them a million dollars to end their relationship? I wouldn't ever willingly hurt her either. I understood it. I wasn't pissed at Jade. I was pissed at the situation.

Did I think she considered taking the money? Not for a fucking second. So, why'd I lose my shit over this? Because I hated my father and everything he stood for. He'd found my weakness and he'd gone after it. I'd drive for a few hours and then pull over and catch some sleep at a hotel. I'd call Jade and work this shit out. For now, I was just going to drive.

Bright lights blinded me, and I used my hand as a shield to block out the brightness. That's when I realized the car in front of me was on the wrong side of the road. I swerved and felt the impact immediately. My body slammed forward, and the sound of skidding tires surrounded me. Metal hitting metal. My phone flew through the air in slow motion, as the car flipped over multiple times. Round and round. And I thought of my girl. And that she'd told me she loved me. And I hadn't said it back.

Love you more.

And everything went dark.

twenty-five

. . .

Jade

TWELVE HOURS. Twelve hours since I'd heard from Cruz. And no one knew where he was. Lennon and I had been on the phone no less than one hundred times this morning. I hadn't slept at all, as I'd been trying to reach Cruz all night. I knew something was wrong. I felt it in my gut. There'd been no word from him, and Lennon hadn't heard anything either. I knew Cruz was mad, but this still wasn't like him. He hadn't taken his father's plane, as Lennon had called to ask. I was in the process of calling every hospital in Austin, and panic was coursing through my veins.

To say I was manic was an understatement. I had Ari on the phone calling police stations. He'd vanished, and I didn't know what else to do. Lennon was calling rental car companies while I continued to check the hospitals. I waited on hold while the lady searched his name and checked all the John Does that were brought in without identification.

Nothing.

"Okay, thank you." My words broke on a sob.

"Good luck," she said.

My phone rang as soon as I ended the call and Lennon's name flashed across the screen.

"Anything?"

"Yes. He rented a car last night. He was planning to drive from Austin to Chicago. He couldn't have gotten all that far, so we need to check all the hospitals on that path. But Jade, it is possible that his phone just died and he's fine. He was pissed off, so maybe he just needs time to cool off." Lennon sounded so hopeful.

I covered my eyes with my hand. "I don't think so. He told me he'd call me in a few hours. Something's wrong. He wouldn't go this long without touching base with us. Something's wrong, Lennon."

"Alright, let's split up the hospitals."

"Okay. I'm looking at the map now. We can check for accidents. Send me the make and model of the rental car. I'll send it to my father and see if he can make some calls. I'll text you a list of hospitals to try next," I said, swiping at my cheeks and frantically typing on my laptop.

"It'll be okay. We're going to find him."

"I feel really bad. I lied to him. I just didn't want to hurt him. But he was so angry when we talked. I told him I loved him, and he didn't say it back. What if he never says it back?" I couldn't contain my sobs, as all the worry bubbled to the surface and I fell apart.

"Don't do that to yourself. My brother loves you more than anything. He's crazy about you. Of course you didn't want to tell him our father is a bigger piece of shit than we already thought. He understands. I promise. He was just angry at Dad. It has nothing to do with you."

"I think he's pretty angry at me too. And I deserve it. We just need to find him."

"Okay. We will. Don't worry. It's going to be fine."

"I'll send you the list," I said before ending the call.

Ari came back in my room to tell me she had no luck with any of the police stations in Austin. We divided up a new list as we tracked the path that Cruz would have taken. I called my father and gave him the make and model of the rental car and brought him up to speed. He said he'd place some calls right away.

I started calling hospitals in Temple, Texas. I was once again put on hold while a woman on the other end searched the system for Cruz Winslow.

"You still there, hon?" she said.

"Yes, I'm here."

"Alright, we don't have anyone by that name. But a young man was brought in around two o'clock this morning. They didn't find any identification at the scene, and he's currently in surgery. He wasn't conscious when he was brought in, so I don't have much to tell you at this time."

I covered my mouth with my hand and glanced down as a text came in from my father.

DAD

There was a head-on collision in Temple, Texas around 1:30 A.M., and one of the cars involved matches the make and model of the rental car Cruz was driving. It doesn't mean it's him, Jade. I'm having them run the plates to find out if it was a rental car or privately owned.

"You still there?" the lady asked on the other end of the line.

"Yes," I said, and the hysteria in my voice caught me off guard. "I think that's him. I'm coming there now."

"You don't want to wait until I can get some more information? I'd hate for you to come all this way if it's not him," she said.

I was tossing clothes in a duffle bag and pulling a hoodie over my head. "It's him."

I ended the call and dialed Lennon's number. "I think I found him. There was a head-on collision in Temple at one-thirty A.M. and a young man was brought into the hospital there shortly after. They don't have identification for him, but I know it's Cruz," I said, pulling my hair into a bun on top of my head.

"Jesus fucking Christ. Go straight to the hanger. I'll have the plane ready to take you there. I'm getting in a car now, and we should get there around the same time," Lennon said, and I didn't miss the panic in his voice.

"Okay. I'm leaving now."

I yelled out to Ari and told her what I'd found out. She grabbed her car keys and we both hurried to the car. I called my father from the road. He offered to go with me, but I wanted to leave immediately, and I told him I'd keep him posted.

The plane ride was a blur. I sat in a daze, trying to piece together how so much could have changed in the last twenty-four hours. Nothing made sense. Cruz had gotten in that rental car because of what his father told him. Because I'd lied to him. The overwhelming sense of shame and guilt flooded me. Ponch called out a few times and asked if I was all right and I nodded. I couldn't find the words to speak.

Because the truth was—I wasn't all right.

And until I knew that Cruz was okay, I wouldn't be all right.

When the plane landed, Lennon had a car there ready to take me to the hospital. When I arrived, I hurried inside to find him in the waiting area.

"Hey," he said.

"Have you seen him? Is it him?"

"I just got here, they said they'd take us back in a minute. The nurse wanted to speak to the doctor first," he said.

The enormous lump in my throat kept my words at bay. I dropped my bag at my feet and Lennon pulled me into his arms and said what he probably thought I needed to hear. "He's going to be okay."

But we didn't know that. Cruz had been brought in unconscious. He was far from fine.

"Okay, I can take you back to see if this is your loved one, and if it is, Dr. Wallace will be in to speak to you about his condition." A tall woman with long blonde hair stood in front of us. She wore light blue scrubs, and she led us down a long hallway.

Monitors were beeping and voices blurred in the background. I used the sleeve of my hoodie to swipe at my face, as the tears made it difficult to see.

She pushed the door open and held out her arm for us to enter. I took one look at him, and a new set of tears found their way down my cheeks. I covered my mouth to muffle the sounds that I could no longer hold back.

Cruz lies there in bed, with cords coming out of his arms, his face was bruised, and he had a large bandage across his forehead. I hurried to the side of the bed and reached for his hand, leaning down to press my cheek against it.

"Holy shit. What the hell happened?" Lennon asked the nurse.

"I don't know the details, but I was told there was a head-on collision and he was brought in by ambulance."

I stroked the hair away from his beautiful face and tried to assess his injuries.

"What surgery did he have?" I croaked.

"I'll go get the doctor so he can fill you in."

Dr. Wallace came in to speak to Lennon and I. Cruz was actually lucky considering the gravity of the accident. Thankfully, he was not ejected from the car, and the airbag had most likely saved his life. They'd had to remove a portion of his spleen, he also had a punctured lung and three broken ribs. He was covered in cuts and bruises, and he hadn't been conscious when they first brought him in, but the doctor insisted that wasn't unusual. He didn't appear to have any traumatic brain injury, and he said we would just have to watch him closely for the next twenty-four hours to see how he progressed. Dr. Wallace was hopeful that he would wake up soon.

Luke, Bailey, Adam, Zach, and Juliette all showed up shortly after we arrived. I sent a group text to my father, Sara, Ari and Sam to let them know what was happening. I never left the chair beside Cruz's bed. It felt like my heart had been ripped from my body as I sat there for hours watching, as he just lies there with no movement.

Late in the evening, Lennon convinced everyone to take off and get some sleep at the hotel across the street. I had no intention of leaving, and the nurse said I was welcome to sleep in the chair next to Cruz. Lennon didn't fight me, and he said he'd keep his phone on him and to call if there was any change. They'd all be back in the morning.

I dozed off a few times and startled when I'd hear voices outside the room, or when someone would come in to check his vitals. My hand rested in Cruz's and something moved, and I jumped. I squinted to see as the room was dark, but the light from the moon peeked through the cracks in the blinds and illuminated his face. Honey browns locked with mine.

"Hey, you're awake," I said with a gasp, leaning forward in my chair so I could stroke his hair.

"Hey, More Jade."

I was overwhelmed with emotion. The fear that I'd lost him. That he wouldn't recover. That I'd lied to him and he'd never forgive me. It all bubbled up and rose to the surface, and I moved closer to him. "Cruz, I'm so sorry. I'm so, so sorry."

"I'm not mad at you, baby. You were just trying to protect me. I get it."

I rested my cheek against the back of his hand. Tears dropped down, landing on his forearm, and I didn't try to stop them. "I should have told you the truth. I'm sorry."

"I know you are. No more secrets, okay?"

"No more secrets," I said.

"What happened? How long have I been out?"

"You were in an accident last night." I glanced down at my phone for the time, and my voice trembled as I told him what happened. "Over twenty-four hours ago. They removed part of your spleen, and you have a punctured lung and a few broken ribs."

"Yeah, I'm sore as hell. Where are we?"

"We're in Temple, Texas," I said, my fingers intertwining with his.

"Jesus. I didn't get very far. I remember seeing a car coming toward me on my side of the road."

"We don't have any details yet, but apparently a few people had called in to report a person driving reckless and swerving between lanes, and the police were right behind him when he crossed over and hit you. The nurse told us he was presumed drunk and given a sobriety test. But we haven't heard anything certain yet. Luckily the police were there, and they were able to get you to the hospital right away."

"Holy shit. Is the other guy okay?" he asked.

I shook my head. "According to the nurse, he's fine. But I'd like to have a few minutes alone with him in a room."

"You going to use your ninja moves on him?" he teased.

"Sure am. I love you."

"Love you more," he said.

The three words I most needed to hear.

twenty-six

· · ·

Cruz

I'D SPENT ALMOST two weeks in the hospital in Temple before Jade and I headed home to Chicago. I'd been here recuperating for another week and a half. The doctor had agreed it would be okay for me to try to perform the last two weeks of the tour, so I could officially transition out of Exiled and close that chapter of my life. We could have just called it done after the accident, but I wanted to do it right and pass the baton to Zach. I owed it to the guys and to the fans. Jade had assured Dr. Wallace that if it was too much, she would make sure I sat out the second half of the set. The girl had been playing nurse since the day I woke up in the hospital, and I fucking loved it. I wasn't used to being cared for the way Jade cared for me. We'd been through a shit ton together, and I was ready for a simpler life with her.

We were flying to Los Angeles tomorrow for two weeks, and then I'd be done touring with the band. Jade and I had put what happened with my father behind us. I knew she'd only been trying to protect me, and I couldn't fault her for that. I hadn't heard from my father since the night of our argument at the hotel. Not during the two weeks I'd been in the hospital, and not since I'd been released. And I was okay with that. My accident had been covered on every news channel, so there was no way he'd missed what happened. But I served my father no purpose when I wasn't on stage performing, and the man had a one-track mind.

"What are you doing out of bed?" Jade huffed when she came into the bedroom. We were staying at the rental house she shared with Ari. Ari's boyfriend Jace would be moving in next week, and Jade would be officially moving out.

"I wanted to sit at the desk and sketch a little. I don't need to lay down, baby. I'm good."

"I know, but we ran a lot of errands today, and I don't want you to overdo it. The next two weeks are going to be a lot for you."

"I'm good. Come here," I said, tugging on her hand and pulling her to sit on my lap.

"I don't want to hurt you, Winslow," she said, squirming around with a laugh.

"It only hurts me when you stay away."

"Is that so?" she asked, settling on my lap and wrapping her arms around my neck.

"It is so."

We hadn't had sex since my accident, and damn if I wasn't horny as hell with my hot nurse waiting on me around the clock. I pushed to my feet, lifting her with me, and dropping her down on the bed.

"What is it that you think you're doing?" She smiled and pushed herself up on her elbows to look at me.

"I'd like to be *doing you*," I said, dropping down and propping myself above her. I stared down at her jade greens.

"You're such a perv." She rolled her eyes.

"A perv that's crazy about his girl." I tipped her all the way back and kissed her neck. Her breaths came hard and fast, and I grazed her ear with my lips as her fingers tangled in my hair.

"I can see that. And I'm crazy about *you*. But I don't want to hurt you."

"I'm going to be performing tomorrow night. I'm also ready to start working out with Gio again. Sex is a walk in the park," I said with a smirk.

"You're not working out with Gio yet. Dr. Wallace said you needed to wait four weeks. You have a few more days."

"So technical, baby."

She laughed and I swear my chest squeezed. Jade Moore had turned me into a big fucking pussy, but I wouldn't tell her that.

"Well, a little workout might be fine." She wriggled her brows.

I took that as my cue and covered her mouth with mine. There was no part of this girl that I didn't love.

I settled between her legs and pressed into her, so she'd know just how much I wanted her. Hell, I always wanted her.

She arched up and I pulled her T-shirt over her head. She reached for mine, and I helped her yank it off and tossed it to the floor. I unbuttoned her jeans and shimmied them down her legs, taking her pink panties right along with them.

Perfection.

I could sketch this girl for the rest of my life and never run out of inspiration. She was that fucking beautiful.

She sat forward and pushed my joggers down and stopped to trace the small scar on my abdomen with her finger where they'd removed part of my spleen. I reached around and found the small scar on the back of her head.

"These are our battle wounds, baby," I said, leaning down to kiss her.

"They led us here."

"Nowhere else I'd rather be." And with those words, I tipped her back and settled above her.

Taking my time. Kissing every inch of her glorious body. I relished the sweet moans that escaped her and kissed my way down her body, burying my face between her thighs.

Nowhere else I'd rather be.

Wasn't that the fucking truth.

———

"More Of Me" was the last song I sang, at my final show as the lead singer of Exiled. It felt fucking good. This song was inspired by my

girl, and I was walking my ass off the stage tonight to start a new life with her. And I was more than ready.

The last two weeks on tour had been epic. We introduced new music, I had Jade by my side, and my body had healed to the point that I was feeling like myself again. When I found my girl waiting for me beside the stage like she always did, I pulled her in my arms and hugged her. Her legs wrapped around my waist, and she kissed me hard.

"I'm proud of you, Winslow." She pulled back to look at me.

"Nothing to be proud of, baby. You and me are just getting started," I said, glancing over her shoulder to see my brother bent down on the floor beside our mother.

Mom wanted to be at my last show, as she'd been more present in our lives this last year than she'd ever been before. Jade turned her head to the side to follow my gaze and she slid down my body.

"Is she okay?"

"I have no idea. Let's go find out," I said.

My mother sat on the floor, her hands covered her face and Lennon was rubbing her back like he was consoling her.

"What's going on?"

When Mom pulled her hands away, tears streaked her face and her eyes were red and puffy.

"It's your father, Cruz," she said, her words broke on a sob. "I just received a call. His body was found a few hours ago in a hotel room not far from the house. He overdosed. He's gone."

"Jesus. Who was there? Who found him?" I asked.

"No one. He was alone. The housekeeper found him."

"What the fuck?" I said, looking up to meet my brother's gaze. He wasn't crying, and he didn't look surprised—but I saw the sadness. The disappointment.

"Are we sure it's him?" I asked.

"It's him." Lennon nodded as he spoke.

"I'm so sorry, Juliette," Jade said, bending down to embrace my mother.

My brother and I stood there like motionless fucking robots, because I don't think either of us knew how to feel.

Our father was dead.

The man was the devil dressed in Armani—but he was still our father.

And the fucking irony was not lost on me. He was the final Winslow to take his addiction too far. The difference—he had nothing to live for. Mom, Lennon, and I…we did. And we'd fight every day to be better. To live well. To fucking contribute to the people in our lives. The people we loved.

My father never did.

He'd never loved anyone more than himself.

And he'd died alone. Just like he'd lived.

"I need to make some calls," my mother said suddenly, as she hurried to her feet.

Lennon, Bailey, Jade, and I went back to the house with her. Though my mother hadn't been with my father when he died, he'd been the love of her life, and I don't think she truly ever got over him. She'd learned how to live without him because it was her only chance at survival—but she'd given him her heart, and I don't believe she ever got it back. And right now, she needed our support.

The days that followed were both difficult and exhausting. We stayed with Mom at my parents' sprawling Santa Monica beach house, and we talked more and shared more than we ever had before. Seeing my mother's strength through her grief gave me hope that she would be okay. She'd made peace with my father's death, and she'd worked hard to tune out all the outside noise. The media was all over this story, and it was hard to escape all the negativity as all of my father's dirty little secrets had surfaced. He'd lived large— and everyone had an opinion on his lifestyle. None of it was a surprise to us, but at the same time, we didn't want to relive it all with everyone's eyes on us. Mom, Lennon, and I had wounds that had yet to heal.

As we sat in the mortuary on the day we put my father to rest, I listened as friends and family members spoke about him. Some shared fond memories of Dad as a young boy, while others talked about the adventures they'd had with him. The grand parties and the over-the-top vacations. The yachts and the private planes and the extraordinary gifts they'd received from him. As I listened, I wondered if any of them truly knew the man I'd had a tumultuous relationship with my entire life. For many, he'd been the life of the party. He'd been generous with his money, because that was the only way he'd known how to show love. Or wield control. I guess I'd never really know what his motivation was.

Maybe I never really knew him at all.

Jade's fingers tightened around mine as we pushed to our feet and made our way out of the mortuary. Mom invited everyone back to our house for a reception, but I wasn't feeling social. I couldn't pinpoint what I felt—it was a combination of sadness, disappointment, and anger. Disappointment over the relationship I shared with my father, and anger that we'd never get the chance to rectify it.

When we got back to the house, I tried to make small talk with the many acquaintances my father had that I'd never even met.

Jade had gone to the restroom and when she returned, there was a blanket draped over her arm. She pushed up on her tiptoes and whispered in my ear, "Come on, Winslow. Let's go sit on the beach."

She always knew what I needed. Knew when I was retreating. And knew how to bring me back.

She spread the blanket out on the sand, and we both dropped down to sit. The waves crashed against the shore, and the sky was covered in shades of whites and grays, as the sun fought to make an appearance on this gloomy day.

"How do you feel?" she asked, running her fingers through my hair, and studying my face.

"I feel okay. I mean, I had a shit relationship with the man. So yeah, I'm disappointed we never got past it. I'm resentful that he sucked at being a father and made no effort to change that. And a part of me feels guilty for not knowing how to feel about him being dead. Right? He's my father. He's gone. And I don't know if I'm sad or angry? That's pretty fucked up."

"That's pretty honest, actually," she said. "And the truth is, it's okay to feel all of those things. Your dad made a lot of mistakes, Cruz. And just because he's gone, it doesn't lessen the damage that he did. So, it's okay to be angry. It's okay to be disappointed. And the fact that you're allowing yourself to feel all those things shows how far you've come. You don't need to numb those feelings anymore. You just—process them. You hurt, and you grieve, and you move forward."

"How'd you get so smart, *More Jade*?" I teased, leaning forward to kiss her.

Her hair was blowing in the breeze, and her black dress was puddled around her legs and her jade gaze locked with mine. "Not smart. Just honest."

"Thanks for being here."

"Nowhere else I'd want to be," she said.

"You know this story is going to be in the press for weeks. I'm done with the band, and we have some time before you start medical school. I know we wanted to go to New York and get settled in our new place, but how would you feel about getting away? Just you and me. We could go to Europe for a few weeks. I'd love to show you France and London. Maybe go to Italy. Everything will be waiting for us back home after."

There was no hesitation. "I'd go anywhere with you, Winslow. Let's do it."

I pulled her to sit on my lap and I wrapped my arms around her, resting my chin on her shoulder. We both stared out at the turquoise sea, as the waves crashed into the shore.

Time away with my girl was exactly what I needed.

twenty-seven

. . .

Jade

I WAS all ready for the big day with a little time to spare. I pulled out Mom's journal and sat back on the bed to read it.

August 10th

> *Dear Journal,*
>
> *How am I a senior in college? What a journey, huh? As I'm getting ready for my first day of my last year of undergrad, I'm thinking back to my first day of class and everything that I wanted to accomplish. I did it all over the last three years, and I'm proud of it. The good, the bad and the ugly. And there have been all of those things. But here's what I've learned. They are all necessary in this great thing called life. Jack and I have been through so much, and it's taught me that you need to go through tough times to truly appreciate the good times. My love for this beautiful, stubborn, hard-working, smart, strong boy has shown me that. He's my person. My best friend. The one I want to do life with. We've had our fair share of disagreements and we'll have many more I'm sure. But there's no one else I'd rather argue with, laugh with or give my heart to.*
>
> *I'm ready for my senior year. Ready for the future. I've interned with the best and brightest in the industry, and I've held my own. I've listened when*

I needed to and spoken up when I felt passionately about something. I've studied abroad and loved it; yet I learned that home is where my heart is. I'm not afraid to say that anymore. It doesn't make me any less driven to want a family and want to be surrounded by the people I love. Because I can pursue all my dreams right here where I want to be.

So, bring it on senior year. Challenge me. Push me. I look forward to it. These last three years have molded me into the person I am today, and I'm proud of it. I'm ready to blow the roof off this last year. My goal? To be in the moment. To be present and appreciate each step I take along the way.

I want to make a difference in this world, and I'm ready to make it happen. Cheers to my last year in college.

Ciao for now,

J.E.

I loved reading Mom's journal, and I dreaded the day it would come to an end. For now, I'd take in all her wisdom with each word she wrote. Thankful that she'd left me her life story to read.

We'd just arrived in New York in time for my white coat ceremony. We'd spent six weeks in France, London, and Italy. It was nice traveling together when we weren't rushing to shows, or on anyone else's schedule. It was just the two of us, and it had been an unbelievable couple of weeks. I'd had my very own built-in tour guide as Cruz had been to all of those places many times. I knew he'd needed the time away. The time to heal after his father's death. Their relationship had not been a strong one, but Steven was still his father, and my boyfriend needed to grieve that loss. We'd spent hours talking about all the things he was feeling, and he'd tried hard to remember the good times he'd shared with his dad, as the bad times still hovered like a dark cloud. But he'd recalled a few memories from his childhood—some of the best being of a trip to Europe that they'd taken as a family. It was important for him to hold on to those as well.

We both didn't want our trip to end, but we needed to get back to New York and settle into our new place before my white coat ceremony and the first day of school for both of us.

Cruz had been accepted to the Creative Writing master's program at NYU. He thought he would want to pursue Art

History, but his passion for writing music had inspired an interest he'd never known was there. NYU had approached him about teaching a songwriting course to beginning writers, and he'd agreed to do a trial class this semester which they worked around his course schedule. That was my boyfriend—so much passion lived beneath that broody, tough exterior. And I loved everything about him.

He'd read me Wuthering Heights while we traveled through Europe, reading a little bit to me each night before we went to bed, and now we were going to make our way through all the classics. His smooth voice lulled me to sleep each night, and now I couldn't imagine drifting off any other way. Life had taken on a simplicity that we'd each craved, and even though we were both pursuing a challenging road in our education, our lives were less complicated now. Cruz's father's death was still in the news, but New York offered us more privacy, and people left us alone for the most part.

It was a big day, and I Ubered over to campus, as Cruz was at the airport picking up Dad, Sara, Sam, and Ari who'd all flown in for my white coat ceremony. I made my way to the table to check-in. We were led to our seats and I introduced myself to the students sitting beside me.

"Hey, I'm Jade."

"Hi, I'm Eva. Nice to meet you. Can you even believe this day is finally here?" she said. Eva was tall with shoulder-length blond hair and a warm smile.

"I know, right? It's hard to believe it's all happening."

"I'm Sean. Nice to meet you guys. Where are you from?" he asked us.

"I'm from North Carolina," Eva said.

"Chicago," I said. "How about you?"

"I'm actually from here. Grew up in Brooklyn."

"That's nice, you'll be close to home." I smiled before waving at a kid who just dropped down next to Sean.

Everyone was friendly and excited to be here. These were the people I'd be spending the next four years with. I leaned back in my seat and thought about the last few years. It had all led me here. The white coat ceremony was the start of a new journey. One I'd dreamt about for as long as I could remember.

Dean Devore spoke. Her words were powerful as she reminded us that we were not just students, but physicians in training. She told us that these next few years would be challenging but we would be surrounded by professors, mentors, and peers who would support us through the process. I glanced over my shoulder at my own little support group who'd always been there to cheer me on. My gaze locked with Cruz's honey browns, and I relaxed.

I was on my way to becoming a doctor. And I was living in New York City with the boy that I loved more than anything. Life was good. Really good. Things had fallen into place. All the highs and lows, the heartache, the disappointment—it was all worth it. And I wouldn't change a thing.

I was going to make a difference in this world, in whatever way I could. I couldn't ask for more than that. And I was ready for all of it.

After the ceremony, Dad insisted on taking everyone to lunch to celebrate.

"Proud of you, kiddo," he said, and I was overcome with emotion. I don't know why. It wasn't like this man hadn't encouraged me and believed in me every step of the way. He'd told me hundreds of times how proud he was of me. But something about the way that he looked at me made my heart squeeze. Making my father proud was one of my greatest accomplishments.

"Thanks, Dad. Couldn't have done it without you. You know that, right?"

"We can agree to disagree on that one." He winked. "I wish Mom was here to see this moment. She'd be so damn proud."

I reached for his hand on the table, placing mine on top of his. "She is here. Has been the whole way."

His eyes were glassy. "I think you're right, Jady bug. And she's damn proud."

"Of both of us," I said.

He nodded. "Alright. Enough of the mushy stuff. This is supposed to be a celebration."

I chuckled and turned back to face the table. Cruz and Sam were laughing about something ridiculous, Ari and Sara were comparing pictures from the white coat ceremony, and my father was beaming down at me. It was a memory I'd carry with me forever.

———

I dropped down on the white slip-covered couch in our new apartment.

"Tell me why we picked a white sofa again?" Cruz said, setting a few boxes of Chinese food on the coffee table and joining me on the couch.

"Because it's a slipcover and we can throw it in the wash."

"We can't wash a black slipcover?" he asked with a smirk.

I laughed. "You can't bleach a black slipcover. And who wants a black couch?"

"Cool people."

"You love this couch," I said, rolling my eyes and trying to hide my smile.

"I love *you*. Don't really give a fuck about the couch."

I glanced around the room, still pinching myself that we were finally here. "I can't believe this is our place."

Cruz and I found a great two-bedroom in the west village. It was much swankier than what I ever imagined living in, but I'd talked Cruz down from getting a penthouse apartment, so we'd met in the middle. We'd purchased a couch, a coffee table, and a bed. The rest we would get over time. We weren't in a hurry. There was no expiration or timeline anymore. No miles between us or trips to plan. This was our new life, and we were together.

Cruz wore black joggers, a vintage rock tee, and military boots. His hair was disheveled and sexy, and he had fully embraced this new life in New York. This city fit him so well. He loved that we walked everywhere to eat and shop, and that we could take public transportation, and of course there were endless museums to visit here. He liked that people weren't following him with cameras, and no one was getting in his business.

"You happy?" he asked.

"Very. How about you? You sure you're ready to give up the rock star life, Professor?"

He laughed and held out a piece of sweet and sour chicken on his chopsticks and I opened my mouth, allowing him to pop it in. "It's been a long time coming. I'm ready. For all of it."

"Yeah? Imagine how all the freshman girls are going to swoon over Cruz Winslow teaching their songwriting course." The class had already had to be broken into two separate blocks as it had filled up within the first ninety seconds of being open for registration.

"Only one girl I want to swoon," he said, dropping his chopsticks on the coffee table and tipping me back on the couch, propping himself above me.

"I'm already swooning, Winslow," I said through a fit of giggles.

"You sure about that?"

"I'm positive," I said, smiling up at him.

He lifted my arm and kissed the little music note tattoo on the inside of my wrist. "So, when can I propose?"

I rolled my eyes. "You're not supposed to ask me, fool."

"Why not? You live by rules. *I don't*. I'd marry you today and put a few babies in you if you'd let me. But we both know you have a plan, and I just need you to give me the thumbs up when it's fucking go-time."

It was difficult to speak through my laughter. "*Go time?* Really? And put a few babies in me? Are you serious right now?"

He looked down at me, his honey browns dancing with mischief. "Dead. Fucking. Serious."

"We just moved in together. I'm starting medical school, you're getting your masters and teaching. Let's just sit on this for a minute." I tangled my fingers in his hair.

"Not really my style, but I'll do it for you."

"Okay." I bit down on my bottom lip. "Thanks for coming to New York with me."

"I'd go anywhere with you. Thanks for waiting for me to stop being a fuck up."

"I'd wait for you forever," I whispered.

His mouth came over mine, and he lifted me in his arms as he pushed to his feet and my legs wrapped around his waist. His lips never left mine as he walked me down the hall to our bedroom.

He dropped me on the bed, and I bounced on the new mattress. I scrambled over to the nightstand and opened the drawer. "I got something for you."

"Is it a sex toy?"

I laughed. "No, you perv. It's a book."

He dropped down beside me on the bed and I handed it to him.

"Pride and Prejudice. Ah, a little Jane Austen. Does Mr. Darcy do it for you?" he rolled me on my back and settled above me.

"Cruz Winslow does it for me." My voice came out all breathy and needy which made us both laugh.

"That's what I like to hear, More Jade."

He kissed my neck, and the book dropped onto the mattress beside us. His mouth came over mine before he pulled away and sat back on his heels and reached for the book.

"You want me to read to you now?" he asked, and I didn't miss the heat in his eyes.

I grabbed the book and tossed it to the side. "Mr. Darcy can wait."

"Is that so? Tell me what you need, baby," he said, leaning over me again.

"More Cruz Winslow."

He laughed. "Not a problem. I'm all yours."

"And I'm all yours," I whispered.

"Damn straight. Always have been, always will be."

His mouth crashed into mine, and I tangled my fingers in his hair. I had everything I ever wanted, and I was looking forward to the future.

And starting our new life together.

And doing it all with Cruz Winslow.

epilogue

. . .

Cruz

Ten years later

IT WAS HALLOWEEN, and my girls were in the bathroom getting ready. Yeah, my wife was *that mom*. The kind of mom we all wished for. She'd been working on Winnie's butterfly costume for weeks. Our little girl had a thing for butterflies, and Jade stayed up late last night to finish constructing the wings.

"Daddy, Daddy, look at me," Winnie said, running toward me down the hall flapping her orange and black wings like she was about to take flight. "I'm a real butterfly."

Winnie just might be the most curious three-year-old on the planet. The girl never stopped asking questions and repeating things we said. She was smart like her mama. Jade and I read to her all the time and took her to museums and on nature hikes—always pointing things out.

Winona Jaqueline Winslow was the light of our lives.

Jade and I got married while she was in her second year of med school. We had a small ceremony on Little Gasparilla Island and flew our closest friends and family out to celebrate with us. Jade had matched for her residency program at the University of Chicago, which brought us back home. After a clerkship in pediatric neurology, my wife had discovered her calling. We found out she was pregnant with Winnie during her third year of residency. I'd landed a teaching gig at the same university, where I now taught both art history and musical composition. Between my mom who now lived in the city full-time and Jade's father and his wife Sara, everyone stepped up to help out with Winnie.

"I didn't even know it was you. I thought a real butterfly had flown in the house," I said, bending down to meet my baby girl's jade green gaze. Light brown curls trailed down her back, and her tiny little hand reached up and cupped my cheek.

"It's me, Daddy. It's Winnie," she said, her eyes searching mine to make sure I understood.

"I can't believe it's you. You're the prettiest butterfly I've ever seen."

"Mama says that butterflies start out as canter-pills before they shed their skin. Did you know that, Daddy?" she asked, and I swear to Christ my chest exploded every time this little girl looked at me like that. Her brows cinched just like her mother's always did, as she concentrated on what she was saying.

"Yep, they're *caterpillars* first. They shed their skin and turn into beautiful butterflies."

"When I was a baby, did I shed my skin before I turned into a big girl?" She scrunched her little nose, as she thought this over, before pinching the skin on her forearm. "No, Daddy. This is the same skin as I always had. I remember it."

"Because you were born a beautiful butterfly, Winnie. You never had to shed your skin," I said, pushing to stand when the doorbell rang.

"'Cause I'm your special girl, right Daddy?"

"You know it," I said, opening the door of our Evanston home.

"Where is she?" Jade's father, Jack and his wife Sara hurried inside, anxious to see Winnie all dressed up.

Halloween wasn't what it used to be for Jack and Jade, not since Winnie had come into the world. It was no longer a day of mourning, but a day of celebration and fun. Winnie ran to the door, flapping her wings. Her tulle skirt fluttering all around her.

"Grampy, Grammie, don't be scared. It's me, Winnie, in here. Mama made me a butterfly costume," she said, and Jack scooped her into his arms.

"Prettiest butterfly I've ever seen," he said.

"Did Mama do your face makeup too?" Sara asked, admiring Jade's handiwork of orange and yellow face paint on Winnie's chubby little cheeks.

"Hey," Jade said, her round belly entering the room ahead of her. She was eight and a half months pregnant with baby number two. We had another little girl on the way, and we couldn't wait.

Things were more manageable now with Jade settled into her own practice, and me having some flexibility in my teaching schedule. I still wrote music for Exiled and occasionally joined them on stage when they performed in the city for old time's sake. Lennon had married Bailey shortly after Jade and I tied the knot, and they had two little boys, Wyatt and Ace, who we adored. They were a few years older than Winnie, and we all got together as often as we could. They had a house not too far from ours, and they'd be joining us to trick-or-treat tonight.

The doorbell rang again, and Jade answered it and gave my mom a hug. They'd grown close over the years, and I was happy that my mother was so involved with Winnie, Wyatt and Ace. She'd stepped up as a grandmother. It had taken Mom years to get over the loss of my father, but she'd remained clean and sober through the healing process, and I was proud of her. She still didn't date, but she'd found a peace in her life that she hadn't had before. And I'd made peace with my father's death as well. Did I have fond memories of the man? No. But I'd let go of all the anger that I'd been holding on to for years, and I'd come to terms with the fact that he was an addict—and his addiction cost him his life, as well as his relationships with the people he loved. I didn't want anger and resentment to be something I carried around with me. Something my little girl would learn from me.

Hell, I'd even made peace with that fucker, Dex. I'd run into him in the city a few years back, and the guy had opened a music school for at-risk teens. He told me he'd had a few slip-ups with his sobriety over the years, but he'd continued to fight it with rehab and meetings, and I couldn't fault the dude. He was trying. And there was something to be said about that. And God knows I'd had my fair share of fuck-ups that I'd been forgiven, so I'd left my hostility for Dex in my rearview. Were we best-friends? Hell no. But I didn't hate him anymore, and that was a step in the right direction.

"So, shall we tell them what you did, and see if they think I'm the crazy one for getting upset about it?" Jade said, her lips turned up in the corners, and her eyes met mine. The woman still did crazy shit to me with just a look. She was fucking beautiful, and I couldn't get enough of her.

"Let's hear it," her father said.

"Well, Cruz took Winnie to her friend Jasmine's birthday party this morning at Chuck E. Cheese while I put the goody bags together for tonight, and he had a little *run-in* with a five-year-old boy." She smirked. My wife loved to give me shit.

"That little shi—er, stinker had it coming," I said, correcting myself because I'd do what I fucking could to preserve the sweetness of my baby girl, and Jade would kick my ass as well. "He scratched Winnie in the face. You can't see the little cut on her cheek under the face paint. He didn't want her to get in the ball pit. I saw the little punk do it. He gouged her face and pushed her on her back," I said, crossing my arms over my chest.

Jack, Sara, and my mom all burst out in laughter. I didn't find it funny.

Yeah, I was the fucking president of the Winnie Winslow fan club, and no one was going to fuck with her on my watch. Period.

"So, what did you do?" my mother asked, acting all judgmental before I even spoke.

"Not enough. I can tell you that. The little punk's mother had the nerve to tell me to let the kids work it out. She said that's how kids deal with things, all while she remained on her cell phone," I said rolling my eyes before continuing. "Listen, I wouldn't tolerate Winnie hurting another kid either and I sure as shi—um, heck, am not about to let some little punk hurt her. She's three years old for God's sake. So, I took her to the table and cleaned her face up. She was bleeding, baby," I said, turning to look at Jade. We'd already argued about it this afternoon when my daughter ran in and told her what happened. Winnie couldn't keep a secret if her life depended on it.

"I told Mama... Daddy was my prince today. He slays *all the dragons* for me. He's a real prince, 'cause that's what real princes do, right Daddy?" Winnie asked, her eyes big as saucers, and I beamed with pride.

"How exactly did he slay this particular dragon?" Jack directed his question to Winnie and then looked up at me with a smirk on his face.

"I'll tell you how. That kid could have cared less that he'd hurt her. He had *zero remorse*. He came running by our table while she was bleeding, and I was cleaning her up. He was yelling at his mom for more tokens. The kid was twice her size, and a bully," I said.

"So, what did you do?" Jade moved closer and looked up at me.

"Well, my leg moved of its own volition, it just shot out—and the kid tripped over my foot and yard sailed across the floor. Served the little punk right. He didn't get hurt, it just bruised is ego. He can thank me later."

"Yep. He can thank Daddy later. Because that's bad manners to push a lady, right Daddy?" Winnie said.

Jade laughed and wrapped her arms around my middle. Her hard, round belly pressed against me, and I tilted her chin up to meet her gaze. "Just protecting our baby girl."

"Are you going to slay all the dragons for her?" she teased.

"I sure am, just like I'll slay all the dragons for you," I said.

"You always have." She pushed up and kissed me, and I had to adjust myself in my jeans, so no one noticed the raging erection beneath my zipper from one small kiss from this woman. My wife had that effect on me.

"Are you doing okay, baby?" I whispered against her ear so only she could hear me. I knew this day was still tough for her, even if she put on a brave face to make it magical for Winnie.

"I'm happy. Really happy," she said, smiling up at me and my chest squeezed.

Damn. The Winslow girls were my kryptonite. And now there was going to be another one I'd need to protect. There was nothing I wouldn't do for them. They were my whole world. Jade had created this life for me that I never knew existed. I woke up every fucking day happy to be alive. Who'd have thought that was possible?

"Me too," I told her.

My brother, Bailey, Wyatt and Ace came barreling through the door. The asshole never knocked. Jade ran over to give everyone a hug and pass out the goody bags she'd made for the kids. She was a fucking rock star. Always had been. She rocked being a wife and a mother, and I'd never wrap my head around the fact that she'd chosen me. I did my special handshake with my two nephews because the dudes were born cool. They'd obviously inherited the cool gene from me, at least that's what I always told Lennon.

The doorbell rang again, and I rolled my eyes. It was grand-fuck-ing-central at our house all the time, and Winnie fluttered around the room relishing the chaos. Jade answered the door and Adam and Tory stepped inside with the twins, followed by Ari, Jace, and their little four-year-old hellion, Felix. Before she could shut the door, Sam and Cara pushed inside with their brood of four boys.

"Daddy, can we go now? I want to ring *all the bells* and get *all the candy*," Winnie said, tugging on my hand.

"Okay, let's move it out," I shouted, and all the kids charged the door with their trick-or-treat bags in hand.

Winnie flapped her wings and Jack grabbed her hand, leading her outside.

"Hey, Winslow," Jade said from the kitchen, as she stood behind the large island.

"Yeah? Come on, baby. We gotta go."

"Can you ask my dad to stay with Winnie?" she said, her hands resting on the counter.

I moved toward my wife, alarm bells going off. Maybe she was trying too hard to make this day okay. I always worried about how hard she pushed herself. "Are you thinking about your mom?"

She smiled. "No, but my water just broke."

I rushed over to her, patting her down like I was checking for weapons, for reasons I don't know. "Are you hurt?"

"No." She broke out in a fit of laughter. "But we need to go to the hospital. Can you bring Winnie back inside so I can say goodbye to her?"

"Yes. Of course. Don't move."

I ran out the front door, shouting for Jack, and everyone turned around. "Jade's water broke. Can you stay with Winnie?"

"Of course. What a day to be born, huh? I'll bet Jaqueline is looking down smiling, making sure this day becomes better and better for this family," Jack said, and I nodded.

"You gotta take care of Mama, right Daddy?"

"Yeah, baby. Can you come say goodbye, so she won't be missing you too much?" I asked, scooping my baby girl in my arms, and jogging back in the house.

"Don't be scared, Mama. Daddy's gonna slay all the dragons for you, right?" Winnie asked, smiling at Jade.

"Yes, sweetie. He slays all the dragons. You stay with Grampy and Grammie, and they'll bring you to the hospital tomorrow to meet your new baby sister, okay? And only two pieces of candy tonight and then brush those teeth real good."

"'Cause the tooth fairy doesn't want me to get those sugar bugs in my teeth, right?"

Jade laughed, and I clutched my chest. This kid was going to kill me with all her sweetness.

"And tomorrow I'll meet my little baby, Presley?" she asked, patting my cheek with her little hand.

Presley Edington Winslow. Baby number two. Jade wanted each of our daughters to have a piece of her mother, so we'd chosen middle names that would honor Jaqueline.

"Tomorrow you'll meet baby Presley," I said.

Jack walked up and hugged his daughter, and I hurried to grab Jade's suitcase from our room. Everyone huddled around the car as I buckled my wife in, and we waved goodbye.

I glanced over at Jade as I backed out of the driveway and tears streamed down her beautiful face. I stopped the car. "Should we call an ambulance? Are you in pain?"

She swiped at her cheeks and shook her head. The corners of her lips turned up. "No. I'm just happy."

I pulled down the street and laughed. "Me too. We sure are lucky, huh?"

"We sure are. I love you, Cruz Winslow," she said, squeezing my hand.

"Love you more."

And I meant it.

I'd never get enough.

Because everything was good as long as I was with her.

More Jade.

THE END

acknowledgments

Greg, Chase & Hannah, thank you for being my biggest supporters and always believing in me. I love you more than Jamie loves Claire! Aye, Sassenach! xo

Pathi, Annette, Natalie, Hannah, Abi, Nicole and Doo, thank you for being the BEST beta readers EVER! Your feedback means the world to me. I would be lost without you!

Thank you, Jena Brignola for bringing yet another gorgeous cover to life!

Sue Grimshaw (Edits by Sue), what a journey we have taken together with this series. I trust you completely and I am so thankful for your guidance and support.

Ellie McLove (My Brother's Editor), thank you for being YOU!! Your comments and feedback make editing so much fun!! Thank you for believing in me and always being so supportive! Now I will have an actual stack of books to bring to Love N Vegas!!

Rosa Sharon (My Brother's Editor) thank you for making this book shine!! I love your feedback and appreciate all that you do for me!

Tamara Cribley (The Deliberate Page), thank you for making me feel so good about putting my books out there in the world!! I love every little detail, and all the gorgeous touches you add in!

Jo and Kylie at Give Me Books Promotions, I would be lost without you. Oh my gosh...the disasters that you have saved me from. I appreciate you both so much, and absolutely LOVE working with you! So excited to meet you at the Four Brits Book Fest!!!

Ashlee (Ashes & Vellichor), once again...you nailed it! I cannot tell you how much it means to me that you always make time to create the MOST BEAUTIFUL graphics and trailers. Thank you for taking this journey with me!

Mom, thank you for your love and support. Love you!

Dad, you really are the reason that I keep chasing my dreams!! Thank you for teaching me to never give up. Love you!

Sandy, thank you for reading and supporting me throughout this journey. Love you!

Eric, there is no one that listens and supports me more than you!! Love you, E$!

Sissy, thank you for making me laugh when I need it most. Do you have to let it linger??? Love you!

Pathi, it doesn't matter how many rewrites I do, how many errors I make, you are always there ready to dig in and read whatever I give you. Thank you for being the best cheerleader and friend throughout this journey!

Natalie (Head in the Clouds, Nose in a Book), I could never thank you enough for all that you do for me. Thank you for taking on the newsletter, the website, and everything in between. Your support means SO MUCH to me!!

Steph, you are the best book event coordinator around! Thank you for supporting me endlessly, and coordinating our maxi dresses, and all the bundt cakes, and charcuterie boards!

Willow, Thank you for being the best sprinting partner around. You always encourage me, answer my endless questions and I can't even wait to be on Living In The Pages!! I appreciate you so much my sweet friend!

To all of the bloggers and bookstagrammers who have posted, shared and supported me—I can't begin to tell you how much it means to me. I love seeing the graphics that you make, and the gorgeous posts that you share. I am forever grateful for your support!

Lisa, Julie, Eric, Jen and Jim, I am very thankful to have such supportive and encouraging siblings in my life. Love you!

Nicole, Sue, Thompson, Pathi, Bell, Natalie, Annette, Carol, Margy, Steph, Mindy, Kristin, Laura, Anne, Abi, Dina, Kelly, Maggie, Leigh Anne, Julie, Nancy, Bev, Leslie, Florence, Tina, Renae, Cindy,

Kelly & Kate, Darleen, Althea, Jess, Ariel, Heather, Shannon, Brandon, Logan, Brock, Caroline, Liva, Kennedy, all the amazing ladies at d'annata boutique and Bloom boutique, and all of my friends who have supported me along this journey…thank you so much!!

Thank you for reading *More Of Us*, book 3 in the Love You More Series. I hope you enjoyed your journey with Jade and Cruz! Please consider leaving a review on Amazon/Goodreads!! They help authors SO MUCH!!

keep up on new releases

Linktree Laurapavlovauthor
Newsletter laurapavlov.com

other books by laura pavlov

Magnolia Falls Series
Loving Romeo
Wild River
Forbidden King
Beating Heart
Finding Hayes

Cottonwood Cove Series
Into the Tide
Under the Stars
On the Shore
Before the Sunset
After the Storm

Honey Mountain Series
Always Mine
Ever Mine
Make You Mine
Simply Mine
Only Mine

The Willow Springs Series
Frayed
Tangled
Charmed
Sealed
Claimed

Montgomery Brothers Series
Legacy
Peacekeeper
Rebel

A Love You More Rock Star Romance
More Jade
More of You
More of Us

The Shine Design Series
Beautifully Damaged
Beautifully Flawed

The G.D. Taylors Series with Willow Aster
Wanted Wed or Alive
The Bold and the Bullheaded
Another Motherfaker
Don't Cry Spilled MILF
Friends with Benefactors

follow me

Website laurapavlov.com
Goodreads @laurapavlov
Instagram @laurapavlovauthor
Facebook @laurapavlovauthor
Pav-Love's Readers @pav-love's readers
Amazon @laurapavlov
BookBub @laurapavlov
TikTok @laurapavlovauthor